LIVE AND LET DIE

Ian Fleming was born in 1908 and educated at Eton. After Sandhurst, and Munich and Geneva Universities, he joined Reuters – making his first mark as a journalist during the famous 1933 Moscow trial of British engineers. He began to understand espionage methods.

After a short spell as a partner in a stockbroking firm, he joined the staff of *The Times* and returned to Moscow. During the war he served with the rank of Commander in the Naval Intelligence Division and in 1945 he joined the Kemsley Newspapers as foreign manager. In Jamaica he built his house, 'Goldeneye', in which to spend his annual leave, and it was here that James Bond was 'conceived'.

Casino Royale was completed on the eve of his marriage to Anne Rothermere in 1952. In all he published thirteen books about the character who became the most famous secret agent ever, and so far eight James Bond adventures have been filmed. Twenty-six million copies of his books have been sold by Pan alone.

During the 1950s Ian Fleming's health began to fail and he died in 1964 at the age of 56.

LIVE AND LET DIE

IAN FLEMING

UNABRIDGED

PAN BOOKS LTD : LONDON

First published 1954 by Jonathan Cape Ltd.
This edition published 1957 by Pan Books Ltd.,
33 Tothill Street, London, S.W.1

ISBN 0 330 10233 8

2nd Printing 1958
3rd Printing 1959
4th Printing 1960
5th Printing 1961
6th Printing 1961
7th Printing 1962
8th Printing 1962
9th Printing 1963
10th Printing 1963
11th Printing 1963
12th Printing 1963
13th Printing 1964
14th Printing 1964
15th Printing 1964
16th Printing 1964
17th Printing 1964
18th Printing 1965
19th Printing 1965
20th Printing 1965
21st Printing 1966
22nd Printing 1969
23rd Printing 1973

Printed in Great Britain by Richard Clay (The Chaucer Press), Ltd., Bungay, Suffolk

LIVE AND LET DIE

'A snorter. From first word to last . . . the reader is compelled to surrender to a superb story-teller.'—*Time & Tide*

'Don't blame me if you get a stroke.'—*Observer*

'Speed . . . tremendous zest . . . communicated excitement. Brrh! How wincingly well Mr Fleming writes.'

—*Sunday Times*

CONTENTS

CHAPTER I

THE RED CARPET

THERE are moments of great luxury in the life of a secret agent. There are assignments on which he is required to act the part of a very rich man; occasions when he takes refuge in good living to efface the memory of danger and the shadow of death; and times when, as was now the case, he is a guest in the territory of an allied Secret Service.

From the moment the BOAC Stratocruiser taxied up to the International Air Terminal at Idlewild, James Bond was treated like royalty.

When he left the aircraft with the other passengers he had resigned himself to the notorious purgatory of the US Health, Immigration and Customs machinery. At least an hour, he thought, of overheated, drab-green rooms smelling of last year's air and stale sweat and guilt and the fear that hangs round all frontiers, fear of those closed doors marked PRIVATE that hide the careful men, the files, the teleprinters chattering urgently to Washington, to the Bureau of Narcotics, Counter Espionage, the Treasury, the FBI.

As he walked across the tarmac in the bitter January wind he saw his own name going over the network: BOND, JAMES. BRITISH DIPLOMATIC PASSPORT 0094567, the short wait and the replies coming back on the different machines: NEGATIVE, NEGATIVE, NEGATIVE. And then, from the FBI: POSITIVE AWAIT CHECK. There would be some hasty traffic on the FBI circuit with the Central Intelligence Agency and then: FBI TO IDLEWILD: BOND OKAY OKAY, and the bland official out front would hand him back his passport with a 'Hope you enjoy your stay, Mr. Bond.'

Bond shrugged his shoulders and followed the other passengers through the wire fence towards the door marked US HEALTH SERVICE.

In his case it was only a boring routine, of course, but he disliked the idea of his dossier being in the possession of any foreign power. Anonymity was the chief tool of his trade. Every thread of his real identity that went on record in any file diminished his value and, ultimately, was a threat to his life. Here in America, where they knew all about him, he felt like a negro whose shadow has been stolen by the witch-doctor. A vital part of himself was in pawn, in the hands of others. Friends, of course, in this instance, but still . . .

'Mr. Bond?'

A pleasant-looking nondescript man in plain clothes had stepped forward from the shadow of the Health Service building.

'My name's Halloran. Pleased to meet you!'

They shook hands.

'Hope you had a pleasant trip. Would you follow me, please?'

He turned to the officer of the Airport police on guard at the door.

'Okay, Sergeant.'

'Okay, Mr. Halloran. Be seeing you.'

The other passengers had passed inside. Halloran turned to the left, away from the building. Another policeman held open a small gate in the high boundary fence.

' 'Bye, Mr. Halloran.'

''Bye, Officer. Thanks.'

Directly outside a black Buick waited, its engine sighing quietly. They climbed in. Bond's two light suitcases were in front next to the driver. Bond couldn't imagine how they had been extracted so quickly from the mound of passengers' luggage he had seen only minutes before being trolleyed over to Customs.

'Okay, Grady. Let's go.'

Bond sank back luxuriously as the big limousine surged forward, slipping quickly into top through the Dynaflow gears.

He turned to Halloran.

'Well, that's certainly one of the reddest carpets I've ever seen. I expected to be at least an hour getting through Immigration. Who laid it on? I'm not used to VIP treatment. Anyway, thanks very much for your part in it all.'

'You're very welcome, Mr. Bond.' Halloran smiled and offered him a cigarette from a fresh pack of Luckies. 'We want to make your stay comfortable. Anything you want, just say so and it's yours. You've got some good friends in Washington. I don't myself know why you're here but it seems the authorities are keen that you should be a privileged guest of the Government. It's my job to see you get to your hotel as quickly and as comfortably as possible and then I'll hand over and be on my way. May I have your passport a moment, please.'

Bond gave it to him. Halloran opened a brief-case on the seat beside him and took out a heavy metal stamp. He turned the pages of Bond's passport until he came to the US Visa, stamped it, scribbled his signature over the dark blue circle of the Department of Justice cypher and gave it back to him. Then he took out his pocket-book and extracted a thick white envelope which he gave to Bond.

'There's a thousand dollars in there, Mr. Bond.' He held up his hand as Bond started to speak. 'And it's Communist money we took in the Schmidt–Kinaski haul. We're using it back at them and you are asked to co-operate and spend this in any way you like on your present assignment. I am advised that it will be considered a very unfriendly act if you refuse. Let's please say no more about it and,' he added, as Bond continued to hold the envelope dubiously in his hand, 'I am also to say that the disposal of this money through your hands has the knowledge and approval of your own Chief.'

Bond eyed him narrowly and then grinned. He put the envelope away in his notecase.

'All right,' he said. 'And thanks. I'll try and spend it where it does most harm. I'm glad to have some working capital. It's certainly good to know it's been provided by the opposition.'

'Fine,' said Halloran; 'and now, if you'll forgive me, I'll just write up my notes for the report I'll have to put in. Have to remember to get a letter of thanks sent to Immigration and Customs and so forth for their co-operation. Routine.'

'Go ahead,' said Bond. He was glad to keep silent and gaze out at his first sight of America since the war. It was no waste of time to start picking up the American idiom again: the advertisements, the new car models and the prices of second-hand ones in the used-car lots; the exotic pungency of the road signs: SOFT SHOULDERS – SHARP CURVES – SQUEEZE AHEAD – SLIPPERY WHEN WET; the standard of driving; the number of women at the wheel, their menfolk docilely beside them; the men's clothes; the way the women were doing their hair; the Civil Defence warnings: IN CASE OF ENEMY ATTACK – KEEP MOVING – GET OFF BRIDGE; the thick rash of television aerials and the impact of TV on hoardings and shop windows; the occasional helicopter; the public appeals for cancer and polio funds: THE MARCH OF DIMES – all the small, fleeting impressions that were as important to his trade as are broken bark and bent twigs to the trapper in the jungle.

The driver chose the Triborough Bridge and they soared across the breath-taking span into the heart of up-town Manhattan, the beautiful prospect of New York hastening towards them until they were down amongst the hooting, teeming, petrol-smelling roots of the stressed-concrete jungle.

Bond turned to his companion.

'I hate to say it,' he said, 'but this must be the fattest atomic-bomb target on the whole face of the globe.'

'Nothing to touch it,' agreed Halloran. 'Keeps me awake nights thinking what would happen.'

They drew up at the best hotel in New York, the St. Regis, at the corner of Fifth Avenue and 55th Street. A saturnine middle-aged man in a dark blue overcoat and black homburg came forward behind the commissionaire. On the sidewalk, Halloran introduced him.

'Mr. Bond, meet Captain Dexter.' He was deferential. 'Can I pass him along to you now, Captain?'

'Sure, sure. Just have his bags sent up. Room 2100. Top floor. I'll go ahead with Mr. Bond and see he has everything he wants.'

Bond turned to say good-bye to Halloran and thank him. For a moment Halloran had his back to him as he said something about Bond's luggage to the commissionaire.

Bond looked past him across 55th Street. His eyes narrowed. A black sedan, a Chevrolet, was pulling sharply out into the thick traffic, right in front of a Checker cab that braked hard, its driver banging his fist down on the horn and holding it there. The sedan kept going, just caught the tail of the green light, and disappeared north up Fifth Avenue.

It was a smart, decisive bit of driving, but what startled Bond was that it had been a negress at the wheel, a fine-looking negress in a black chauffeur's uniform, and through the rear window he had caught a glimpse of the single passenger – a huge grey-black face which had turned slowly towards him and looked directly back at him, Bond was sure of it, as the car accelerated towards the Avenue.

Bond shook Halloran by the hand. Dexter touched his elbow impatiently.

'We'll go straight in and through the lobby to the elevators. Half-right across the lobby. And would you please keep your hat on, Mr. Bond.'

As Bond followed Dexter up the steps into the hotel he reflected that it was almost certainly too late for these precautions. Hardly anywhere in the world will you find a negress driving a car. A negress acting as a chauffeur is still more extraordinary. Barely conceivable even in Harlem, but that was certainly where the car was from.

And the giant shape in the back seat? That grey-black face? Mister Big?

'Hm,' said Bond to himself as he followed the slim back of Captain Dexter into the elevator.

The elevator slowed up for the twenty-first floor.

'We've got a little surprise ready for you, Mr. Bond,' said Captain Dexter, without, Bond thought, much enthusiasm.

They walked down the corridor to the corner room.

The wind sighed outside the passage windows and Bond had a fleeting view of the tops of other skyscrapers and, beyond, the stark fingers of the trees in Central Park. He felt far out of touch with the ground and for a moment a strange feeling of loneliness and empty space gripped his heart.

Dexter unlocked the door of No. 2100 and shut it behind them. They were in a small lighted lobby. They left their hats and coats on a chair and Dexter opened the door in front of them and held it for Bond to go through.

He walked into an attractive sitting-room decorated in Third Avenue 'Empire' – comfortable chairs and a broad sofa in pale yellow silk, a fair copy of an Aubusson on the floor, pale grey walls and ceiling, a bow-fronted French sideboard with bottles and glasses and a plated ice-bucket, a wide window through which the winter sun poured out of a Swiss-clear sky. The central heating was just bearable.

The communicating door with the bedroom opened.

'Arranging the flowers by your bed. Part of the famous CIA "Service With a Smile".' The tall thin young man came forward with a wide grin, his hand outstretched, to where Bond stood rooted with astonishment.

'Felix Leiter! What the hell are you doing here?' Bond grasped the hard hand and shook it warmly. 'And what the hell are you doing in my bedroom, anyway? God! it's good to see you. Why aren't you in Paris? Don't tell me they've put you on this job?'

Leiter examined the Englishman affectionately.

'You've said it. That's just exactly what they have done. What a break! At least, it is for me. CIA thought we did all right together on the Casino job[1] so they hauled me away from the Joint Intelligence chaps in Paris, put me through the works in Washington and here I am. I'm sort of liaison between the Central Intelligence Agency and our friends of the F B I.' He waved towards Captain Dexter, who was watching this unprofessional ebullience without enthusiasm. 'It's their case, of course, at least the American end of it is, but as you know there are some big overseas angles which are C I A's territory, so we're running it joint. Now you're here to handle the Jamaican end for the British and the team's complete. How does it look to you? Sit down and let's have a drink. I ordered lunch directly I got the word you were downstairs and it'll be on its way.' He went over to the sideboard and started mixing a Martini.

'Well, I'm damned,' said Bond. 'Of course that old devil M never told me. He just gives one the facts. Never tells one any good news. I suppose he thinks it might influence one's decision to take a case or not. Anyway, it's grand.'

Bond suddenly felt the silence of Captain Dexter. He turned to him.

'I shall be very glad to be under your orders here, Captain,' he said tactfully. 'As I understand it, the case breaks pretty neatly into two halves. The first half lies wholly on American territory. Your jurisdiction, of course. Then it looks as if we shall have to follow it into the Caribbean. Jamaica. And I understand I am to take over outside United States territorial waters. Felix here will marry up the two halves so far as your government is concerned. I shall report to London through C I A while I'm here, and

[1] This terrifying gambling case is described in the author's *Casino Royale*.

direct to London, keeping CIA informed, when I move to the Caribbean. Is that how you see it?'

Dexter smiled thinly. 'That's just about it, Mr. Bond. Mr. Hoover instructs me to say that he's very pleased to have you along. As our guest,' he added. 'Naturally we are not in any way concerned with the British end of the case and we're very happy that CIA will be handling that with you and your people in London. Guess everything should go fine. Here's luck,' and he lifted the cocktail Leiter had put into his hand.

They drank the cold hard drink appreciatively, Leiter with a faintly quizzical expression on his hawk-like face.

There was a knock on the door. Leiter opened it to let in the bellboy with Bond's suitcases. He was followed by two waiters pushing trolleys loaded with covered dishes, cutlery and snow-white linen, which they proceeded to lay out on a folding table.

'Soft-shell crabs with tartare sauce, flat beef Hamburgers, medium-rare, from the charcoal grill, french-fried potatoes, broccoli, mixed salad with thousand-island dressing, ice-cream with melted butterscotch and as good a Liebfraumilch as you can get in America. Okay?'

'It sounds fine,' said Bond with a mental reservation about the melted butterscotch.

They sat down and ate steadily through each delicious course of American cooking at its rare best.

They said little, and it was only when the coffee had been brought and the table cleared away that Captain Dexter took the fifty-cent cigar from his mouth and cleared his throat decisively.

'Mr. Bond,' he said, 'now perhaps you would tell us what you know about this case.'

Bond slit open a fresh pack of King Size Chesterfields with his thumb-nail and, as he settled back in his comfortable chair in the warm luxurious room, his mind went back two weeks to the bitter raw day in early January when he had walked out of his Chelsea flat into the dreary half-light of a London fog.

CHAPTER II

INTERVIEW WITH M

THE grey Bentley convertible, the 1933 4½-litre with the Amherst-Villiers supercharger, had been brought round a few minutes earlier from the garage where he kept it and the engine had kicked directly he pressed the self-starter. He had turned on the twin fog lights and had driven gingerly along King's Road and then up Sloane Street into Hyde Park.

M's Chief of Staff had telephoned at midnight to say that M wanted to see Bond at nine the next morning. 'Bit early in the day,' he had apologized, 'but he seems to want some action from somebody. Been brooding for weeks. Suppose he's made up his mind at last.'

'Any line you can give me over the telephone?'

'A for Apple and C for Charlie,' said the Chief of Staff, and rang off.

That meant that the case concerned Stations A and C, the sections of the Secret Service dealing respectively with the United States and the Caribbean. Bond had worked for a time under Station A during the war, but he knew little of C or its problems.

As he crawled beside the kerb up through Hyde Park, the slow drumbeat of his two-inch exhaust keeping him company, he felt excited at the prospect of his interview with M, the remarkable man who was then, and still is, head of the Secret Service. He had not looked into those cold, shrewd eyes since the end of the summer. On that occasion M had been pleased.

'Take some leave,' he had said. 'Plenty of leave. Then get some new skin grafted over the back of that hand. "Q" will put you on to the best man and fix a date. Can't have you going round with that damn Russian trade-mark on you. See if I can find you a good target when you've got cleaned up. Good luck.'

The hand had been fixed, painlessly but slowly. The thin scars, the single Russian letter which stands for SCH, the first letter of *Spion*, a spy, had been removed and as Bond thought of the man with the stiletto who had cut them he clenched his hands on the wheel.

What was happening to the brilliant organization of which the man with the knife had been an agent, the Soviet organ of vengeance, SMERSH, short for *Smyert Spionam* – Death to Spies? Was it still as powerful, still as efficient? Who controlled it now that Beria was gone? After the great gambling case in which he had been involved at Royale-les-Eaux, Bond had sworn to get back at them. He had told M as much at that last interview. Was this appointment with M to start him on his trail of revenge?

Bond's eyes narrowed as he gazed into the murk of Regents Park and his face in the faint dashlight was cruel and hard.

He drew up in the mews behind the gaunt high building, handed his car over to one of the plain-clothes drivers from the pool and walked round to the main entrance. He was taken up in the lift to the top floor and along the thickly carpeted corridor he knew so well to the door next to M's. The Chief of Staff was waiting for him and at once spoke to M on the intercom.

'007's here now, Sir.'

'Send him in.'

The desirable Miss Moneypenny, M's all-powerful private secretary, gave him an encouraging smile and he walked through the double doors. At once the green light came on, high on the wall in the room he had left. M was not to be disturbed as long as it burned.

A reading lamp with a green glass shade made a pool of light across the red leather top of the broad desk. The rest of the room was darkened by the fog outside the windows.

'Morning, 007. Let's have a look at the hand. Not a bad job. Where did they take the skin from?'

'High up on the forearm, Sir.'

'Hm. Hairs'll grow a bit thick. Crooked too. However. Can't be helped. Looks all right for the time being. Sit down.'

Bond walked round to the single chair which faced M across the desk. The grey eyes looked at him, through him.

'Had a good rest?'

'Yes thank you, Sir.'

'Ever seen one of these?' M abruptly fished something out of his waistcoat pocket. He tossed it half way across the desk towards Bond. It fell with a faint clang on the red leather and lay, gleaming richly, an inch-wide, hammered gold coin.

Bond picked it up, turned it over, weighed it in his hand.

'No, Sir. Worth about five pounds, perhaps.'

'Fifteen to a collector. It's a Rose Noble of Edward IV.'

M fished again in his waistcoat pocket and tossed more magnificent gold coins on to the table in front of Bond. As he did so, he glanced at each one and identified it.

'Double Excellente, Spanish, Ferdinand and Isabella,

1510; Ecu au Soleil, French, Charles IX, 1574; Double Ecu d'or, French, Henry IV, 1600; Double Ducat, Spanish, Philip II, 1560; Ryder, Dutch, Charles d'Egmond, 1538; Quadruple, Genoa, 1617; Double louis, à la mèche courte, French, Louis XIV, 1644. Worth a lot of money melted down. Much more to collectors, ten to twenty pounds each. Notice anything common to them all?'

Bond reflected. 'No, Sir.'

'All minted before 1650. Bloody Morgan, the pirate, was Governor and Commander-in-Chief of Jamaica from 1675 to 1688. The English coin is the joker in the pack. Probably shipped out to pay the Jamaica garrison. But for that and the dates, these could have come from any other treasure-trove put together by the great pirates – L'Ollonais, Pierre le Grand, Sharp, Sawkins, Blackbeard. As it is, and both Spinks and the British Museum agree, this is almost certainly part of Bloody Morgan's treasure.'

M paused to fill his pipe and light it. He didn't invite Bond to smoke and Bond would not have thought of doing so uninvited.

'And the hell of a treasure it must be. So far nearly a thousand of these and similar coins have turned up in the United States in the last few months. And if the Special Branch of the Treasury, and the F B I, have traced a thousand, how many more have been melted down or disappeared into private collections? And they keep on coming in, turning up in banks, bullion merchants, curio shops, but mostly pawnbrokers of course. The F B I are in a proper fix. If they put these on the police notices of stolen property they know the source will dry up. They'd be melted down into gold bars and channelled straight into the black bullion market. Have to sacrifice the rarity value of the coins, but the gold would go straight underground. As it is, someone's using the negroes – porters, sleeping-car attendants, truck-drivers – and getting the money well spread over the States. Quite innocent people. Here's a typical case.' M opened a brown folder bearing the Top Secret red star and selected a single sheet of paper. Through the reverse side, as M held it up, Bond could see the engraved heading : 'Department of Justice. Federal Bureau of Investigations.' M read from it :

'Zachary Smith, 35, Negro, Member of the Sleeping Car Porters Brotherhood, address 90b West 126th Street, New York City.' (M looked up : 'Harlem,' he said.) 'Subject was identified by Arthur Fein of Fein Jewels Inc., 870 Lenox Avenue, as having offered for sale on November 21st last four gold coins of the sixteenth and seventeenth century (details attached). Fein offered a hundred dollars which was accepted. Interrogated later, Smith said they had been sold to him in Seventh Heaven Bar-B-Q (a well-known Harlem bar) for twenty dollars each by a negro he had never seen before or since. Vendor had said they were worth fifty dollars each at Tiffany's, but that he, the vendor, wanted ready cash and Tiffany's was too far anyway. Smith bought one for twenty dollars and on finding that a neighbouring pawnbroker would offer him twenty-five dollars for it, returned to the bar and purchased the remaining three for sixty dollars. The next morning he took them to Fein's. Subject has no criminal record.'

M returned the paper to the brown folder.

'That's typical,' he said. 'Several times they've caught up with the next link, the middle man who bought them a bit cheaper and they find that he bought a handful, in one case a hundred of them, from some man who presumably got them cheaper still. All these larger transactions have taken place in Harlem or Florida. Always the next man in the link was an unknown negro, in all cases a white-collar man, prosperous, educated, who said he guessed they were treasure-trove, Blackbeard's treasure.

'This Blackbeard story would stand up to most investigations,' continued M, 'because there is reason to believe that part of his hoard was dug up around Christmas Day, 1928, at a place called Plum Point. It's a narrow neck of land in Beaufort County, North Carolina, where a stream called Bath Creek flows into the Pamlico River. Don't think I'm an expert,' he smiled, 'you can read all about this in the dossier. So, in theory, it would be quite reasonable for those lucky treasure-hunters to have hidden the loot until everyone had forgotten the story and then thrown it fast on the market. Or else they could have sold it en bloc at the time, or later, and the purchaser has just decided to cash in. Anyway it's a good enough cover except on two counts.'

M paused and relit his pipe.

'Firstly, Blackbeard operated from about 1690 to 1710 and it's improbable that none of his coin should have been minted later than 1650. Also, as I said before, it's very unlikely that his treasure would contain Edward IV Rose Nobles, since there's no record of an English treasure-ship being captured on its way to Jamaica. The Brethren of the Coast wouldn't take them on. Too heavily escorted. There were much easier pickings if you were sailing in those days "on the plundering account" as they called it.

'Secondly,' and M looked at the ceiling and then back at Bond, 'I know where the treasure is. At least I'm pretty sure I do. And it's not in America. It's in Jamaica, and it is Bloody Morgan's, and I guess it's one of the most valuable treasure-troves in history.'

'Good Lord,' said Bond. 'How . . . where do we come into it?"

M held up his hand. 'You'll find all the details in here,' he let his hand come down on the brown folder. 'Briefly, Station C has been interested in a Diesel yacht, the *Secatur*, which has been running from a small island on the North Coast of Jamaica through the Florida Keys into the Gulf of Mexico, to a place called St. Petersburg. Sort of pleasure resort, near Tampa. West Coast of Florida. With the help of the FBI we've traced the ownership of this boat and of the island to a man called Mr. Big, a negro gangster. Lives in Harlem. Ever heard of him?'

'No,' said Bond.

'And curiously enough,' M's voice was softer and quieter, 'a twenty-dollar bill which one of these casual negroes had paid for a gold coin and whose number he had noted for Peaka Peow, the Numbers game, was paid out by one of Mr. Big's lieutenants. And it was paid,' M pointed the stem of his pipe at Bond, 'for information received, to an FBI double-agent who is a member of the Communist Party.'

Bond whistled softly.

'In short,' continued M, 'we suspect that this Jamaican treasure is being used to finance the Soviet espionage system, or an important part of it, in America. And our suspicion becomes a certainty when I tell you who this Mr. Big is.'

Bond waited, his eyes fixed on M's.

'Mr. Big,' said M, weighing his words, 'is probably the most powerful negro criminal in the world. He is,' and he enumerated carefully, 'the head of the Black Widow Voodoo cult and believed by that cult to be the Baron Samedi himself. (You'll find all about that here,' he tapped the folder, 'and it'll frighten the daylights out of you.) He is also a Soviet agent. And finally he is, and this will particularly interest you, Bond, a known member of SMERSH.'

'Yes,' said Bond slowly, 'I see now.'

'Quite a case,' said M, looking keenly at him. 'And quite a man, this Mr. Big.'

'I don't think I've ever heard of a great negro criminal before,' said Bond, 'Chinamen, of course, the men behind the opium trade. There've been some big-time Japs, mostly in pearls and drugs. Plenty of negroes mixed up in diamonds and gold in Africa, but always in a small way. They don't seem to take to big business. Pretty law-abiding chaps I should have thought except when they've drunk too much.'

'Our man's a bit of an exception,' said M. 'He's not pure negro. Born in Haiti. Good dose of French blood. Trained in Moscow, too, as you'll see from the file. And the negro races are just beginning to throw up geniuses in all the professions – scientists, doctors, writers. It's about time they turned out a great criminal. After all, there are 250,000,000 of them in the world. Nearly a third of the white population. They've got plenty of brains and ability and guts. And now Moscow's taught one of them the technique.'

'I'd like to meet him,' said Bond. Then he added, mildly, 'I'd like to meet any member of SMERSH.'

'All right then, Bond. Take it away.' M handed him the thick brown folder. 'Talk it over with Plender and Damon. Be ready to start in a week. It's a joint CIA and FBI job. For God's sake don't step on the FBI's toes. Covered with corns. Good luck.'

Bond had gone straight down to Commander Damon, Head of Station A, an alert Canadian who controlled the link with the Central Intelligence Agency, America's Secret Service.

Damon looked up from his desk. 'I see you've bought it,' he said, looking at the folder. 'Thought you would. Sit down,' he waved to an armchair beside the electric fire. 'When you've waded through it all, I'll fill in the gaps.'

CHAPTER III

A VISITING-CARD

AND now it was ten days later and the talk with Dexter and Leiter had not added much, reflected Bond as he awoke slowly and luxuriously in his bedroom at the St. Regis the morning after his arrival in New York.

Dexter had had plenty of detail on Mr. Big, but nothing that threw any new light on the case. Mr. Big was forty-five years old, born in Haiti, half negro and half French. Because of the initial letters of his fanciful name, Buonaparte Ignace Gallia, and because of his huge height and bulk, he came to be called, even as a youth, 'Big Boy' or just 'Big'. Later this became 'The Big Man' or 'Mr. Big', and his real names lingered only on a parish register in Haiti and on his dossier with the F B I. He had no known vices except women, whom he consumed in quantities. He didn't drink or smoke and his only Achilles heel appeared to be a chronic heart disease which had, in recent years, imparted a greyish tinge to his skin.

The Big Boy had been initiated into Voodoo as a child, earned his living as a truck-driver in Port au Prince, then emigrated to America and worked successfully for a hi-jacking team in the Legs Diamond gang. With the end of Prohibition he had moved to Harlem and bought half-shares in a small nightclub and a string of coloured call-girls. His partner was found in a barrel of cement in the Harlem River in 1938 and Mr. Big automatically became sole proprietor of the business. He was called up in 1943 and, because of his excellent French, came to the notice of the Office of Strategic Services, the wartime secret service of America, who trained him with great thoroughness and put him into Marseilles as an agent against the Pétain collaborationists. He merged easily with African negro dock-hands, and worked well, providing good and accurate naval intelligence. He operated closely with a Soviet spy who was doing a similar job for the Russians. At the end of the war he was demobilized in France (and decorated by the Americans and the French) and then he disappeared for five years, probably to Moscow. He returned to Harlem in 1950 and soon came to the notice of the FBI as a suspected Soviet agent. But he never incriminated himself or fell into any of the traps laid by the FBI. He bought up three nightclubs and a prosperous chain of Harlem brothels. He seemed to have unlimited funds and paid all his lieutenants a flat rate of twenty thousand dollars a year. Accordingly, and as a result of weeding by murder, he was expertly and diligently served. He was known to have originated an underground Voodoo temple in Harlem and to have established a link between it and the main cult in Haiti. The rumour had started that he was the Zombie or living corpse of Baron Samedi himself, the dreaded Prince of Darkness, and he fostered the story so that now it was accepted through all the lower strata of the negro world. As a result, he commanded real fear, strongly substantiated by the immediate and often mysterious deaths of anyone who crossed him or disobeyed his orders.

Bond had questioned Dexter and Leiter very closely on the evidence connecting the giant negro with SMERSH. It certainly seemed conclusive.

In 1951, by the promise of one million dollars in gold

and a safe refuge after six months' work for them, the FBI had at last persuaded a known Soviet agent of the MWD to turn double. All went well for a month and the results exceeded the highest expectations. The Russian spy held the appointment of an economic expert on the Soviet delegation to the United Nations. One Saturday, he had gone to take the subway to Pennsylvania Station en route for the Soviet week-end rest camp at Glen Cove, the former Morgan estate on Long Island.

A huge negro, positively identified from photographs as The Big Man, had stood beside him on the platform as the train came in and was seen walking towards the exit even before the first coach had come to a standstill over the bloody vestiges of the Russian. He had not been seen to push the man, but in the crowd it would not have been difficult. Spectators said it could not have been suicide. The man screamed horribly as he fell and he had had (melancholy touch!) a bag of golf clubs over his shoulder. The Big Man, of course, had had an alibi as solid as Fort Knox. He had been held and questioned, but was quickly sprung by the best lawyer in Harlem.

The evidence was good enough for Bond. He was just the man for SMERSH, with just the training. A real, hard weapon of fear and death. And what a brilliant set-up for dealing with the smaller fry of the negro underworld and for keeping a coloured information network well up to the mark! – the fear of Voodoo and the supernatural, still deeply, primevally ingrained in the negro subconscious! And what genius to have, as a beginning, the whole transport system of America under surveillance, the trains, the porters, the truck-drivers, the stevedores! To have at his disposal a host of key men who would have no idea that the questions they answered had been asked by Russia. Small-time professional men who, if they thought at all, would guess that the information on freights and schedules was being sold to rival transport concerns.

Not for the first time, Bond felt his spine crawl at the cold, brilliant efficiency of the Soviet machine, and at the fear of death and torture which made it work and of which the supreme engine was SMERSH – SMERSH, the very whisper of death.

Now, in his bedroom at the St. Regis, Bond shook away his thoughts and jumped impatiently out of bed. Well, there was one of them at hand, ready for the crushing. At Royale he had only caught a glimpse of his man. This time it would be face to face. Big Man? Then let it be a giant, a homeric slaying.

Bond walked over to the window and pulled back the curtains. His room faced north, towards Harlem. Bond gazed for a moment towards the northern horizon, where another man would be in his bedroom asleep, or perhaps awake and thinking conceivably of him, Bond, whom he had seen with Dexter on the steps of the hotel. Bond looked at the beautiful day and smiled. And no man, not even Mr. Big, would have liked the expression on his face.

Bond shrugged his shoulders and walked quickly to the telephone.

'St. Regis Hotel. Good morning,' said a voice.

'Room Service, please,' said Bond.

'Room Service? I'd like to order breakfast. Half a pint of orange juice, three eggs, lightly scrambled, with bacon, a double portion of café Espresso with cream. Toast. Marmalade. Got it?'

The order was repeated back to him. Bond walked out

into the lobby and picked up the five pounds' weight of newspapers which had been placed quietly inside the door earlier in the morning. There was also a pile of parcels on the hall table which Bond disregarded.

The afternoon before he had had to submit to a certain degree of Americanization at the hands of the F B I. A tailor had come and measured him for two single-breasted suits in dark blue light-weight worsted (Bond had firmly refused anything more dashing) and a haberdasher had brought chilly white nylon shirts with long points to the collars. He had had to accept half a dozen unusually patterned foulard ties, dark socks with fancy clocks, two or three 'display kerchiefs' for his breast pocket, nylon vests and pants (called T-shirts and shorts), a comfortable light-weight camel-hair overcoat with over-buttressed shoulders, a plain grey snap-brim Fedora with a thin black ribbon and two pairs of hand-stitched and very comfortable black Moccasin 'casuals'.

He also acquired a 'Swank' tie-clip in the shape of a whip, an alligator-skin billfold from Mark Cross, a plain Zippo lighter, a plastic 'Travel-Pak' containing razor, hairbrush and toothbrush, a pair of horn-rimmed glasses with plain lenses, various other oddments and, finally, a light-weight Hartmann 'Skymate' suitcase to contain all these things.

He was allowed to retain his own Beretta .25 with the skeleton grip and the chamois leather shoulder-holster, but all his other possessions were to be collected at midday and forwarded down to Jamaica to await him.

He was given a military haircut and was told that he was a New Englander from Boston and that he was on holiday from his job with the London office of the Guaranty Trust Company. He was reminded to ask for the 'check' rather than the 'bill', to say 'cab' instead of 'taxi' and (this from

Leiter) to avoid words of more than two syllables. ('You can get through any American conversation,' advised Leiter, 'with "Yeah", "Nope" and "Sure".') The English word to be avoided at all costs, added Leiter, was 'Ectually'. Bond had said that this word was not part of his vocabulary.

Bond looked grimly at the pile of parcels which contained his new identity, stripped off his pyjamas for the last time ('We mostly sleep in the raw in America, Mr. Bond') and gave himself a sizzling cold shower. As he shaved he examined his face in the glass. The thick comma of black hair above his right eyebrow had lost some of its tail and his hair was trimmed close across the temples. Nothing could be done about the thin vertical scar down his right cheek, although the FBI had experimented with 'Cover-Mark', or about the coldness and hint of anger in his grey-blue eyes, but there was the mixed blood of America in the black hair and high cheekbones and Bond thought he might get by – except, perhaps, with women.

Naked, Bond walked out into the lobby and tore open some of the packages. Later, in white shirt and dark blue trousers, he went into the sitting-room, pulled a chair up to the writing-desk near the window and opened *The Travellers Tree*, by Patrick Leigh Fermor.[1]

This extraordinary book had been recommended to him by M.

'It's by a chap who knows what he's talking about,' he said, 'and don't forget that he was writing about what was happening in Haiti in 1950. This isn't medieval black-magic stuff. It's being practised every day.'

Bond was half way through the section on Haiti.

[1] This, one of the great travel books, is published by John Murray at 25s.

> The next step [he read] is the invocation of evil denizens of the Voodoo pantheon – such as Don Pedro, Kitta, Mondongue, Bakalou and Zandor – for harmful purposes, for the reputed practice (which is of Congolese origin) of turning people into zombies in order to use them as slaves, the casting of maleficent spells, and the destruction of enemies. The effects of the spell, of which the outward form may be an image of the intended victim, a miniature coffin or a toad, are frequently stiffened by the separate use of poison. Father Cosme enlarged on the superstitions that maintain that men with certain powers change themselves into snakes; on the 'Loups-Garoups' that fly at night in the form of vampire bats and suck the blood of children; on men who reduce themselves to infinitesimal size and roll about the countryside in calabashes. What sounded far more sinister were a number of mystico-criminal secret societies of wizards, with nightmarish titles – 'les Mackanda', named after the poison campaign of the Haitian hero; 'les Zobop', who were also robbers; the 'Mazanxa', the 'Caporelata' and the 'Vlinbindingue'. These, he said, were the mysterious groups whose gods demand – instead of a cock, a pigeon, a goat, a dog, or a pig, as in the normal rites of Voodoo – the sacrifice of a 'cabrit sans cornes'. This hornless goat, of course, means a human being. . . .

Bond turned over the pages, occasional passages combining to form an extraordinary picture in his mind of a dark religion and its terrible rites.

> . . . Slowly, out of the turmoil and the smoke and the shattering noise of the drums, which, for a time, drove

everything except their impact from the mind, the details began to detach themselves. . . .

. . . Backwards and forwards, very slowly, the dancers shuffled, and at each step their chins shot out and their buttocks jerked upwards, while their shoulders shook in double time. Their eyes were half closed and from their mouths came again and again the same incomprehensible words, the same short line of chanted song, repeated after each iteration, half an octave lower. At a change in the beat of the drums, they straightened their bodies, and flinging their arms in the air while their eyes rolled upwards, spun round and round. . . .

. . . At the edge of the crowd we came upon a little hut, scarcely larger than a dog kennel: 'Le caye Zombi'. The beam of a torch revealed a black cross inside and some rags and chains and shackles and whips: adjuncts used at the Ghédé ceremonies, which Haitian ethnologists connect with the rejuvenation rites of Osiris recorded in the Book of the Dead. A fire was burning, in which two sabres and a large pair of pincers were standing, their lower parts red with the heat: 'le Feu Marinette', dedicated to a goddess who is the evil obverse of the bland and amorous Maîtresse Erzulie Fréda Dahomin, the Goddess of Love.

Beyond, with its base held fast in a socket of stone, stood a large black wooden cross. A white death's head was painted near the base, and over the crossbar were pulled the sleeves of a very old morning coat. Here also rested the brim of a battered bowler hat, through the torn crown of which the top of the cross projected. This totem, with which every peristyle must be equipped, is not a lampoon of the central event of the

Christian faith, but represents the God of the Cemeteries and the Chief of the Legion of the Dead, Baron Samedi. The Baron is paramount in all matters immediately beyond the tomb. He is Cerberus and Charon as well as Aeacus, Rhadamanthus and Pluto. . .

. . . The drums changed and the Houngenikon came dancing on to the floor, holding a vessel filled with some burning liquid from which sprang blue and yellow flames. As he circled the pillar and spilt three flaming libations, his steps began to falter. Then, lurching backwards with the same symptoms of delirium that had manifested themselves in his forerunner, he flung down the whole blazing mass. The houncis caught him as he reeled, and removed his sandals and rolled his trousers up, while the kerchief fell from his head and laid bare his young woolly skull. The other houncis knelt to put their hands in the flaming mud, and rub it over their hands and elbows and faces. The Houngan's bell and 'açon' rattled officiously and the young priest was left by himself, reeling and colliding against the pillar, helplessly catapulting across the floor, and falling among the drums. His eyes were shut, his forehead screwed up and his chin hung loose. Then, as though an invisible fist had dealt him a heavy blow, he fell to the ground and lay there, with his head stretching backwards in a rictus of anguish until the tendons of his neck and shoulders projected like roots. One hand clutched at the other elbow behind his hollowed back as though he were striving to break his own arm, and his whole body, from which the sweat was streaming, trembled and shuddered like a dog in a dream. Only the whites of his eyes were visible as, although his eye-sockets were now wide open, the pupils had vanished under the lids. Foam collected on his lips. . . .

. . . Now the Houngan, dancing a slow step and brandishing a cutlass, advanced from the fireside, flinging the weapon again and again into the air, and catching it by the hilt. In a few minutes he was holding it by the blunted end of the blade. Dancing slowly towards him, the Houngenikon reached out and grasped the hilt. The priest retired, and the young man, twirling and leaping, spun from side to side of the 'tonnelle'. The ring of spectators rocked backwards as he bore down upon them whirling the blade over his head, with the gaps in his bared teeth lending to his mandril face a still more feral aspect. The 'tonnelle' was filled for a few seconds with genuine and unmitigated terror. The singing had turned to a universal howl and the drummers, rolling and lolling with the furious and invisible motion of their hands, were lost in a transport of noise.

Flinging back his head, the novice drove the blunt end of the cutlass into his stomach. His knees sagged, and his head fell forward. . . .

There came a knock on the door and a waiter came in with breakfast. Bond was glad to put the dreadful tale aside and re-enter the world of normality. But it took him minutes to forget the atmosphere, heavy with terror and the occult, that had surrounded him as he read.

With breakfast came another parcel, about a foot square, expensive-looking, which Bond told the waiter to put on the sideboard. Some afterthought of Leiter's, he supposed. He ate his breakfast with enjoyment. Between mouthfuls he looked out of the wide window and reflected on what he had just read.

It was only when he had swallowed his last mouthful of coffee and had lit his first cigarette of the day that he suddenly became aware of the tiny noise in the room behind him.

It was a soft, muffled ticking, unhurried, metallic. And it came from the direction of the sideboard.

'Tick-tock . . . tick-tock . . . tick-tock.'

Without a moment's hesitation, without caring that he looked a fool, he dived to the floor behind his armchair and crouched, all his senses focused on the noise from the square parcel. 'Steady,' he said to himself. 'Don't be an idiot. It's just a clock.' But why a clock? Why should he be given a clock? Who by?

'Tick-tock . . . tick-tock . . . tick-tock.'

It had become a huge noise against the silence of the room. It seemed to be keeping time with the thumping of Bond's heart. 'Don't be ridiculous. That Voodoo stuff of Leigh Fermor's has put your nerves on edge. Those drums. . . .'

'Tick-tock . . . tick-tock . . . tick – '

And then, suddenly, the alarm went off with a deep, melodious, urgent summons.

'Tongtongtongtongtongtong. . . .'

Bond's muscles relaxed. His cigarette was burning a hole in the carpet. He picked it up and put it in his mouth. Bombs in alarm clocks go off when the hammer first comes down on the alarm. The hammer hits a pin in a detonator, the detonator fires the explosive and WHAM. . . .

Bond raised his head above the back of the chair and watched the parcel.

'Tongtongtongtongtong. . . .'

The muffled gonging went on for half a minute, then it started to slow down.

'tong . . tong . . . tong . . . . tong . . . . . tong . . . .

'C-R-A-C-K. . . .'

It was not louder than a 12-bore cartridge, but in the confined space it was an impressive explosion.

The parcel, in tatters, had fallen to the ground. The glasses and bottles on the sideboard were smashed and there was a black smudge of smoke on the grey wall behind them. Some pieces of glass tinkled on to the floor. There was a strong smell of gunpowder in the room.

Bond got slowly to his feet. He went to the window and opened it. Then he dialled Dexter's number. He spoke levelly.

'Pineapple. . . . No, a small one . . . only some glasses . . . okay, thanks . . . of course not . . . 'bye.'

He skirted the debris, walked through the small lobby to the door leading into the passage, opened it, hung the DON'T DISTURB sign outside, locked it, and went through into his bedroom.

By the time he had finished dressing there was a knock on the door.

'Who is it?" he called.

'Okay. Dexter.'

Dexter hustled in, followed by a sallow young man with a black box under his arm.

'Trippe, from Sabotage,' announced Dexter.

They shook hands and the young man at once went on his knees beside the charred remnants of the parcel.

He opened his box and took out some rubber gloves and a handful of dentist's forceps. With his tools he painstakingly extracted small bits of metal and glass from the charred parcel and laid them out on a broad sheet of blotting paper from the writing-desk.

While he worked, he asked Bond what had happened.

'About a half-minute alarm? I see. Hullo, what's this?' He delicately extracted a small aluminium container such as is used for exposed film. He put it aside.

After a few minutes he sat up on his haunches.

'Half-minute acid capsule,' he announced. 'Broken by the first hammer-stroke of the alarm. Acid eats through thin copper wire. Thirty seconds later wire breaks, releases plunger on to cap of this.' He held up the base of a cartridge. '4-bore elephant gun. Black powder. Blank. No shot. Lucky it wasn't a grenade. Plenty of room in the parcel. You'd have been damaged. Now let's have a look at this.' He picked up the aluminium cylinder, unscrewed it, extracted a small roll of paper, and unravelled it with his forceps.

He carefully flattened it out on the carpet, holding its corners down with four tools from his black box. It contained three typewritten sentences. Bond and Dexter bent forward.

'THE HEART OF THIS CLOCK HAS STOPPED TICKING,' they read. 'THE BEATS OF YOUR OWN HEART ARE NUMBERED. I KNOW THAT NUMBER AND I HAVE STARTED TO COUNT.'

The message was signed '1234567 . . . ?'

They stood up.

'Hm,' said Bond. 'Bogeyman stuff.'

'But how the hell did he know you were here?' asked Dexter.

Bond told him of the black sedan on 55th Street.

'But the point is,' said Bond, 'how did he know what I was here *for*? Shows he's got Washington pretty well sewn up. Must be a leak the size of the Grand Canyon somewhere.'

'Why should it be Washington?' asked Dexter testily. 'Anyway,' he controlled himself with a forced laugh, 'Hell and damnation. Have to make a report to Headquarters on this. So long, Mr. Bond. Glad you came to no harm.'

'Thanks,' said Bond. 'It was just a visiting-card. I must return the compliment.'

CHAPTER IV

THE BIG SWITCHBOARD

WHEN Dexter and his colleague had gone, taking the remains of the bomb with them, Bond took a damp towel and rubbed the smoke-mark off the wall. Then he rang for the waiter and, without explanation, told him to put the broken glass on his check and clear away the breakfast things. Then he took his hat and coat and went out on the street.

He spent the morning on Fifth Avenue and on Broadway, wandering aimlessly, gazing into the shop windows and watching the passing crowds. He gradually assimilated the casual gait and manners of a visitor from out of town, and when he tested himself out in a few shops and asked the way of several people he found that nobody looked at him twice.

He had a typical American meal at an eating house called 'Gloryfried Ham-N-Eggs' ('The Eggs We Serve Tomorrow Are Still in the Hens') on Lexington Avenue and then took a cab downtown to police headquarters, where he was due to meet Leiter and Dexter at 2.30.

A Lieutenant Binswanger of Homicide, a suspicious and crusty officer in his late forties, announced that Commissioner Monahan had said that they were to have complete co-operation from the Police Department. What could he do for them? They examined Mr. Big's police record, which more or less duplicated Dexter's information, and they were shown the records and photographs of most of his known associates.

They went over the reports of the US Coastguard Service on the comings and goings of the yacht *Secatur* and also the comments of the US Customs Service, who had kept a close watch on the boat each time she had docked at St. Petersburg.

These confirmed that the yacht had put in at irregular intervals over the previous six months and that she always tied up in the Port of St. Petersburg at the wharf of the 'Ourobouros Worm and Bait Shippers Inc.', an apparently innocent concern whose main business was to sell live bait to fishing clubs throughout Florida, the Gulf of Mexico and further afield. The company also had a profitable side-line in sea-shells and coral for interior decoration, and a further sideline in tropical aquarium fish—particularly rare poisonous species for the research departments of medical and chemical foundations.

According to the proprietor, a Greek sponge-fisher from the neighbouring Tarpon Springs, the *Secatur* did big business with his company, bringing in cargoes of queen conchs and other shells from Jamaica and also highly prized varieties of tropical fish. These were purchased by Ourobouros Inc., stored in their warehouse and sold in bulk to wholesalers and retailers up and down the coast. The name of the Greek was Papagos. No criminal record.

The FBI, with the help of Naval Intelligence, had tried listening in to the *Secatur*'s wireless. But she kept off the air except for short messages before she sailed from Cuba or Jamaica and then transmitted *en clair* in a language which was unknown and completely indecipherable. The last notation on the file was to the effect that the operator was talking in 'Language', the secret Voodoo speech only used by initiates, and that every effort would be made to hire an expert from Haiti before the next sailing.

'More gold been turning up lately,' announced Lieutenant Binswanger as they walked back to his office from the Identification Bureau across the street. ''Bout a hundred coins a week in Harlem and New York alone. Want us to do anything about it? If you're right and these are Commie funds, they must be pulling it in pretty fast while we sit on our asses doin' nothing.'

'Chief says to lay off,' said Dexter. 'Hope we'll see some action before long.'

'Well, the case is all yours,' said Binswanger grudgingly. 'But the Commissioner sure don't like having this bastard crappin' away on his own front doorstep while Mr. Hoover sits down in Washington well to leeward of the stink. Why don't we pull him in on tax evasion or misuse of the mails or parkin' in front of a hydrant or sumpn? Take him down to the Tombs and give 'em the works? If the Feds won't do it, we'd be glad to oblige.'

'D'you want a race riot?' objected Dexter sourly. 'There's nothing against him and you know it, and we know it. If he wasn't sprung in half an hour by that black mouthpiece of his, those Voodoo drums would start beating from here to the Deep South. When they're full of that stuff we all know what happens. Remember '35 and '43? You'd have to call out the Militia. We didn't ask for the case. The President gave it us and we've got to stick with it.'

They were back in Binswanger's drab office. They picked up their coats and hats.

'Anyway, thanks for the help, Lootenant,' said Dexter

with forced cordiality, as they made their farewells. 'Been most valuable.'

'You're welcome,' said Binswanger stonily. 'Elevator's to your right.' He closed the door firmly behind them.

Leiter winked at Bond behind Dexter's back. They rode down to the main entrance on Centre Street in silence.

On the sidewalk, Dexter turned to them.

'Had some instructions from Washington this morning,' he said unemotionally. 'Seems I'm to look after the Harlem end, and you two are to go down to St. Petersburg tomorrow. Leiter's to find out what he can there and then move right on to Jamaica with you, Mr. Bond. That is,' he added, 'if you'd care to have him along. It's your territory.'

'Of course,' said Bond. 'I was going to ask if he could come anyway.'

'Fine,' said Dexter. 'Then I'll tell Washington everything's fixed. Anything else I can do for you? All communications with FBI, Washington, of course. Leiter's got the names of our men in Florida, knows the Signals routine and so forth.'

'If Leiter's interested and if you don't mind,' said Bond, 'I'd like very much to get up to Harlem this evening and have a look round. Might help to have some idea of what it looks like in Mr. Big's back yard.'

Dexter reflected.

'Okay,' he said finally. 'Probably no harm. But don't show yourselves too much. And don't get hurt,' he added. 'There's no one to help you up there. And don't go stirring up a lot of trouble for us. This case isn't ripe yet. Until it is, our policy with Mr. Big is "live and let live".'

Bond looked quizzically at Captain Dexter.

'In my job,' he said, 'when I come up against a man like this one, I have another motto. It's "live and let die".'

Dexter shrugged his shoulders. 'Maybe,' he said, 'but you're under my orders here, Mr. Bond, and I'd be glad if you'd accept them.'

'Of course,' said Bond, 'and thanks for all your help. Hope you have luck with your end of the job.'

Dexter flagged a cab. They shook hands.

' 'Bye, fellers,' said Dexter briefly. 'Stay alive.' His cab pulled out into the uptown traffic.

Bond and Leiter smiled at each other.

'Able guy, I should say,' said Bond.

'They're all that in his show,' said Leiter. 'Bit inclined to be stuffed shirts. Very touchy about their rights. Always bickering with us or with the police. But I guess you have much the same problem in England.'

'Oh of course,' said Bond. 'We're always rubbing MI 5 up the wrong way. And they're always stepping on the corns of the Special Branch. Scotland Yard,' he explained. 'Well, how about going up to Harlem tonight?'

'Suits me,' said Leiter. 'I'll drop you at the St. Regis and pick you up again about six-thirty. Meet you in the King Cole Bar, on the ground floor. Guess you want to take a look at Mr. Big,' he grinned. 'Well, so do I, but it wouldn't have done to tell Dexter so.' He flagged a Yellow Cab.

'St. Regis Hotel. Fifth at 55th.'

They climbed into the overheated tin box reeking of last week's cigar-smoke.

Leiter wound down a window.

'Whaddya want ter do?' asked the driver over his shoulder. 'Gimme pneumony?'

'Just that,' said Leiter, 'if it means saving us from this gas chamber.'

'Wise guy, hn?' said the driver, crashing tinnily through his gears. He took the chewed end of a cigar from behind his ear and held it up. 'Two bits for three,' he said in a hurt voice.

'Twenty-four cents too much,' said Leiter. The rest of the drive was passed in silence.

They parted at the hotel and Bond went up to his room. It was four o'clock. He asked the telephone operator to call him at six. For a while he looked out of the window of his bedroom. To his left, the sun was setting in a blaze of colour. In the skyscrapers the lights were coming on, turning the whole town into a golden honeycomb. Far below the streets were rivers of neon lighting, crimson, blue, green. The wind sighed sadly outside in the velvet dusk, lending his room still more warmth and security and luxury. He drew the curtains and turned on the soft lights over his bed. Then he took off his clothes and climbed between the fine percale sheets. He thought of the bitter weather in the London streets, the grudging warmth of the hissing gas-fire in his office at Headquarters, the chalked-up menu on the pub he had passed on his last day in London: 'Giant Toad & 2 Veg.'

He stretched luxuriously. Very soon he was asleep.

Up in Harlem, at the big switchboard, 'The Whisper' was dozing over his racing form. All his lines were quiet. Suddenly a light shone on the right of the board – an important light.

'Yes, Boss,' he said softly into his headphone. He couldn't have spoken any louder if he had wished to. He had been born on 'Lung Block', on Seventh Avenue, at 142nd Street, where death from TB is twice as high as anywhere in New York. Now, he only had part of one lung left.

'Tell all "Eyes",' said a slow, deep voice, 'to watch out from now on. Three men.' A brief description of Leiter, Bond and Dexter followed. 'May be coming in this evening or tomorrow. Tell them to watch particularly on First to Eight and the other Avenues. The night spots too, in case they're missed coming in. They're not to be molested. Call me when you get a sure fix. Got it?'

'Yes, Sir, Boss,' said The Whisper, breathing fast. The voice went quiet. The operator took the whole handful of plugs, and soon the big switchboard was alive with winking lights. Softly, urgently, he whispered on into the evening.

At six o'clock Bond was awakened by the soft burr of the telephone. He took a cold shower and dressed carefully. He put on a garishly striped tie and allowed a broad wedge of bandana to protrude from his breast pocket. He slipped the chamois leather holster over his shirt so that it hung three inches below his left armpit. He whipped at the mechanism of the Beretta until all eight bullets lay on the bed. Then he packed them back into the magazine, loaded the gun, put up the safety-catch and slipped it into the holster.

He picked up the pair of Moccasin casuals, felt their toes and weighed them in his hand. Then he reached under the bed and pulled out a pair of his own shoes he had carefully kept out of the suitcase full of his belongings the FBI had taken away from him that morning.

He put them on and felt better equipped to face the evening.

Under the leather, the toe-caps were lined with steel.

At six twenty-five he went down to the King Cole Bar and chose a table near the entrance and against the wall. A few minutes later Felix Leiter came in. Bond hardly recognized him. His mop of straw-coloured hair was now jet black and he wore a dazzling blue suit with a white shirt and a black-and-white polka-dot tie.

Leiter sat down with a broad grin.

'I suddenly decided to take these people seriously,' he explained. 'This stuff's only a rinse. It'll come off in the morning. I hope,' he added.

Leiter ordered medium-dry Martinis with a slice of lemon peel. He stipulated House of Lords gin and Martini Rossi. The American gin, a much higher proof than English gin, tasted harsh to Bond. He reflected that he would have to be careful what he drank that evening.

'We'll have to keep on our toes, where we're going,' said Felix Leiter, echoing his thoughts. 'Harlem's a bit of a jungle these days. People don't go up there any more like they used to. Before the war, at the end of an evening, one used to go to Harlem just as one goes to Montmartre in Paris. They were glad to take one's money. One used to go to the Savoy Ballroom and watch the dancing. Perhaps pick up a high-yaller and risk the doctor's bills afterwards. Now that's all changed. Harlem doesn't like being stared at any more. Most of the places have closed and you go to the others strictly on sufferance. Often you get tossed out on your ear, simply because you're white. And you don't get any sympathy from the police either.'

Leiter extracted the lemon peel from his Martini and chewed it reflectively. The bar was filling up. It was warm and companionable – a far cry, Leiter reflected, from the inimical, electric climate of the negro pleasure-spots they would be drinking in later.

'Fortunately,' continued Leiter, 'I like the negroes and they know it somehow. I used to be a bit of an aficionado of Harlem. Wrote a few pieces on Dixieland Jazz for the *Amsterdam News*, one of the local papers. Did a series for the North American Newspaper Alliance on the negro theatre about the time Orson Welles put on his *Macbeth* with an all-negro cast at the Lafayette. So I know my way about up there. And I admire the way they're getting on in the world, though God knows I can't see the end of it.'

They finished their drinks and Leiter called for the check.

'Of course there are some bad ones,' he said. 'Some of the worst anywhere. Harlem's the capital of the negro world. In any half a million people of any race you'll get plenty of stinkeroos. The trouble with our friend Mr. Big is that he's the hell of a good technician, thanks to his O S S and Moscow training. And he must be pretty well organized up there.'

Leiter paid. He shrugged his shoulders.

'Let's go,' he said. 'We'll have ourselves some fun and try and get back in one piece. After all, this is what we're paid for. We'll take a bus on Fifth Avenue. You won't find many cabs that want to go up there after dark.'

They walked out of the warm hotel and took the few steps to the bus stop on the Avenue.

It was raining. Bond turned up the collar of his coat and gazed up the Avenue to his right, towards Central Park, towards the dark citadel that housed The Big Man.

Bond's nostrils flared slightly. He longed to get in there after him. He felt strong and compact and confident. The evening awaited him, to be opened and read, page by page, word by word.

In front of his eyes, the rain came down in swift, slanting strokes – italic script across the unopened black cover that hid the secret hours that lay ahead.

CHAPTER V

NIGGER HEAVEN

At the bus stop at the corner of Fifth and Cathedral Parkway three negroes stood quietly under the light of a street lamp. They looked wet and bored. They were. They had been watching the traffic on Fifth since the call went out at four-thirty.

'Yo next, Fatso,' said one of them as the bus came up out of the rain and stopped with a sigh from the great vacuum brakes.

'Ahm tahd,' said the thick-set man in the mackintosh. But he pulled his hat down over his eyes and climbed aboard, slotted his coins and moved down the bus, scanning the occupants. He blinked as he saw the two white men, walked on and took the seat directly behind them.

He examined the backs of their necks, their coats and hats and their profiles. Bond sat next to the window. The negro saw the reflection of his scar in the dark glass.

He got up and moved to the front of the bus without looking back. At the next stop he got off the bus and made straight for the nearest drugstore. He shut himself into the paybox.

Whisper questioned him urgently, then broke the connection.

He plugged in on the right of the board.

'Yes?' said the deep voice.

'Boss, one of them's just come in on Fifth. The Limey

with the scar. Got a friend with him, but he don't seem to fit the dope on the other two.' Whisper passed on an accurate description of Leiter. 'Coming north, both of them,' he gave the number and probable timing of the bus.

There was a pause.

'Right,' said the quiet voice. 'Call off all Eyes on the other avenues. Warn the night spots that one of them's inside and get this to Tee-Hee Johnson, McThing, Blabbermouth Foley, Sam Miami and The Flannel. . . .'

The voice spoke for five minutes.

'Got that? Repeat.'

'Yes, Sir, Boss,' said The Whisper. He glanced at his shorthand pad and whispered fluently and without a pause into the mouthpiece.

'Right.' The line went dead.

His eyes bright, The Whisper took up a fistful of plugs and started talking to the town.

From the moment that Bond and Leiter walked under the canopy of Sugar Ray's on Seventh Avenue at 123rd Street there was a team of men and women watching them or waiting to watch them, speaking softly to The Whisper at the big switchboard on the Riverside Exchange, handing them on towards the rendezvous. In a world where they were naturally the focus of attention, neither Bond nor Leiter felt the hidden machine nor sensed the tension around them.

In the famous night-spot the stools against the long bar were crowded, but one of the small booths against the wall was empty and Bond and Leiter slipped into the two seats with the narrow table between them.

They ordered Scotch-and-soda – Haig and Haig Pinch-bottle. Bond looked the crowd over. It was nearly all men.

There were two or three whites, boxing fans or reporters for the New York sports columns, Bond decided. The atmosphere was warmer, louder than downtown. The walls were covered with boxing photographs, mostly of Sugar Ray Robinson and of scenes from his great fights. It was a cheerful place, doing great business.

'He was a wise guy, Sugar Ray,' said Leiter. 'Let's hope we both know when to stop when the time comes. He stashed plenty away and now he's adding to his pile on the music halls. His percentage of this place must be worth a packet and he owns a lot of real estate around here. He works hard still, but it's not the sort of work that sends you blind or gives you a haemorrhage of the brain. He quit while he was still alive.'

'He'll probably back a Broadway show and lose it all.' said Bond. 'If I quit now and went in for fruit-farming in Kent, I'd most likely hit the worst weather since the Thames froze over, and be cleaned out. One can't plan for everything.'

'One can try,' said Leiter. 'But I know what you mean – better the frying-pan you know than the fire you don't. It isn't a bad life when it consists of sitting in a comfortable bar drinking good whisky. How do you like this corner of the jungle?' He leant forward. 'Just listen in to the couple behind you. From what I've heard they're straight out of "Nigger Heaven".'

Bond glanced carefully over his shoulder.

The booth behind him contained a handsome young negro in an expensive fawn suit with exaggerated shoulders. He was lolling back against the wall with one foot up on the bench beside him. He was paring the nails of his left hand with a small silver pocket-knife, occasionally glancing in bored fashion towards the animation at the bar. His head rested on the back of the booth just behind Bond and a whiff of expensive hair-straightener came from him. Bond took in the artificial parting traced with a razor across the left side of the scalp, through the almost straight hair which was a tribute to his mother's constant application of the hot comb since childhood. The plain black silk tie and the white shirt were in good taste.

Opposite him, leaning forward with concern on her pretty face, was a sexy little negress with a touch of white blood in her. Her jet-black hair, as sleek as the best permanent wave, framed a sweet almond-shaped face with rather slanting eyes under finely drawn eyebrows. The deep purple of her parted, sensual lips was thrilling against the bronze skin. All that Bond could see of her clothes was the bodice of a black satin evening dress, tight and revealing across the firm, small breasts. She wore a plain gold chain round her neck and a plain gold band round each thin wrist.

She was pleading anxiously and paid no heed to Bond's quick embracing glance.

'Listen and see if you can get the hang of it,' said Leiter. 'It's straight Harlem – Deep South with a lot of New York thrown in.'

Bond picked up the menu and leant back in the booth, studying the Special Fried Chicken Dinner at $3.75.

'Cmon, honey,' wheedled the girl. 'How come yuh-all's actin' so tahd tonight?'

'Guess ah jist nacherlly gits tahd listenin' at yuh,' said the man languidly. 'Why'nt yuh hush yo' mouff'n let me 'joy mahself 'n peace 'n qui-yet.'

'Is yuh wan' me tuh go 'way, honey?'

'Yuh kin suit yo sweet self.'

'Aw, honey,' pleaded the girl. 'Don' ack mad at me, honey. Ah was fixin' tuh treat yuh tonight. Take yuh tuh Smalls Par'dise, mebbe. See dem high-yallers shakin' 'n truckin'. Dat Birdie Johnson, da maitre d', he permis me a ringside whenebber Ah come nex'.'

The man's voice suddenly sharpened. 'Wha' dat Birdie he mean tuh yuh, hey?' he asked suspiciously. 'Perzackly,' he paused to let the big word sink in, 'perzackly wha' goes 'tween yuh 'n dat lowdown ornery wuthless Nigguh? Yuh sleepin' wid him mebbe? Guess Ah gotta study 'bout dat little situayshun 'tween yuh an' Birdie Johnson. Mebbe git mahself a betterer gal. Ah jist don' lak gals which runs off ever' which way when Ah jist happen be busticated temporaneously. Yesmam. Ah gotta study 'bout dat little situayshun.' He paused threateningly. 'Sure have,' he added.

'Aw, honey,' the girl was anxious. ' 'dey ain't no use tryin' tuh git mad at me. Ah done nuthen tuh give yuh recasion tuh ack dat way. Ah jist thunk you mebbe preshiate a ringside at da Par'dise 'nstead of settin' hyah countin' yo troubles. Why, honey, yuh all knows Ah wudden fall fo' dat richcrat ack' of Birdie Johnson. No sir. He don' mean nuthen tuh me. Him duh wusstes' man 'n Harlem, dawg bite me effn he ain't. All da same, he permis me da bestess seats 'nda house 'n Ah sez let's us go set 'n dem, 'n have us a beer 'n a good time. Cmon, honey. Let's git out of hyah. Yuh done look so swell 'n Ah jist wan' mah frens tuh see usn together.'

'Yuh done look okay yoself, honeychile,' said the man, mollified by the tribute to his elegance, 'an' dat's da troof. But Ah mus' spressify dat yuh stays close up tuh me an keeps yo eyes offn dat lowdown trash 'n his hot pants. 'N Ah may say,' he added threateningly, 'dat ef Ah ketches yuh makin' up tuh dat dope Ah'll jist nachrally whup da hide off'n yo sweet ass.'

'Shoh ting, honey,' whispered the girl excitedly.

Bond heard the man's foot scrape off the seat to the ground.

'Cmon, baby, lessgo. Waiduh!'

Bond put down the menu. 'Got the gist of it,' he said. 'Seems they're interested in much the same things as everyone else – sex, having fun, and keeping up with the Jones's. Thank God they're not genteel about it.'

'Some of them are,' said Leiter. 'Tea-cups, aspidistras and tut-tutting all over the place. The Methodists are almost their strongest sect. Harlem's riddled with social distinctions, the same as any other big city, but with all the colour variations added. Come on,' he suggested, 'let's go and get ourselves something to eat.'

They finished their drinks and Bond called for the check.

'All this evening's on me,' he said. 'I've got a lot of money to get rid of and I've brought three hundred dollars of it along with me.'

'Suits me,' said Leiter, who knew about Bond's thousand dollars.

As the waiter was picking up the change, Leiter suddenly said, 'Know where The Big Man's operating tonight?'

The waiter showed the whites of his eyes.

He leant forward and flicked the table down with his napkin.

'I've got a wife'n kids, Boss,' he muttered out of the corner of his mouth. He stacked the glasses on his tray and went back to the bar.

'Mr. Big's got the best protection of all,' said Leiter. 'Fear.'

They went out on to Seventh Avenue. The rain had stopped, but 'Hawkins', the bone-chilling wind from the north which the negroes greet with a reverent 'Hawkins is here', had come instead to keep the streets free of their usual crowds. Leiter and Bond moved with the trickle of couples on the sidewalk. The looks they got were mostly contemptuous or frankly hostile. One or two men spat in the gutter when they had passed.

Bond suddenly felt the force of what Leiter had told him. They were trespassing. They just weren't wanted. Bond felt the uneasiness that he had known so well during the war, when he had been working for a time behind the enemy lines. He shrugged the feeling away.

'We'll go to Ma Frazier's, further up the Avenue,' said Leiter. 'Best food in Harlem, or at any rate it used to be.'

As they went along Bond gazed into the shop windows.

He was struck by the number of barbers' saloons and 'beauticians'. They all advertised various forms of hair-straightener – 'Apex Glossatina, for use with the hot comb', 'Silky Strate. Leaves no redness, no burn' – or nostrums for bleaching the skin. Next in frequency were the haberdashers and clothes shops, with fantastic men's snakeskin shoes, shirts with small aeroplanes as a pattern, peg-top trousers with inch-wide stripes, zoot suits. All the book shops were full of educational literature – how to learn this, how to do that – and comics. There were several shops devoted to lucky charms and various occultisms – *Seven Keys to Power*, 'The Strangest book ever written', with sub-titles such as: 'If you are CROSSED, shows you how to remove and cast it back.' 'Chant your desires in the Silent Tongue.' 'Cast a Spell on Anyone, no matter where.' 'Make any person Love you.' Among the charms were 'High John the Conqueror Root', 'Money Drawing Brand Oil', 'Sachet Powders, Uncrossing Brand', 'Incense, Jinx removing Brand', and the 'Lucky Whamie Hand Charm, giving Protection from Evil. Confuses and Baffles Enemies'.

Bond reflected it was no wonder that the Big Man found Voodooism such a powerful weapon on minds that still recoiled at a white chicken's feather or crossed sticks in the road – right in the middle of the shining capital city of the Western world.

'I'm glad we came up here,' said Bond. 'I'm beginning to get the hang of Mr. Big. One just doesn't catch the smell of all this in a country like England. We're a superstitious lot there of course – particularly the Celts – but here one can almost hear the drums.'

Leiter grunted. 'I'll be glad to get back to my bed,' he said. 'But we need to size up this guy before we decide how to get at him.'

Ma Frazier's was a cheerful contrast to the bitter streets. They had an excellent meal of Little Neck Clams and Fried Chicken Maryland with bacon and sweet corn. 'We've got to have it,' said Leiter. 'It's the national dish.'

It was very civilized in the warm restaurant. Their waiter seemed glad to see them and pointed out various celebrities, but when Leiter slipped in a question about Mr. Big the waiter seemed not to hear. He kept away from them until they called for their bill.

Leiter repeated the question.

'Sorry, Sah,' said the waiter briefly. 'Ah cain't recall a gemmun of dat name.'

By the time they left the restaurant it was ten-thirty and the Avenue was almost deserted. They took a cab to the

Savoy Ballroom, had a Scotch-and-soda, and watched the dancers.

'Most modern dances were invented here,' said Leiter. 'That's how good it is. The Lindy Hop, Truckin', the Susie Q, the Shag. All started on that floor. Every big American band you've ever heard of is proud that it once played here – Duke Ellington, Louis Armstrong, Cab Calloway, Noble Sissle, Fletcher Henderson. It's the Mecca of jazz and jive.'

They had a table near the rail round the huge floor. Bond was spellbound. He found many of the girls very beautiful. The music hammered its way into his pulse until he almost forgot what he was there for.

'Gets you, doesn't it?' said Leiter at last. 'I could stay here all night. Better move along. We'll miss out Small's Paradise. Much the same as this, but not quite in the same class. Think I'll take you to "Yeah Man", back on Seventh. After that we must get moving to one of Mr. Big's own joints. Trouble is, they don't open till midnight. I'll pay a visit to the washroom while you get the check. See if I can get a line on where we're likely to find him tonight. We don't want to have to go to all his places.'

Bond paid the check and met Leiter downstairs in the narrow entrance hall.

Leiter drew him outside and they walked up the street looking for a cab.

'Cost me twenty bucks,' said Leiter, 'but the word is he'll be at The Boneyard. Small place on Lenox Avenue. Quite close to his headquarters. Hottest strip in town. Girl called G-G Sumatra. We'll have another drink at "Yeah Man" and hear the piano. Move on at about twelve-thirty.'

The big switchboard, now only a few blocks away, was almost quiet. The two men had been checked in and out of Sugar Ray's, Ma Frazier's and the Savoy Ballroom. Midnight had them entering 'Yeah Man'. At twelve-thirty the final call came and then the board was silent.

Mr. Big spoke on the house-phone. First to the head waiter.

'Two white men coming in in five minutes. Give them the Z table.'

'Yes, Sir, Boss,' said the head waiter. He hurried across the dance-floor to a table away on the right, obscured from most of the room by a wide pillar. It was next to the Service entrance but with a good view of the floor and the band opposite.

It was occupied by a party of four, two men and two girls.

'Sorry folks,' said the head waiter. 'Been a mistake. Table's reserved. Newspaper men from downtown.'

One of the men began to argue.

'Move, Bud,' said the head waiter crisply. 'Lofty, show these folks to table F. Drinks is on the house. Sam,' he beckoned to another waiter, 'clear the table. Two covers.' The party of four moved docilely away, mollified by the prospect of free liquor. The head waiter put a Reserved sign on table Z, surveyed it and returned to his post at his table-plan on the high desk beside the curtained entrance.

Meanwhile Mr. Big had made two more calls on the house-phone. One to the Master of Ceremonies.

'Lights out at the end of G-G's act.'

'Yes, Sir, Boss,' said the MC with alacrity.

The other call was to four men who were playing craps in the basement. It was a long call, and very detailed.

CHAPTER VI

TABLE Z

At twelve forty-five Bond and Leiter paid off their cab and walked in under the sign which announced 'The Boneyard' in violet and green neon.

The thudding rhythm and the sour-sweet smell rocked them as they pushed through the heavy curtains inside the swing door. The eyes of the hat-check girls glowed and beckoned.

'Have you reserved, Sir?' asked the head waiter.

'No,' said Leiter. 'We don't mind sitting at the bar.'

The head waiter consulted his table-plan. He seemed to decide. He put his pencil firmly through a space at the end of the card.

'Party hasn't shown. Guess Ah cain't hold their res'vation all night. This way, please.' He held his card high over his head and led them round the small crowded dance-floor. He pulled out one of the two chairs and removed the 'Reserved' sign.

'Sam,' he called a waiter over. 'Look after these gemmums order.' He moved away.

They ordered Scotch-and-soda and chicken sandwiches.

Bond sniffed. 'Marihuana,'' he commented.

'Most of the real hep-cats smoke reefers,' explained Leiter. 'Wouldn't be allowed most places.'

Bond looked round. The music had stopped. The small four-piece band, clarinet, double-bass, electric guitar and drums, was moving out of the corner opposite. The dozen or so couples were walking and jiving to their tables and the crimson light was turned off under the glass dance-floor. Instead, pencil-thin lights in the roof came on and hit coloured glass witchballs, larger than footballs, that hung at intervals round the wall. They were of different hues, golden, blue, green, violet, red. As the beams of light hit them, they glowed like coloured suns. The walls, varnished black, mirrored their reflections as did the sweat on the ebony faces of the men. Sometimes a man sitting between two lights showed cheeks of different colour, green on one side, perhaps, and red on the other. The lighting made it impossible to distinguish features unless they were only a few feet away. Some of the lights turned the girls' lipstick black, others lit their whole faces in a warm glow on one side and gave the other profile the luminosity of a drowned corpse.

The whole scene was macabre and livid, as if El Greco had done a painting by moonlight of an exhumed graveyard in a burning town.

It was not a large room, perhaps sixty foot square. There were about fifty tables and the customers were packed in like black olives in a jar. It was hot and the air was thick with smoke and the sweet, feral smell of two hundred negro bodies. The noise was terrific – an undertone of the jabber of negroes enjoying themselves without restraint, punctuated by sharp bursts of noise, shouts and high giggles, as loud voices called to each other across the room.

'Sweet Jeessus, look who's hyar. . . .'

'Where you been keepin yoself, baby. . . .'

'Gawd's troof. It's Pinkus. . . . Hi Pinkus. . . .'

'Cmon over. . . .'

'Lemme be . . . Lemme be, I'se telling ya . . .' (The noise of a slap.)

'Where's G-G. Cmon G-G. Strut yo stuff. . . .'

From time to time a man or girl would erupt on to the dance-floor and start a wild solo jive. Friends would clap the rhythm. There would be a burst of catcalls and whistles. If it was a girl, there would be cries of 'Strip, strip, strip,' 'Get hot, baby!' 'Shake it, shake it,' and the MC would come out and clear the floor amidst groans and shouts of derision.

The sweat began to bead on Bond's forehead. Leiter leant over and cupped his hands. 'Three exits. Front. Service behind us. Behind the band.' Bond nodded. At that moment he felt it didn't matter. This was nothing new to Leiter, but for Bond it was a close-up of the raw material on which The Big Man worked, the clay in his hands. The evening was gradually putting flesh on the dossiers he had read in London and New York. If the evening ended now, without any closer sight of Mr. Big himself, Bond still felt his education in the case would be almost complete. He took a deep draught of his whisky. There was a burst of applause. The MC had come out on to the dance-floor, a tall negro in immaculate tails with a red carnation in his button hole. He stood, holding up his hands. A single white spotlight caught him. The rest of the room went dark.

There was silence.

'Folks,' announced the MC with a broad flash of gold and white teeth. 'This is it.'

There was excited clapping.

He turned to the left of the floor, directly across from Leiter and Bond.

He flung out his right hand. Another spot came on.

'Mistah Jungles Japhet 'n his drums.'

A crash of applause, catcalls, whistles.

Four grinning negroes in flame-coloured shirts and peg-top white trousers were revealed, squatting astride four tapering barrels with rawhide membranes. The drums were of different sizes. The negroes were all gaunt and stringy. The one sitting astride the bass drum rose briefly and shook clasped hands at the spectators.

'Voodoo drummers from Haiti,' whispered Leiter.

There was silence. With the tips of their fingers the drummers began a slow, broken beat, a soft rumba shuffle.

'And now, friends,' announced the MC, still turned towards the drums, 'G-G . . .' he paused, 'SUMATRA.'

The last word was a yell. He began to clap. There was pandemonium in the room, a frenzy of applause. The door behind the drums burst open and two huge negroes, naked except for gold loincloths, ran out on to the floor carrying between them, her arms round their necks, a tiny figure, swathed completely in black ostrich feathers, a black domino across her eyes.

They put her down in the middle of the floor. They bowed down on either side of her until their foreheads met the ground. She took two paces forward. With the spot-light off them, the two negroes melted away into the shadows and through the door.

The MC had disappeared. There was absolute silence save for the soft thud of the drums.

The girl put her hand up to her throat and the cloak of black feathers came away from the front of her body and spread out into a five-foot black fan. She swirled it slowly behind her until it stood up like a peacock's tail. She was naked except for a brief vee of black lace and a black sequin star in the centre of each breast and the thin black domino across her eyes. Her body was small, hard, bronze, beautiful. It was slightly oiled and glinted in the white light.

The audience was silent. The drums began to step up the tempo. The bass drum kept its beat dead on the timing of the human pulse.

The girl's naked stomach started slowly to revolve in time with the rhythm. She swept the black feathers across and behind her again, and her hips started to grind in time with the bass drum. The upper part of her body was motionless. The black feathers swirled again, and now her feet were shifting and her shoulders. The drums beat louder. Each part of her body seemed to be keeping a different time. Her lips were bared slightly from her teeth. Her nostrils began to flare. Her eyes glinted hotly through the diamond slits. It was a sexy, pug-like face – *chienne* was the only word Bond could think of.

The drums thudded faster, a complexity of interlaced rhythms. The girl tossed the big fan off the floor, held her arms up above her head. Her whole body began to shiver. Her belly moved faster. Round and round, in and out. Her legs straddled. Her hips began to revolve in a wide circle. Suddenly she plucked the sequin star off her right breast and threw it into the audience. The first noise came from the spectators, a quiet growl. Then they were silent again. She plucked off the other star. Again the growl and then silence. The drums began to crash and roll. Sweat poured off the drummers. Their hands fluttered like grey flannel on the pale membranes. Their eyes were bulging, distant. Their heads were slightly bent to one side as if they were listening. They hardly glanced at the girl. The audience panted softly, liquid eyes bulging and rolling.

The sweat was shining all over her now. Her breasts and stomach glistened with it. She broke into great shuddering jerks. Her mouth opened and she screamed softly. Her hands snaked down to her sides and suddenly she had torn away the strip of lace. She threw it into the audience. There was nothing now but a single black G-string. The drums went into a hurricane of sexual rhythm. She screamed softly again and then, her arms stretched before her as a balance, she started to lower her body down to the floor and up again. Faster and faster. Bond could hear the audience panting and grunting like pigs at the trough. He felt his own hands gripping the tablecloth. His mouth was dry.

The audience began to shout at her. 'Cmon, G-G. Take it away, Baby. Cmon. Grind Baby, grind.'

She sank to her knees and as the rhythm slowly died so she too went into a last series of juddering spasms, mewing softly.

The drums came down to a slow tom-tom beat and shuffle. The audience howled for her body. Harsh obscenities came from different corners of the room.

The MC came on to the floor. A spot went on him.

'Okay, folks, okay.' The sweat was pouring off his chin. He spread his arms in surrender.

'Da G-G AGREES !'

There was a delighted howl from the audience. Now she would be quite naked. 'Take it off, G-G. Show yoself Baby. Cmon, cmon.'

The drums growled and stuttered softly.

'But, mah friends,' yelled the MC, 'she stipperlates – With da lights OUT !'

There was a frustrated groan from the audience. The whole room was plunged in darkness.

Must be an old gag, thought Bond to himself.

Suddenly all his senses were alert.

The howling of the mob was disappearing, rapidly. At the same time he felt cold air on his face. He felt as if he was sinking.

'Hey,' shouted Leiter. His voice was close but it sounded hollow.

Christ! thought Bond.

Something snapped shut above his head. He put his hand out behind him. It touched a moving wall a foot from his back.

'Lights,' said a voice, quietly.

At the same time both his arms were gripped. He was pressed down in his chair.

Opposite him, still at the table, sat Leiter, a huge negro grasping his elbows. They were in a tiny square cell. To right and left were two more negroes in plain clothes with guns trained on them.

There was the sharp hiss of a hydraulic garage lift and the table settled quietly to the floor. Bond glanced up. There was the faint join of a broad trap-door a few feet above their heads. No sound came through it.

One of the negroes grinned.

'Take it easy, folks. Enjoy da ride?'

Leiter let out one single harsh obscenity. Bond relaxed his muscles, waiting.

'Which is da Limey?' asked the negro who had spoken. He seemed to be in charge. The pistol he held trained lazily on Bond's heart was very fancy. There was a glint of mother-of-pearl between his black fingers on the stock and the long octagonal barrel was finely chased.

'Dis one, Ah guess,' said the negro who was holding Bond's arm. 'He got da scar.'

The negro's grip on Bond's arm was terrific. It was as if he had two fierce tourniquets applied above the elbows. His hands were beginning to go numb.

The man with the fancy gun came round the corner of the table. He shoved the muzzle of his gun into Bond's stomach. The hammer was back.

'You oughtn't to miss at that range,' said Bond.

'Shaddap,' said the negro. He frisked Bond expertly with his left hand – legs, thighs, back, sides. He dug out Bond's gun and handed it to the other armed man.

'Give dat to da Boss, Tee-Hee,' he said. 'Take da Limey up. Yuh go 'long wid em. Da other guy stays wid me.'

'Yassuh,' said the man called Tee-Hee, a paunchy negro in a chocolate shirt and lavender-coloured peg-top trousers.

Bond was hauled to his feet. He had one foot hooked under a leg of the table. He yanked hard. There was a crash of glass and silverware. At the same moment, Leiter kicked out backwards round the leg of his chair. There was a satisfactory 'klonk' as his heel caught his guard's shin. Bond did the same but missed. There was a moment of chaos, but neither of the guards slackened his grip. Leiter's guard picked him bodily out of the chair as if he had been a child, faced him to the wall and slammed him into it. It nearly smashed Leiter's nose. The guard swung him round. Blood was streaming down over his mouth.

The two guns were still trained unwaveringly on them. It had been a futile effort, but for a split second they had regained the initiative and effaced the sudden shock of capture.

'Don' waste yo breff,' said the negro who had been giving the orders. 'Take da Limey away.' He addressed Bond's guard. 'Mr. Big's waiten'.' He turned to Leiter.

'Yo kin tell yo fren' goodbye,' he said. 'Yo is unlikely be seein' yoselves agin.'

Bond smiled at Leiter. 'Lucky we made a date for the police to meet us here at two,' he said. 'See you at the line-up.'

Leiter grinned back. His teeth were red with blood. 'Commissioner Monahan's going to be pleased with this bunch. Be seeing you.'

'Crap,' said the negro with conviction. 'Get goin'.'

Bond's guard whipped him round and shoved him against a section of the wall. It opened on a pivot into a long bare passage. The man called Tee-Hee pushed past them and led the way.

The door swung to behind them.

CHAPTER VII

MISTER BIG

THEIR footsteps echoed down the stone passage. At the end there was a door. They went through into another long passage lit by an occasional bare bulb in the roof. Another door and they found themselves in a large warehouse. Cases and bales were stacked in neat piles. There were runways for overhead cranes. From the markings on the crates it seemed to be a liquor store. They followed an aisle across to an iron door. The man called Tee-Hee rang a bell. There was absolute silence. Bond guessed they must have walked at least a block away from the night club.

There was a clang of bolts and the door opened. A negro in evening dress with a gun in his hand stepped aside and they went through into a carpeted hallway.

'Yo kin go on in, Tee-Hee,' said the man in evening dress.

Tee-Hee knocked on a door facing them, opened it and led the way through.

In a high-backed chair, behind an expensive desk, Mr. Big sat looking quietly at them.

'Good morning, Mister James Bond.' The voice was deep and soft. 'Sit down.'

Bond's guard led him across the thick carpet to a low armchair in leather and tubular steel. He released Bond's arms and Bond sat down and faced The Big Man across the wide desk.

It was a blessed relief to be rid of the two vice-like hands. All sensation had left Bond's forearms. He let them hang beside him and welcomed the dull pain as the blood started to flow again.

Mr. Big sat looking at him, his huge head resting against the back of the tall chair. He said nothing.

Bond at once realized that the photographs had conveyed nothing of this man, nothing of the power and the intellect which seemed to radiate from him, nothing of the over-size features.

It was a great football of a head, twice the normal size and very nearly round. The skin was grey-black, taut and shining like the face of a week-old corpse in the river. It was hairless, except for some grey-brown fluff above the ears. There were no eyebrows and no eyelashes and the eyes were extraordinarily far apart so that one could not focus on them both, but only on one at a time. Their gaze was very steady and penetrating. When they rested on something, they seemed to devour it, to encompass the whole of it. They bulged slightly and the irises were golden round black pupils which were now wide. They were animal eyes, not human, and they seemed to blaze.

The nose was wide without being particularly negroid. The nostrils did not gape at you. The lips were only slightly everted, but thick and dark. They opened only when the man spoke and then they opened wide and drew back from the teeth and the pale pink gums.

There were few wrinkles or creases on the face, but there were two deep clefts above the nose, the clefts of concentration. Above them the forehead bulged slightly before merging with the polished, hairless crown.

Curiously, there was nothing disproportionate about the

monstrous head. It was carried on a wide, short neck supported by the shoulders of a giant. Bond knew from the records that he was six and a half foot tall and weighed twenty stone, and that little of it was fat. But the total impression was awe-inspiring, even terrifying, and Bond could imagine that so ghastly a misfit must have been bent since childhood on revenge against fate and against the world that hated because it feared him.

The Big Man was draped in a dinner-jacket. There was a hint of vanity in the diamonds that blazed on his shirt-front and at his cuffs. His huge flat hands rested half-curled on the table in front of him. There were no signs of cigarettes or an ash-tray and the smell of the room was neutral. There was nothing on the desk save a large intercom with about twenty switches and, incongruously, a very small ivory riding-crop with a long thin white lash.

Mr. Big gazed with silent and deep concentration across the table at Bond.

After inspecting him carefully in return, Bond glanced round the room.

It was full of books, spacious and restful and very quiet, like the library of a millionaire.

There was one high window above Mr. Big's head but otherwise the walls were solid with bookshelves. Bond turned round in his chair. More bookshelves, packed with books. There was no sign of a door, but there might have been any number of doors faced with dummy books. The two negroes who had brought him to the room stood rather uneasily against the wall behind his chair. The whites of their eyes showed. They were not looking at Mr. Big, but at a curious effigy which stood on a table in an open space of floor to the right, and slightly behind Mr. Big.

Even with his slight knowledge of Voodoo, Bond recognized it at once from Leigh Fermor's description.

A five-foot white wooden cross stood on a raised white pedestal. The arms of the cross were thrust into the sleeves of a dusty black frock-coat whose tails hung down behind the table towards the floor. Above the neck of the coat a battered bowler hat gaped at him, its crown pierced by the vertical bar of the cross. A few inches below the rim, round the neck of the cross, resting on the cross-bar, was a deep starched clergyman's collar.

At the base of the white pedestal, on the table, lay an old pair of lemon-coloured gloves. A short malacca stick with a gold knob, its ferrule resting beside the gloves, rose against the left shoulder of the effigy. Also on the table was a battered black top hat.

This evil scarecrow gazed out across the room – God of the Cemeteries and Chief of the Legion of the Dead – Baron Samedi. Even to Bond it seemed to carry a dreadful gaping message.

Bond looked away, back to the great grey-black face across the desk.

Mr. Big spoke.

'I want you, Tee-Hee.' His eyes shifted. 'You can go, Miami.'

'Yes, Sir, Boss,' they both said together.

Bond heard a door open and close.

Silence fell again. At first, Mr. Big's eyes had been focused sharply on Bond. They had examined him minutely. Now, Bond noticed that though the eyes rested on him they had become slightly opaque. They gazed upon Bond without perception. Bond had the impression that the brain behind them was occupied elsewhere.

Bond was determined not to be disconcerted. Feeling had returned to his hands and he moved them towards his body to reach for his cigarettes and lighter.

Mr. Big spoke.

'You may smoke, Mister Bond. In case you have any other intentions you may care to lean forward and inspect the keyhole of the drawer in this desk facing your chair. I shall be ready for you in a moment.'

Bond leant forward. It was a large keyhole. In fact, Bond estimated, .45 centimetres in diameter. Fired, Bond supposed, by a foot-switch under the desk. What a bunch of tricks this man was. Puerile. Puerile? Perhaps, after all, not to be dismissed so easily. The tricks – the bomb, the disappearing table – had worked neatly, efficiently. They had not been just empty conceits, designed to impress. Again, there was nothing absurd about this gun. Rather painstaking, perhaps, but, he had to admit, technically sound.

He lit a cigarette and gratefully drew the smoke deep into his lungs. He did not feel particularly worried by his position. He refused to believe he would come to any harm. It would be a clumsy affair to have him disappear a couple of days after he arrived from England unless a very expert accident could be contrived. And Leiter would have to be disposed of at the same time. That would be altogether too much for their two Services and Mr. Big must know it. But he was worried about Leiter in the hands of those clumsy black apes.

The Big Man's lips rolled slowly back from his teeth.

'I have not seen a member of the Secret Service for many years, Mister Bond. Not since the war. Your Service did well in the war. You have some able men. I learn from my friends that you are high up in your Service. You have a double-o number, I believe – 007, if I remember right. The significance of that double-o number, they tell me, is that you have had to kill a man in the course of some assignment. There cannot be many double-o numbers in a Service which does not use assassination as a weapon. Whom have you been sent over to kill here, Mister Bond? Not me by any chance?'

The voice was soft and even, without expression. There was a slight mixture of accents, American and French, but the English was almost pedantically accurate, without a trace of slang.

Bond remained silent. He assumed that Moscow had signalled his description.

'It is necessary for you to reply, Mister Bond. The fate of both of you depends upon your doing so. I have confidence in the sources of my information. I know much more than I have said. I shall easily detect a lie.'

Bond believed him. He chose a story he could support and which would cover the facts.

'There are English gold coins circulating in America. Edward IV Rose Nobles,' he said. 'Some have been sold in Harlem. The American Treasury asked for assistance in tracing them since they must come from a British source. I came up to Harlem to see for myself, with a representative of the American Treasury, who I hope is now safely on his way back to his hotel.'

'Mr. Leiter is a representative of the Central Intelligence Agency, not of the Treasury,' said Mr. Big without emotion. 'His position at this moment is extremely precarious.'

He paused and seemed to reflect. He looked past Bond.

'Tee-Hee.'

'Yassuh, Boss.'

'Tie Mister Bond to his chair.'

Bond half rose to his feet.

'Don't move, Mister Bond,' said the voice softly. 'You have a bare chance of survival if you stay where you are.'

Bond looked at The Big Man, at the golden, impassive eyes.

He lowered himself back into his chair. Immediately a broad strap was passed round his body and buckled tight. Two short straps went round his wrists and tied them to the leather and metal arms. Two more went round his ankles. He could hurl himself and the chair to the floor, but otherwise he was powerless.

Mr. Big pressed down a switch on the intercom.

'Send in Miss Solitaire,' he said and centred the switch again.

There was a moment's pause and then a section of the bookcase to the right of the desk swung open.

One of the most beautiful women Bond had ever seen came slowly in and closed the door behind her. She stood just inside the room and stood looking at Bond, taking him in slowly inch by inch, from his head to his feet. When she had completed her detailed inspection, she turned to Mr. Big.

'Yes?' she inquired flatly.

Mr. Big had not moved his head. He addressed Bond.

'This is an extraordinary woman, Mister Bond,' he said in the same quiet soft voice, 'and I am going to marry her because she is unique. I found her in a cabaret, in Haiti, where she was born. She was doing a telepathic act which I could not understand. I looked into it and I still could not understand. There was nothing to understand. It was telepathy.'

Mr. Big paused.

'I tell you this to warn you. She is my inquisitor. Torture is messy and inconclusive. People tell you what will ease the pain. With this girl it is not necessary to use clumsy methods. She can divine the truth in people. That is why she is to be my wife. She is too valuable to remain at liberty. And,' he continued blandly, 'it will be interesting to see our children.'

Mr. Big turned towards her and gazed at her impassively.

'For the time being she is difficult. She will have nothing to do with men. That is why, in Haiti, she was called "Solitaire".'

'Draw up a chair,' he said quietly to her. 'Tell me if this man lies. Keep clear of the gun,' he added.

The girl said nothing but took a chair similar to Bond's from beside the wall and pushed it towards him. She sat down almost touching his right knee. She looked into his eyes.

Her face was pale, with the pallor of white families that have lived long in the tropics. But it contained no trace of the usual exhaustion which the tropics impart to the skin and hair. The eyes were blue, alight and disdainful, but, as they gazed into his with a touch of humour, he realized they contained some message for him personally. It quickly vanished as his own eyes answered. Her hair was blue-black and fell heavily to her shoulders. She had high cheekbones and a wide, sensual mouth which held a hint of cruelty. Her jawline was delicate and finely cut. It showed decision and an iron will which were repeated in the straight, pointed nose. Part of the beauty of the face lay in its lack of compromise. It was a face born to command. The face of the daughter of a French Colonial slave-owner.

She wore a long evening dress of heavy white matt silk

whose classical line was broken by the deep folds which fell from her shoulders and revealed the upper half of her breasts. She wore diamond earrings, square-cut in broken bands, and a thin diamond bracelet on her left wrist. She wore no rings. Her nails were short and without enamel.

She watched his eyes on her and nonchalantly drew her forearms together in her lap so that the valley between her breasts deepened.

The message was unmistakable and an answering warmth must have showed on Bond's cold, drawn face, for suddenly The Big Man picked up the small ivory whip from the desk beside him and lashed across at her, the thong whistling through the air and landing with a cruel bite across her shoulders.

Bond winced even more than she did. Her eyes blazed for an instant and then went opaque.

'Sit up,' said The Big Man softly, 'you forget yourself.'

She sat slowly more upright. She had a pack of cards in her hands and she started to shuffle them. Then, out of bravado perhaps, she sent him yet another message – of complicity and of more than complicity.

Between her hands, she faced the knave of hearts. Then the queen of spades. She held the two halves of the pack in her lap so that the two court cards looked at each other. She brought the two halves of the pack together until they kissed. Then she riffled the cards and shuffled them again.

At no moment of this dumb show did she look at Bond and it was all over in an instant. But Bond felt a glow of excitement and a quickening of the pulse. He had a friend in the enemy's camp.

'Are you ready, Solitaire?' asked The Big Man.

'Yes, the cards are ready,' said the girl, in a low, cool voice.

'Mister Bond, look into the eyes of this girl and repeat the reason for your presence here which you gave me just now.'

Bond looked into her eyes. There was no message. They were not focused on his. They looked through him.

He repeated what he had said.

For a moment he felt an uncanny thrill. Could this girl tell? If she could tell, would she speak for him or against him?

For a moment there was dead silence in the room. Bond tried to look indifferent. He gazed up at the ceiling – then back at her.

Her eyes came back into focus. She turned away from him and looked at Mr. Big.

'He speaks the truth,' she said coldly.

CHAPTER VIII

NO SENSAYUMA

MR. BIG reflected for a moment. He seemed to decide. He pressed a switch on the intercom.

'Blabbermouth?'

'Yassuh, Boss.'

'You're holding that American, Leiter.'

'Yassuh.'

'Hurt him considerably. Ride him down to Bellevue Hospital and dump him nearby. Got that?'

'Yassuh.'

'Don't be seen.'

'Nossuh.'

Mr. Big centred the switch.

'God damn your bloody eyes,' said Bond viciously. 'The CIA won't let you get away with this!'

'You forget, Mister Bond. They have no jurisdiction in America. The American Secret Service has no power in America – only abroad. And the FBI are no friends of theirs. Tee-Hee, come here.'

'Yassuh, Boss.' Tee-Hee came and stood beside the desk.

Mr. Big looked across at Bond.

'Which finger do you use least, Mister Bond?'

Bond was startled by the question. His mind raced.

'On reflection, I expect you will say the little finger of the left hand,' continued the soft voice. 'Tee-Hee, break the little finger of Mr. Bond's left hand.'

The negro showed the reason for his nickname.

'Hee-hee,' he gave a falsetto giggle. 'Hee-hee.'

He walked jauntily over to Bond. Bond clutched madly at the arms of his chair. Sweat started to break out on his forehead. He tried to imagine the pain so that he could control it.

The negro slowly unhinged the little finger of Bond's left hand, immovably bound to the arm of his chair.

He held the tip between finger and thumb and very deliberately started to bend it back, giggling inanely to himself.

Bond rolled and heaved, trying to upset the chair, but Tee-Hee put his other hand on the chair-back and held it there. The sweat poured off Bond's face. His teeth started to bare in an involuntary rictus. Through the increasing pain he could just see the girl's eyes wide upon him, her red lips slightly parted.

The finger stood upright, away from the hand. Started to bend slowly backwards towards his wrist. Suddenly it gave. There was a sharp crack.

'That will do,' said Mr. Big.

Tee-Hee released the mangled finger with reluctance.

Bond uttered a soft animal groan and fainted.

'Da guy ain't got no sensayuma,' commented Tee-Hee.

Solitaire sat limply back in her chair and closed her eyes.

'Did he have a gun?' asked Mr. Big.

'Yassuh.' Tee-Hee took Bond's Beretta out of his pocket and slipped it across the desk. The Big Man picked it up and looked at it expertly. He weighed it in his hand, testing the feel of the skeleton grip. Then he pumped the shells out on to the desk, verified that he had also emptied the chamber and slid it over towards Bond.

'Wake him up,' he said, looking at his watch. It said three o'clock.

Tee-Hee went behind Bond's chair and dug his nails into the lobes of Bond's ears.

Bond groaned and lifted his head.

His eyes focused on Mr. Big and he uttered a string of obscenities.

'Be thankful you're not dead,' said Mr. Big without emotion. 'Any pain is preferable to death. Here is your gun. I have the shells. Tee-Hee, give it back to him.'

Tee-Hee took it off the desk and slipped it back into Bond's holster.

'I will explain to you briefly,' continued The Big Man, 'why it is that you are not dead; why you have been permitted to enjoy the sensation of pain instead of adding to the pollution of the Harlem River from the folds of what is jocularly known as a cement overcoat.'

He paused for a moment and then spoke.

'Mister Bond, I suffer from boredom. I am a prey to what the early Christians called "accidie", the deadly lethargy that envelops those who are sated, those who have no more desires. I am absolutely pre-eminent in my chosen profession, trusted by those who occasionally employ my talents, feared and instantly obeyed by those whom I myself employ. I have, literally, no more worlds to conquer within my chosen orbit. Alas, it is too late in my life to change that orbit for another one, and since power is the goal of all ambition, it is unlikely that I could possibly acquire more power in another sphere than I already possess in this one.'

Bond listened with part of his mind. With the other half he was already planning. He sensed the presence of

Solitaire, but he kept his eyes off her. He gazed steadily across the table at the great grey face with its unwinking golden eyes.

The soft voice continued.

'Mister Bond, I take pleasure now only in artistry, in the polish and finesse which I can bring to my operations. It has become almost a mania with me to impart an absolute rightness, a high elegance, to the execution of my affairs. Each day, Mister Bond, I try and set myself still higher standards of subtlety and technical polish so that each of my proceedings may be a work of art, bearing my signature as clearly as the creations of, let us say, Benvenuto Cellini. I am content, for the time being, to be my only judge, but I sincerely believe, Mister Bond, that the approach to perfection which I am steadily achieving in my operations will ultimately win recognition in the history of our times.'

Mr. Big paused. Bond saw that his great yellow eyes were wide, as if he saw visions. He's a raving megalomaniac, thought Bond. And all the more dangerous because of it. The fault in most criminal minds was that greed was their only impulse. A dedicated mind was quite another matter. This man was no gangster. He was a menace. Bond was fascinated and slightly awestruck.

'I accept anonymity for two reasons,' continued the low voice. 'Because the nature of my operations demands it and because I admire the self-negation of the anonymous artist. If you will allow the conceit, I see myself sometimes as one of those great Egyptian fresco painters who devoted their lives to producing masterpieces in the tombs of kings, knowing that no living eye would ever see them.'

The great eyes closed for a moment.

'However, let us return to the particular. The reason,

Mister Bond, why I have not killed you this morning is because it would give me no aesthetic pleasure to blow a hole in your stomach. With this engine,' he gestured towards the gun trained on Bond through the desk drawer, 'I have already blown many holes in many stomachs, so I am quite satisfied that my little mechanical toy is a sound technical achievement. Moreover, as no doubt you rightly surmise, it would be a nuisance for me to have a lot of busybodies around here asking questions about the disappearance of yourself and your friend Mr. Leiter. Not more than a nuisance; but for various reasons I wish to concentrate on other matters at the present time.

'So,' Mr. Big looked at his watch, 'I decided to leave my card upon each of you and to give you one more solemn warning. You must leave the country today, and Mr. Leiter must transfer to another assignment. I have quite enough to bother me without having a lot of agents from Europe added to the considerable strength of local busybodies with which I have to contend.

'That is all,' he concluded. 'If I see you again, you will die in a manner as ingenious and appropriate as I can devise on that day.

'Tee-Hee, take Mister Bond to the garage. Tell two of the men to take him to Central Park and throw him in the ornamental water. He may be damaged but not killed if he resists. Understood?'

'Yassuh, Boss,' said Tee-Hee, giggling in a high falsetto.

He undid Bond's ankles, then his wrists. He took Bond's injured hand and twisted it right up his back. Then with his other hand he undid the strap round his waist. He yanked Bond to his feet.

'Giddap,' said Tee-Hee.

Bond gazed once more into the great grey face.

'Those who deserve to die,' he paused, 'die the death they deserve. Write that down,' he added. 'It's an original thought.'

Then he glanced at Solitaire. Her eyes were bent on the hands in her lap. She didn't look up.

'Git goin,' said Tee-Hee. He turned Bond round towards the wall and pushed him forward, twisting Bond's wrist up his back until his forearm was almost dislocated. Bond uttered a realistic groan and his footsteps faltered. He wanted Tee-Hee to believe that he was cowed and docile. He wanted the torturing grip to ease just a little on his left arm. As it was, any sudden movement would only result in his arm being broken.

Tee-Hee reached over Bond's shoulder and pressed on one of the books in the serried shelves. A large section opened on a central pivot. Bond was pushed through and the negro kicked the heavy section back into place. It closed with a double click. From the thickness of the door, Bond guessed it would be sound-proof. They were faced by a short carpeted passage ending in some stairs that led downwards. Bond groaned.

'You're breaking my arm,' he said. 'Look out. I'm going to faint.'

He stumbled again, trying to measure exactly the negro's position behind him. He remembered Leiter's injunction: 'Shins, groin, stomach, throat. Hit 'em anywhere else and you'll just break your hand.'

'Shut yo mouf,' said the negro, but he pulled Bond's hand an inch or two down his back.

This was all Bond needed.

They were half way down the passage with only a few

feet more to the top of the stairs. Bond faltered again, so that the negro's body bumped into his. This gave him all the range and direction he needed.

He bent a little and his right hand, straight and flat as a board, whipped round and inwards. He felt it thud hard into the target. The negro screamed shrilly like a wounded rabbit. Bond felt his left arm come free. He whirled round, pulling out his empty gun with his right hand. The negro was bent double, his hands between his legs, uttering little panting screams. Bond whipped the gun down hard on the back of the woolly skull. It gave back a dull klonk as if he had hammered on a door, but the negro groaned and fell forward on his knees, throwing out his hands for support. Bond got behind him and with all the force he could put behind the steel-capped shoe, he gave one mighty kick below the lavender-coloured seat of the negro's pants.

A final short scream was driven out of the man as he sailed the few feet to the stairs. His head hit the side of the iron banisters and then, a twisting wheel of arms and legs, he disappeared over the edge, down into the well. There was a short crash as he caromed off some obstacle, then a pause, then a mingled thud and crack as he hit the ground. Then silence.

Bond wiped the sweat out of his eyes and stood listening. He thrust his wounded left hand into his coat. It was throbbing with pain and swollen to almost twice its normal size. Holding his gun in his right hand, he walked to the head of the stairs and slowly down, moving softly on the balls of his feet.

There was only one floor between him and the spread-eagled body below. When he reached the landing, he stopped again and listened. Quite close, he could hear the high-pitched whine of some form of fast wireless transmitter. He verified that it came from behind one of the two doors on the landing. This must be Mr. Big's communications centre. He longed to carry out a quick raid. But his gun was empty and he had no idea how many men he would find in the room. It could only have been the earphones on their ears that had prevented the operators from hearing the sounds of Tee-Hee's fall. He crept on down.

Tee-Hee was either dead or dying. He lay spread-eagled on his back. His striped tie lay across his face like a squashed adder. Bond felt no remorse. He frisked the body for a gun and found one stuck in the waistband of the lavender trousers, now stained with blood. It was a Colt .38 Detective Special with a sawn barrel. All chambers were loaded. Bond slipped the useless Beretta back in its holster. He nestled the big gun into his palm and smiled grimly.

A small door faced him, bolted on the inside. Bond put his ear to it. The muffled sound of an engine reached him. This must be the garage. But the running engine? At that time of the morning? Bond ground his teeth. Of course. Mr. Big would have spoken on the intercom and warned them that Tee-Hee was bringing him down. They must be wondering what was holding him. They were probably watching the door for the negro to emerge.

Bond thought for a moment. He had the advantage of surprise. If only the bolts were well-oiled.

His left hand was almost useless. With the Colt in his right, he tested the first bolt with the edge of his damaged hand. It slipped easily back. So did the second. There remained only a press-down handle. He eased it down and pulled the door softly towards him.

It was a thick door and the noise of the engine got louder

as the crack widened. The car must be just outside. Any further movement of the door would betray him. He whipped it open and stood facing sideways like a fencer so as to offer as small a target as possible. The hammer lay back on his gun.

A few feet away stood a black sedan, its engine running. It faced the open double doors of the garage. Bright arc-lights lit up the shining bodywork of several other cars. There was a big negro at the wheel of the sedan and another stood near him, leaning against the rear door. No one else was in view.

At sight of Bond the negroes' mouths fell open in astonishment. A cigarette dropped from the mouth of the man at the wheel. Then they both dived for their guns.

Instinctively, Bond shot first at the man standing, knowing he would be quickest on the draw.

The heavy gun roared hollowly in the garage.

The negro clutched his stomach with both hands, staggered two steps towards Bond, and collapsed on his face, his gun clattering on to the concrete.

The man at the wheel screamed as Bond's gun swung on to him. Hampered by the wheel the negro's shooting hand was still inside his coat.

Bond shot straight into the screaming mouth and the man's head crashed against the side window.

Bond ran round the car and opened the door. The negro sprawled horribly out. Bond threw his revolver on to the driving-seat and yanked the body out on to the ground. He tried to avoid the blood. He got into the seat and blessed the running engine and the steering-wheel gear-lever. He slammed the door, rested his injured hand on the left of the wheel and crashed the lever forward.

The hand-brake was still on. He had to lean under the wheel to release it with his right hand.

It was a dangerous pause. As the heavy car surged forward out of the wide doors there was the boom of a gun and a bullet hammered into the bodywork. He tore the wheel round right-handed and there was another shot that missed high. Across the street a window splintered.

The flash came from low down near the floor and Bond guessed that the first negro had somehow managed to reach his gun.

There were no other shots and no sound came from the blank faces of the buildings behind him. As he went through the gears he could see nothing in the driving-mirror except the broad bar of light from the garage shining out across the dark empty street.

Bond had no idea where he was or where he was heading. It was a wide featureless street and he kept going. He found himself driving on the left-hand side and quickly swerved over to the right. His hand hurt terribly but the thumb and forefinger helped to steady the wheel. He tried to remember to keep his left side away from the blood on the door and window. The endless street was populated only by the little ghosts of steam that wavered up out of the gratings in the asphalt that gave access to the piped heat system of the city. The ugly bonnet of the car mowed them down one by one, but in the driving-mirror Bond could see them rising again behind him in a diminishing vista of mildly gesticulating white wraiths.

He kept the big car at fifty. He came to some red traffic lights and jumped them. Several more dark blocks and then there was a lighted avenue. There was traffic and he paused until the lights went green. He turned left and was rewarded by a succession of green lights, each one sweeping him on and further away from the enemy. He checked at an intersection and read the signs. He was on Park Avenue and 116th Street. He slowed again at the next street. It was 115th. He was heading downtown, away from Harlem, back into the City. He kept going. He turned off at 60th Street. It was deserted. He switched off the engine and left the car opposite a fire hydrant. He took the gun off the seat, shoved it down the waistband of his trousers and walked back to Park Avenue.

A few minutes later he flagged a prowling cab and then suddenly he was walking up the steps of the St. Regis.

'Message for you, Mr. Bond,' said the night porter. Bond kept his left side away from him. He opened the message with his right hand. It was from Felix Leiter, timed at four a.m. 'Call me at once,' it said.

Bond walked to the elevator and was carried up to his floor. He let himself into 2100 and went through into the sitting-room.

So both of them were alive. Bond fell into a chair beside the telephone.

'God Almighty,' said Bond with deep gratitude. 'What a break.'

CHAPTER IX

TRUE OR FALSE?

BOND looked at the telephone, then he got up and walked over to the sideboard. He put a handful of wilted ice-cubes into a tall glass, poured in three inches of Haig and Haig and swilled the mixture round in the glass to cool and dilute it. Then he drank down half the glass in one long swallow. He put the glass down and eased himself out of his coat. His left hand was so swollen that he could only just get it through the sleeve. His little finger was still crooked back and the pain was vicious as it scraped against the cloth. The finger was nearly black. He pulled down his tie and undid the top of his shirt. Then he picked up his glass, took another deep swallow, and walked back to the telephone.

Leiter answered at once.

'Thank God,' said Leiter with real feeling. 'What's the damage?"

'Broken finger,' said Bond. 'How about you?'

'Blackjack. Knocked out. Nothing serious. They started off by considering all sorts of ingenious things. Wanted to couple me to the compressed-air pump in the garage. Start on the ears and then proceed elsewhere. When no instructions came from The Big Man they got bored and I got to arguing the finer points of Jazz with Blabbermouth, the man with the fancy six-shooter. We got on to Duke Ellington and agreed that we liked our band-leaders to be percussion men, not wind. We agreed the piano or the drums held the band together better than any other solo instrument – Jelly-roll Morton, for instance. Apropos the Duke, I told him the crack about the clarinet – "an ill woodwind that nobody blows good". That made him laugh fit to bust. Suddenly we were friends. The other man – The Flannel, he was called – got sour and Blabbermouth told him he could go off duty, he'd look after me. Then The Big Man rang down.'

'I was there,' said Bond. 'It didn't sound so hot.'

'Blabbermouth was worried as hell. He wandered round the room talking to himself. Suddenly he used the black-jack, hard, and I went out. Next thing I knew we were outside Bellevue Hospital. About half after three. Blabbermouth was very apologetic, said it was the least he could have done. I believe him. He begged me not to give him away. Said he was going to report that he'd left me half dead. Of course I promised to leak back some very lurid details. We parted on the best of terms. I got some treatment at the Emergency ward and came home. I was worried to Hell an' gone about you, but after a while the telephone started ringing. Police and F B I. Seems The Big Man has complained that some fool Limey went berserk at The Boneyard early this morning, shot three of his men – two chauffeurs and a waiter, if you please – stole one of his cars and got away, leaving his overcoat and hat in the cloakroom. The Big Man's yelling for action. Of course I warned off the dicks and the F B I, but they're madder'n hell and we've got to get out of town at once. It'll miss the mornings but it'll be splashed all over the afternoon blatts and Radio and TV'll have it. Apart from all that, Mr. Big will be after you like a nest of hornets. Anyway, I've got some plans fixed. Now you tell, and God, am I glad to hear your voice!'

Bond gave a detailed account of all that had happened. He forgot nothing. When he had finished, Leiter gave a low whistle.

'Boy,' he said with admiration. 'You certainly made a dent in The Big Man's machine. But were you lucky. That Solitaire dame certainly seems to have saved your bacon. D'you think we can use her?'

'Could if we could get near her,' said Bond. 'I should think he keeps her pretty close.'

'We'll have to think about that another day,' said Leiter. 'Now we'd better get moving. I'll hang up and call you back in a few minutes. First I'll get the police surgeon round to you right away. Be along in a quarter of an hour or so. Then I'll talk to the Commissioner myself and sort out some of the police angles. They can stall a bit by discovering the car. The FBI'll have to tip off the radio and newspaper boys so that at least we can keep your name out of it and all this Limey talk. Otherwise we shall have the British Ambassador being hauled out of bed and parades by the National Association for the Advancement of Coloured People and God knows what all. Leiter chuckled down the telephone. 'Better have a word with your chief in London. It's about half after ten their time. You'll need a bit of protection. I can look after the CIA, but the FBI have got a bad attack of "see-here-young-man" this morning. You'll need some more clothes. I'll see to that. Keep awake. We'll get plenty of sleep in the grave. Be calling you.'

He hung up. Bond smiled to himself. Hearing Leiter's cheerful voice and knowing everything was being taken care of had wiped away his exhaustion and his black memories.

He picked up the telephone and talked to the Overseas operator. Ten minutes' delay, she said.

Bond walked into his bedroom and somehow got out of his clothes. He gave himself a very hot shower and then an ice-cold one. He shaved and managed to pull on a clean shirt and trousers. He put a fresh clip in his Beretta and wrapped the Colt in his discarded shirt and put it in his suitcase. He was half way through his packing when the telephone rang.

He listened to the zing and echo on the line, the chatter of distant operators, the patches of Morse from aircraft and ships at sea, quickly suppressed. He could see the big, grey building near Regents Park and imagine the busy switchboard and the cups of tea and a girl saying, 'Yes, this is Universal Export,' the address Bond had asked for, one of the covers used by agents for emergency calls on open lines from abroad. She would tell the Supervisor, who would take the call over.

'You're connected, caller,' said the Overseas operator. 'Go ahead, please. New York calling London.'

Bond heard the calm English voice. 'Universal Export. Who's speaking, please?'

'Can I speak to the Managing Director,' said Bond. 'This is his nephew James speaking from New York.'

'Just a moment, please.' Bond could follow the call to Miss Moneypenny and see her press the switch on the intercom. 'It's New York, Sir,' she would say. 'I think it's 007.' 'Put him through,' M would say.

'Yes?' said the cold voice that Bond loved and obeyed.

'It's James, Sir,' said Bond. 'I may need a bit of help over a difficult consignment.'

'Go ahead,' said the voice.

'I went uptown to see our chief customer last night,' said Bond. 'Three of his best men went sick while I was there.'

'How sick?' asked the voice.

'As sick as can be, Sir,' said Bond. 'There's a lot of 'flu about.'

'Hope you didn't catch any.'

'I've got a slight chill, Sir,' said Bond, 'but absolutely nothing to worry about. I'll write to you about it. The trouble is that with all this 'flu about Federated think I will do better out of town.' (Bond chuckled to himself at the thought of M's grin.) 'So I'm off right away with Felicia.'

'Who?' asked M.

'Felicia,' Bond spelled it out. 'My new secretary from Washington.'

'Oh, yes.'

'Thought I'd try that factory you advised at San Pedro.'

'Good idea.'

'But Federated may have other ideas and I hoped you'd give me your support.'

'I quite understand,' said M. 'How's business?'

'Rather promising, Sir. But tough going. Felicia will be typing my full report today.'

'Good,' said M. 'Anything else?'

'No, that's all, Sir. Thanks for your support.'

'That's all right. Keep fit. Goodbye.'

'Goodbye, Sir.'

Bond put down the telephone. He grinned. He could imagine M calling in the Chief of Staff. '007's already tangled up with the FBI. Dam' fool went up to Harlem last night and bumped off three of Mr. Big's men. Got hurt himself, apparently, but not much. Got to get out of town with Leiter, the CIA man. Going down to St. Petersburg. Better warn A and C. Expect we'll have Washington round our ears before the day's over. Tell A to say I fully sympathize, but that 007 has my full confidence and I'm sure he acted in self-defence. Won't happen again, and so forth. Got that?' Bond grinned again as he thought of Damon's exasperation at having to dish out a lot of soft soap to Washington when he probably had plenty of other Anglo-American snarls to disentangle.

The telephone rang. It was Leiter again.

'Now listen,' he said. 'Everybody's calming down somewhat. Seems the men you got were a pretty nasty trio – Tee-Hee Johnson, Sam Miami and a man called McThing. All wanted on various counts. The FBI's covering up for you. Reluctantly of course, and the Police are stalling like mad. The FBI big brass had already asked my Chief for you to be sent home – got him out of bed, if you please – mostly jealousy, I guess – but we've killed all that. Same time, we've both got to quit town at once. That's all fixed too. We can't go together, so you're taking the train and I'll fly. Jot this down.'

Bond cradled the telephone against his shoulder and reached for a pencil and paper. 'Go ahead,' he said.

'Pennsylvania Station. Track 14. Ten-thirty this morning. "The Silver Phantom". Through train to St. Petersburg via Washington, Jacksonville and Tampa. I've got you a compartment. Very luxurious. Car 245, Compartment H. Ticket'll be on the train. Conductor will have it. In the name of Bryce. Just go to Gate 14 and down to the train. Then straight to your compartment and lock yourself in till the train starts. I'm flying down in an hour by Eastern, so you'll be alone from now on. If you get stuck call Dexter, but don't be surprised if he bites your head off. Train gets in around midday tomorrow. Take a cab and go to the Everglades Cabanas, Gulf Boulevard West, on Sunset Beach.

That's on a place called Treasure Island where all the beach hotels are. Connected with St. Petersburg by a causeway. Cabby'll know it.

'I'll be waiting for you. Got all that? And for God's sake watch out. And I mean it. The Big Man'll get you if he possibly can and a police escort to the train would only put the finger on you. Take a cab and keep out of sight. I'm sending you up another hat and a fawn raincoat. The check's taken care of at the St. Regis. That's the lot. Any questions?'

'Sounds fine,' said Bond. 'I've talked to M and he'll square Washington if there's any trouble. Look after yourself too,' he added. 'You'll be next on the list after me. See you tomorrow. So long.'

'I'll watch out,' said Leiter. ''Bye.'

It was half-past six and Bond pulled back the curtains in the sitting-room and watched the dawn come up over the city. It was still dark down in the caverns below but the tips of the great concrete stalagmites were pink and the sun lit up the windows floor by floor as if an army of descending janitors was at work in the buildings.

The police surgeon came, stayed for a painful quarter of an hour and left.

'Clean fracture,' he had said. 'Take a few days to heal. How did you come by it?'

'Caught it in a door,' said Bond.

'You ought to keep away from doors,' commented the surgeon. 'They're dangerous things. Ought to be forbidden by law. Lucky you didn't catch your neck in this one.'

When he had gone, Bond finished packing. He was wondering how soon he could order breakfast when the telephone rang.

Bond was expecting a harsh voice from the Police or the FBI. Instead, a girl's voice, low and urgent, asked for Mr. Bond.

'Who's calling?' asked Bond, gaining time. He knew the answer.

'I know it's you,' said the voice, and Bond could feel that it was right up against the mouthpiece. 'This is Solitaire.' The name was scarcely breathed into the telephone.

Bond waited, all his senses pricked to what might be the scene at the other end of the line. Was she alone? Was she speaking foolishly on a house-phone with extensions to which other listeners were now coldly, intently glued? Or was she in a room with only Mr. Big's eyes bent carefully on her, a pencil and pad beside him so that he could prompt the next question?

'Listen,' said the voice. 'I've got to be quick. You must trust me. I'm in a drugstore, but I must get back at once to my room. Please believe me.'

Bond had his handkerchief out. He spoke into it. 'If I can reach Mr. Bond what shall I tell him?'

'Oh damn you,' said the girl with what sounded like a genuine touch of hysteria. 'I swear by my mother, by my unborn children. I've got to get away. And so have you. You've got to take me. I'll help you. I know a lot of his secrets. But be quick. I'm risking my life here talking to you.' She gave a sob of exasperation and panic. 'For God's sake trust me. You must. You must!'

Bond still paused, his mind working furiously.

'Listen,' she spoke again, but this time dully, almost hopelessly. 'If you don't take me, I shall kill myself. Now will you? Do you want to murder me?'

If it was acting, it was too good acting. It was still an

unpardonable gamble, but Bond decided. He spoke directly into the telephone, his voice low.

'If this is a double-cross, Solitaire, I'll get at you and kill you if it's the last thing I do. Have you got a pencil and paper?'

'Wait,' said the girl, excitedly. 'Yes, yes.'

If it had been a plant, reflected Bond, all that would have been ready.

'Be at Pennsylvania Station at ten-twenty exactly. The Silver Phantom to . . .' he hesitated. '. . . to Washington. Car 245, Compartment H. Say you're Mrs. Bryce. Conductor has the ticket in case I'm not there already. Go straight to the compartment and wait for me. Got that?'

'Yes,' said the girl, 'and thank you, thank you.'

'Don't be seen,' said Bond. 'Wear a veil or something.'

'Of course,' said the girl. 'I promise. I really promise. I must go.' She rang off.

Bond looked at the dead receiver, then put it down on the cradle. 'Well,' he said aloud. 'That's torn it.'

He got up and stretched. He walked to the window and looked out, seeing nothing. His thoughts raced. Then he shrugged and turned back to the telephone. He looked at his watch. It was seven-thirty.

'Room Service, good morning,' said the golden voice.

'Breakfast, please,' said Bond. 'Pineapple juice, double. Cornflakes and cream. Shirred eggs with bacon. Double portion of Café Espresso. Toast and marmalade.'

'Yes, Sir,' said the girl. She repeated the order. 'Right away.'

'Thank you.'

'You're welcome.'

Bond grinned to himself.

'The condemned man made a hearty breakfast,' he reflected. He sat down by the window and gazed up at the clear sky, into the future.

Up in Harlem, at the big switchboard, The Whisper was talking to the town again, passing Bond's description again to all Eyes: 'All de railroads, all de airports. Fifth Avenue an' 55th Street doors of da San Regis. Mr. Big sez we gotta chance da highways. Pass it down da line. All de railroads, all de airports. . . .'

CHAPTER X

THE SILVER PHANTOM

BOND, the collar of his new raincoat up round his ears, was missed as he came out of the entrance of the St. Regis Drugstore on 55th Street, which has a connecting door into the hotel.

He waited in the entrance and leaped at a cruising cab, hooking the door open with the thumb of his injured hand and throwing his light suitcase in ahead of him. The cab hardly checked. The negro with the collecting-box for the Coloured Veterans of Korea and his colleague fumbling under the bonnet of his stalled car stayed on the job until, much later, they were called off by a man who drove past and sounded two shorts and a long on his horn.

But Bond was immediately spotted as he left his cab at the drive-in to the Pennsylvania Station. A lounging negro with a wicker basket walked quickly into a call-box. It was ten-fifteen.

Only fifteen minutes to go and yet, just before the train started, one of the waiters in the diner reported sick and was hurriedly replaced by a man who had received a full and careful briefing on the telephone. The chef swore there was something fishy, but the new man said a word or two to him and the chef showed the whites of his eyes and went silent, surreptitiously touching the lucky bean that hung round his neck on a string.

Bond had walked quickly through the great glass-covered concourse and through Gate 14 down to his train.

It lay, a quarter of a mile of silver carriages, quietly in the dusk of the underground station. Up front, the auxiliary generators of the 4000 horsepower twin Diesel electric units ticked busily. Under the bare electric bulbs the horizontal purple and gold bands, the colours of the Seaboard Railroad, glowed regally on the streamlined locomotives. The engineman and fireman who would take the great train on the first two hundred mile lap into the south lolled in the spotless aluminium cabin, twelve feet above the track, watching the ammeter and the air-pressure dial, ready to go.

It was quiet in the great concrete cavern below the city and every noise threw an echo.

There were not many passengers. More would be taken on at Newark, Philadelphia, Baltimore and Washington. Bond walked a hundred yards, his feet ringing on the empty platform, before he found Car 245, towards the rear of the train. A Pullman porter stood at the door. He wore spectacles. His black face was bored but friendly. Below the windows of the carriage, in broad letters of brown and gold, was written 'Richmond, Fredericksburg and Potomac', and below that 'Bellesylvania', the name of the Pullman car. A thin wisp of steam rose from the couplings of the central heating near the door.

'Compartment H,' said Bond.

'Mr. Bryce, Suh? Yassuh. Mrs. Bryce just come aboard. Straight down da cyar.'

Bond stepped on to the train and turned down the drab olive green corridor. The carpet was thick. There was the usual American train-smell of old cigar-smoke. A notice said 'Need a second pillow? For any extra comfort ring for your Pullman Attendant. His name is,' then a printed card, slipped in : 'Samuel D. Baldwin.'

H was more than half-way down the car. There was a respectable-looking American couple in E, otherwise the rooms were empty. The door of H was closed. He tried it and it was locked.

'Who's that?' asked a girl's voice, anxiously.

'It's me,' said Bond.

The door opened. Bond walked through, put down his bag and locked the door behind him.

She was in a black tailor-made. A wide-mesh veil came down from the rim of a small black straw hat. One gloved hand was up to her throat and through the veil Bond could see that her face was pale and her eyes were wide with fear. She looked rather French and very beautiful.

'Thank God,' she said.

Bond gave a quick glance round the room. He opened the lavatory door and looked in. It was empty.

A voice on the platform outside called 'Board!' There was a clang as the attendant pulled up the folding iron step and shut the door and then the train was rolling quietly down the track. A bell clanged monotonously as they passed the automatic signals. There was a slight clatter from the wheels as they crossed some points and then the train began to accelerate. For better or for worse, they were on their way.

'Which seat would you like?' asked Bond.

'I don't mind,' she said anxiously. 'You choose.'

Bond shrugged and sat down with his back to the engine. He preferred to face forwards.

She sat down nervously facing him. They were still in

the long tunnel that takes the Philadelphia lines out of the city.

She took off her hat and unpinned the broad-mesh veil and put them on the seat beside her. She took some hair-pins out of the back of her hair and shook her head so that the heavy black hair fell forward. There were blue shadows under her eyes and Bond reflected that she too must have gone without sleep that night.

There was a table between them. Suddenly she reached forward and pulled his right hand towards her on the table. She held it in both her hands and bent forward and kissed it. Bond frowned and tried to pull his hand away, but for a moment she held it tight in both of hers.

She looked up and her wide blue eyes looked candidly into his.

'Thank you,' she said. 'Thank you for trusting me. It was difficult for you.' She released his hand and sat back.

'I'm glad I did,' said Bond inadequately, his mind trying to grapple with the mystery of this woman. He dug in his pocket for his cigarettes and lighter. It was a new pack of Chesterfields and with his right hand he scrabbled at the cellophane wrapper.

She reached over and took the pack from him. She slit it with her thumb-nail, took out a cigarette, lit it and handed it to him. Bond took it from her and smiled into her eyes, tasting the hint of lipstick from her mouth.

'I smoke about three packs a day,' he said. 'You're going to be busy.'

'I'll just help with the new packs,' she said. 'Don't be afraid I'm going to fuss over you the whole way to St. Petersburg.'

Bond's eyes narrowed and the smile went out of them.

'You don't believe I thought we were only going as far as Washington,' she said. 'You weren't very quick on the telephone this morning. And anyway, Mr. Big was certain you would make for Florida. I heard him warning his people down there about you. He spoke to a man called "The Robber", long distance. Said to watch the airport at Tampa and the trains. Perhaps we ought to get off the train earlier, at Tarpon Springs or one of the small stations up the coast. Did they see you getting on the train?'

'Not that I know of,' said Bond. His eyes had relaxed again. 'How about you? Have any trouble getting away?'

'It was my day for a singing lesson. He's trying to make a torch singer out of me. Wants me to go on at The Boneyard. One of his men took me to my teacher as usual and was due to pick me up again at midday. He wasn't surprised I was having a lesson so early. I often have breakfast with my teacher so as to get away from Mr. Big. He expects me to have all my meals with him.' She looked at her watch. He noted cynically that it was an expensive one – diamonds and platinum, Bond guessed. 'They'll be missing me in about an hour. I waited until the car had gone, then I walked straight out again and called you. Then I took a cab downtown. I bought a toothbrush and a few other things at a drugstore. Otherwise I've got nothing except my jewellery and the mad money I've always kept hidden from him. About five thousand dollars. So I won't be a financial burden.' She smiled. 'I thought I'd get my chance one day.' She gestured towards the window. 'You've given me a new life. I've been shut up with him and his nigger gangsters for nearly a year. This is heaven.'

The train was running through the unkempt barren plains and swamps between New York and Trenton. It wasn't an attractive prospect. It reminded Bond of some of the stretches on the pre-war Trans-Siberian Railway except for the huge lonely hoardings advertising the current Broadway shows and the occasional dumps of scrap-iron and old motor cars.

'I hope I can find you something better than that,' he said smiling. 'But don't thank me. We're quits now. You saved my life last night. That is,' he added looking at her curiously, 'if you really have got second sight.'

'Yes,' she said, 'I have. Or something very like it. I can often see what's going to happen, particularly to other people. Of course I embroider on it and when I was earning my living doing it in Haiti it was easy to turn it into a good cabaret act. They're riddled with Voodoo and superstitions there and they were quite certain I was a witch. But I promise that when I first saw you in that room I knew you had been sent to save me. I,' she blushed, 'I saw all sorts of things.'

'What sort of things?'

'Oh I don't know,' she said, her eyes dancing. 'Just things. Anyway, we'll see. But it's going to be difficult,' she added seriously, 'and dangerous. For both of us.' She paused. 'So will you please take good care of us?'

'I'll do my best,' said Bond. 'The first thing is for us both to get some sleep. Let's have a drink and some chicken sandwiches and then we'll get the porter to put our beds down. You mustn't be embarrassed,' he added, seeing her eyes recoil. 'We're in this together. We have to spend twenty-four hours in a double bedroom together, and it's no good being squeamish. Anyway, you're Mrs. Bryce,' he grinned, 'and you must just act like her. Up to a point anyway,' he added.

She laughed. Her eyes speculated. She said nothing but rang the bell below the window.

The conductor arrived at the same time as the Pullman attendant. Bond ordered Old Fashioneds, and stipulated 'Old Grandad' Bourbon, chicken sandwiches, and decaffeined 'Sanka' coffee so that their sleep would not be spoilt.

'I have to collect another fare from you, Mr. Bryce,' said the conductor.

'Of course,' said Bond. Solitaire made a movement towards her handbag. 'It's all right, darling,' said Bond, pulling out his notecase. 'You've forgotten you gave me your money to look after before we left the house.'

'Guess the lady'll need plenty for her summer frocks,' said the conductor. 'Shops is plenty expensive in St. Pete. Plenty hot down there too. You folks been to Florida before?"

'We always go at this time of year,' said Bond.

'Hope you have a pleasant trip,' said the conductor.

When the door shut behind him, Solitaire laughed delightedly.

'You can't embarrass me,' she said. 'I'll think up something really fierce if you're not careful. To begin with, I'm going in there,' she gestured towards the door behind Bond's head. 'I must look terrible.'

'Go ahead, darling,' laughed Bond as she disappeared.

Bond turned to the window and watched the pretty clapboard houses slip by as they approached Trenton. He loved trains and he looked forward with excitement to the rest of the journey.

The train was slowing down. They slid past sidings full of empty freight cars bearing names from all over the States – 'Lackawanna', 'Chesapeake and Ohio' 'Lehigh Valley', 'Seaboard Fruit Express', and the lilting 'Acheson, Topeka and Santa Fe' – names that held all the romance of the American railroads.

'British Railways?' thought Bond. He sighed and turned his thoughts back to the present adventure.

For better or worse he had decided to accept Solitaire, or rather, in his cold way, to make the most of her. There were many questions to be answered but now was not the time to ask them. All that immediately concerned him was that another blow had been struck at Mr. Big – where it would hurt most, in his vanity.

As for the girl, as a girl, he reflected that it was going to be fun teasing her and being teased back and he was glad that they had already crossed the frontiers into comradeship and even intimacy.

Was it true what The Big Man had said, that she would have nothing to do with men? He doubted it. She seemed open to love and to desire. At any rate he knew she was not closed to him. He wanted her to come back and sit down opposite him again so that he could look at her and play with her and slowly discover her. Solitaire. It was an attractive name. No wonder they had christened her that in the sleazy nightclubs of Port au Prince. Even in her present promise of warmth towards him there was much that was withdrawn and mysterious. He sensed a lonely childhood on some great decaying plantation, an echoing 'Great House' slowly falling into disrepair and being encroached on by the luxuriance of the tropics. The parents dying, and the property being sold. The companionship of a servant or two and an equivocal life in lodgings in the capital. The beauty which was her only asset and the struggle against the shady propositions to be a 'governess', a 'companion', a 'secretary', all of which meant respectable prostitution. Then the dubious, unknown steps into the world of entertainment. The evening stint at the nightclub with the mysterious act which, among people dominated by magic, must have kept many away from her and made her a person to be feared. And then, one evening, the huge man with the grey face sitting at a table by himself. The promise that he would put her on Broadway. The chance of a new life, of an escape from the heat and the dirt and the solitude.

Bond turned brusquely away from the window. A romantic picture, perhaps. But it must have been something like that.

He heard the door unlock. The girl came back and slid into the seat opposite him. She looked fresh and gay. She examined him carefully.

'You have been wondering about me,' she said. 'I felt it. Don't worry. There is nothing very bad to know. I will tell you all about it some day. When we have time. Now I want to forget about the past. I will just tell you my real name. It is Simone Latrelle, but you can call me what you like. I am twenty-five. And now I am happy. I like this little room. But I am hungry and sleepy. Which bed will you have?'

Bond smiled at the question. He reflected.

'It's not very gallant,' he said, 'but I think I'd better have the bottom one. I'd rather be close to the floor – just in case. Not that there's anything to worry about,' he added, seeing her frown, 'but Mr. Big seems to have a pretty long arm, particularly in the negro world. And that includes the railroads. Do you mind?'

'Of course not,' she said. 'I was going to suggest it. And you couldn't climb into the top one with your poor hand.'

Their lunch arrived, brought from the diner by a preoccupied negro waiter. He seemed anxious to be paid and get back to his work.

When they had finished and Bond rang for the Pullman porter, he also seemed distrait and avoided looking at Bond. He took his time getting the beds made up. He made much show of not having enough room to move around in.

Finally, he seemed to pluck up courage.

'Praps Mistress Bryce like set down nex' door while Ah git the room fixed,' he said, looking over Bond's head. 'Nex' room goin' to be empty all way to St. Pete.' He took out a key and unlocked the communicating door without waiting for Bond's reply.

At a gesture from Bond, Solitaire took the hint. He heard her lock the door into the corridor. The negro bumped the communicating door shut.

Bond waited for a moment. He remembered the negro's name.

'Got something on your mind, Baldwin?' he asked.

Relieved, the attendant turned and looked straight at him.

'Sho' have, Mister Bryce. Yassuh.' Once started, the words came in a torrent. 'Shouldn be tellin' yuh this, Mister Bryce, but dere's plenty trouble 'n this train this trip. Yuh gotten yoself a henemy 'n dis train, Mister Bryce. Yassuh. Ah hears tings which Ah don' like at all. Cain't say much.

Get mahself 'n plenty trouble. But yuh all want to watch yo step plenty good. Yassuh. Certain party got da finger 'n yuh, Mister Bryce, 'n dat man is bad news. Better take dese hyah,' he reached in his pocket and brought out two wooden window wedges. 'Push dem under the doors,' he said. 'Ah cain't do nuthen else. Git mah throat cut. But Ah don' like any foolin' aroun' wid da customers 'n my cyar. Nossuh.'

Bond took the wedges from him. 'But . . .'

'Cain't help yuh no more, Sah,' said the negro with finality, his hand on the door. 'Ef yuh ring fo me dis evenin', Ah'll fetch yo dinner. Doan yuh go lettin' any person else in the room.'

His hand came out to take the twenty-dollar bill. He crumpled it into his pocket.

'Ah'll do all Ah can, Sah,' he said. 'But dey'll git me ef Ah don' watch it. Sho will.' He went out and quickly shut the door behind him.

Bond thought for a moment then he opened the communicating door. Solitaire was reading.

'He's fixed everything,' he said. 'Took a long time about it. Wanted to tell me all his life-story as well. I'll keep out of your way until you've climbed up to your nest. Call me when you're ready.'

He sat down next door in the seat she had left and watched the grim suburbs of Philadelphia showing their sores, like beggars, to the rich train.

No object in frightening her until it had to be. But the new threat had come sooner than he expected, and her danger if the watcher on the train discovered her identity would be as great as his.

She called and he went in.

The room was in darkness save for his bed-light, which she had turned on.

'Sleep well,' she said.

Bond got out of his coat. He quietly slipped the wedges firmly under both doors. Then he lay down carefully on his right side on the comfortable bed and without a thought for the future fell into a deep sleep, lulled by the pounding gallop of the train.

A few cars away, in the deserted diner, a negro waiter read again what he had written on a telegraph blank and waited for the ten-minute stop at Philadelphia.

CHAPTER XI

ALLUMEUSE

THE crack train thundered on through the bright afternoon towards the south. They left Pennsylvania behind, and Maryland. There came a long halt at Washington, where Bond heard through his dreams the measured clang of the warning bells on the shunting engines and the soft think-speak of the public-address system on the station. Then on into Virginia. Here the air was already softer and the dusk, only five hours away from the bright frosty breath of New York, smelled almost of spring.

An occasional group of negroes, walking home from the fields, would hear the distant rumble on the silent sighing silver rails and one would pull out his watch and consult it and announce, 'Hyah comes da Phantom. Six o'clock. Guess ma watch is right on time.' 'Sho nuff,' one of the others would say as the great beat of the Diesels came nearer and the lighted coaches streaked past and on towards North Carolina.

They awoke around seven to the hasty ting of a grade-crossing alarm bell as the big train nosed its way out of the fields into the suburbs of Raleigh. Bond pulled the wedges from under the doors before he turned on the lights and rang for the attendant.

He ordered dry Martinis and when the two little 'personalized' bottles appeared with the glasses and the ice they seemed so inadequate that he at once ordered four more.

They argued over the menu. The fish was described as being 'Made From Flaky Tender Boneless Filets' and the chicken as 'Delicious French Fried to a Golden Brown, Served Disjointed'.

'Eyewash,' said Bond, and they finally ordered scrambled eggs and bacon and sausages, a salad, and some of the domestic Camembert that is one of the most welcome surprises on American menus.

It was nine o'clock when Baldwin came to clear the dishes away. He asked if there was anything else they wanted.

Bond had been thinking. 'What time do we get into Jacksonville?' he asked.

'Aroun' five 'n the morning, Suh.'

'Is there a subway on the platform?'

'Yassuh. Dis cyar stops right alongside.'

'Could you have the door open and the steps down pretty quick?'

The negro smiled. 'Yassuh. Ah kin take good care of that.'

Bond slipped him a ten-dollar bill. 'Just in case I miss you when we arrive in St. Petersburg,' he said.

The negro grinned. 'Ah greatly preeshiate yo kindness, Suh. Good night, Suh. Good night, Mam.'

He went out and closed the door.

Bond got up and pushed the wedges firmly under the two doors.

'I see,' said Solitaire. 'So it's like that.'

'Yes,' said Bond. 'I'm afraid so.' He told her of the warning he had had from Baldwin.

'I'm not surprised,' said the girl when he had finished. 'They must have seen you coming into the station. He's got a whole team of spies called "The Eyes" and when they're put out on a job it's almost impossible to get by them. I wonder who he's got on the train. You can be certain it's a negro, either a Pullman attendant or someone in the diner. He can make these people do absolutely anything he likes.'

'So it seems,' said Bond. 'But how does it work? What's he got on them?'

She looked out of the window into the tunnel of darkness through which the lighted train was burning its thundering path. Then she looked back across the table into the cool wide grey-blue eyes of the English agent. She thought: how can one explain to someone with that certainty of spirit, with that background of common sense, brought up with clothes and shoes among the warm houses and the lighted streets? How can one explain to someone who hasn't lived close to the secret heart of the tropics, at the mercy of their anger and stealth and poison; who hasn't experienced the mystery of the drums, seen the quick workings of magic and the mortal dread it inspires? What can he know of catalepsy, and thought-transference and the sixth sense of fish, of birds, of negroes; the deadly meaning of a white chicken's feather, a crossed stick in the road, a little leather bag of bones and herbs? What of Mialism, of shadow-taking, of the death by swelling and the death by wasting?

She shivered and a whole host of dark memories clustered round her. Above all, she remembered that first time in the Houmfor where her black nurse had once taken her as a child. 'It do yuh no harm, Missy. Dis powerful good juju. Care fe yuh res 'f yo life.' And the disgusting old man and the filthy drink he had given her. How her nurse had held her jaws open until she had drunk the last drop and how she had lain awake screaming every night for a week. And how her nurse had been worried and then suddenly she had slept all right until, weeks later, shifting on her pillow, she had felt something hard and had dug it out from the pillow-case, a dirty little packet of muck. She had thrown it out of the window, but in the morning she could not find it. She had continued to sleep well and she knew it must have been found by the nurse and secreted somewhere under the floorboards.

Years later, she had found out about the Voodoo drink – a concoction of rum, gunpowder, grave-dirt and human blood. She almost retched as the taste came back to her mouth.

What could this man know of these things or of her half-belief in them?

She looked up and found Bond's eyes fixed quizzically on her.

'You're thinking I shan't understand,' he said. 'And you're right up to a point. But I know what fear can do to people and I know that fear can be caused by many things. I've read most of the books on Voodoo and I believe that it works. I don't think it would work on me because I stopped being afraid of the dark when I was a child and I'm not a good subject for suggestion or hypnotism. But I know the jargon and you needn't think I shall laugh at it. The scientists and doctors who wrote the books don't laugh at it.'

Solitaire smiled. 'All right,' she said. 'Then all I need tell you is that they believe The Big Man is the Zombie of Baron Samedi. Zombies are bad enough by themselves. They're animated corpses that have been made to rise from the dead and obey the commands of the person who controls them. Baron Samedi is the most dreadful spirit in the whole of Voodooism. He is the spirit of darkness and death. So for Baron Samedi to be in control of his own Zombie is a very dreadful conception. You know what Mr. Big looks like. He is huge and grey and he has great psychic power. It is not difficult for a negro to believe that he is a Zombie and a very bad one at that. The step to Baron Samedi is simple. Mr. Big encourages the idea by having the Baron's fetish at his elbow. You saw it in his room.'

She paused. She went on quickly, almost breathlessly: 'And I can tell you that it works and that there's hardly a negro who has seen him and heard the story who doesn't believe it and who doesn't regard him with complete and absolute dread. And they are right,' she added. 'And you would say so too if you knew the way he deals with those who haven't obeyed him completely, the way they are tortured and killed.'

'Where does Moscow come in?' asked Bond. 'Is it true he's an agent of SMERSH?'

'I don't know what SMERSH is,' said the girl, 'but I know he works for Russia, at least I've heard him talking Russian to people who come from time to time. Occasionally he's had me in to that room and asked me afterwards what I thought of his visitors. Generally it seemed to me they were telling the truth although I couldn't understand what they said. But don't forget I've only known him for a year and he's fantastically secretive. If Moscow does use him they've got hold of one of the most powerful men in America. He can find out almost anything he wants to and if he doesn't get what he wants somebody gets killed.'

'Why doesn't someone kill him?' asked Bond.

'You can't kill him,' she said. 'He's already dead. He's a Zombie.'

'Yes, I see,' said Bond slowly. 'It's quite an impressive arrangement. Would you try?'

She looked out of the window, then back at him.

'As a last resort,' she admitted unwillingly. 'But don't forget I come from Haiti. My brain tells me I could kill him, but . . .' She made a helpless gesture with her hands. '. . . my instinct tells me I couldn't.'

She smiled at him docilely. 'You must think me a hopeless fool,' she said.

Bond reflected. 'Not after reading all those books,' he admitted. He put his hand across the table and covered hers with it. 'When the time comes,' he said, smiling, 'I'll cut a cross in my bullet. That used to work in the old days.'

She looked thoughtful. 'I believe that if anybody can do it, you can,' she said. 'You hit him hard last night in exchange for what he did to you.' She took his hand in hers and pressed it. 'Now tell me what I must do.'

'Bed,' said Bond. He looked at his watch. It was ten o'clock. 'Might as well get as much sleep as we can. We'll slip off the train at Jacksonville and chance being spotted. Find another way down to the Coast.'

They got up. They stood facing each other in the swaying train.

Suddenly Bond reached out and took her in his right arm. Her arms went round his neck and they kissed passionately. He pressed her up against the swaying wall and held her there. She took his face between her two hands and held it away, panting. Her eyes were bright and hot. Then she brought his lips against hers again and kissed him long and lasciviously, as if she was the man and he the woman.

Bond cursed the broken hand that prevented him exploring her body, taking her. He freed his right hand and put it between their bodies, feeling her hard breasts, each with its pointed stigma of desire. He slipped it down her back until it came to the cleft at the base of her spine and he let it rest there, holding the centre of her body hard against him until they had kissed enough.

She took her arms away from around his neck and pushed him away.

'I hoped I would one day kiss a man like that,' she said. 'And when I first saw you, I knew it would be you.'

Her arms were down by her sides and her body stood there, open to him, ready for him.

'You're very beautiful,' said Bond. 'You kiss more wonderfully than any girl I have ever known.' He looked down at the bandages on his left hand. 'Curse this arm,' he said. 'I can't hold you properly or make love to you. It hurts too much. That's something else Mr. Big's got to pay for.'

She laughed.

She took a handkerchief out of her bag and wiped the lipstick off his mouth. Then she brushed the hair away from his forehead, and kissed him again, lightly and tenderly.

'It's just as well,' she said. 'There are too many other things on our minds.'

The train rocked him back against her.

He put his hand on her left breast and kissed her white throat. Then he kissed her mouth.

He felt the pounding of his blood softening. He took her

by the hand and drew her out into the middle of the little swaying room.

He smiled. 'Perhaps you're right,' he said. 'When the time comes I want to be alone with you, with all the time in the world. Here there is at least one man who will probably disturb our night. And we'll have to be up at four in the morning anyway. So there simply isn't time to begin making love to you now. You get ready for bed and I'll climb up after you and kiss you good night.'

They kissed once more, slowly, then he stepped away.

'We'll just see if we have company next door,' he said.

He softly pulled the wedge away from under the communicating door and gently turned the lock. He took the Beretta out of its holster, thumbed back the safety-catch and gestured to her to pull open the door so that she was behind it. He gave the signal and she wrenched it quickly open. The empty compartment yawned sarcastically at them

Bond smiled at her and shrugged his shoulders.

'Call me when you're ready,' he said and went in and closed the door.

The door to the corridor was locked. The room was identical with theirs. Bond went over it very carefully for vulnerable points. There was only the air-conditioning vent in the ceiling and Bond, who was prepared to consider any possibility, dismissed the employment of gas in the system. It would slay all the other occupants of the car. There only remained the waste pipes in the small lavatory and while these certainly could be used to insert some death-dealing medium from the underbelly of the train, the operator would have to be a daring and skilled acrobat. There was no ventilating grill into the corridor.

Bond shrugged his shoulders. If anyone came, it would be through the doors. He would just have to stay awake.

Solitaire called for him. The room smelled of Balmain's 'Vent Vert'. She was leaning on her elbow and looking down at him from the upper berth.

The bedclothes were pulled up round her shoulder. Bond guessed that she was naked. Her black hair fell away from her head in a dark cascade. With only the reading-lamp on behind her, her face was in shadow. Bond climbed up the little aluminium ladder and leant towards her. She reached towards him and suddenly the bedclothes fell away from her shoulders.

'Damn you,' said Bond. 'You . . .'

She put her hand over his mouth.

' "Allumeuse" is the nice word for it,' she said. 'It is fun for me to be able to tease such a strong silent man. You burn with such an angry flame. It is the only game I have to play with you and I shan't be able to play it for long. How many days until your hand is well again?'

Bond bit hard into the soft hand over his mouth. She gave a little scream.

'Not many,' said Bond. 'And then one day when you're playing your little game you'll suddenly find yourself pinned down like a butterfly.'

She put her arms round him and they kissed, long and passionately.

Finally she sank back among the pillows.

'Hurry up and get well,' she said. 'I'm tired of my game already.'

Bond climbed down to the floor and pulled her curtains across the berth.

'Try and get some sleep now,' he said. 'We've got a long day tomorrow.'

She murmured something and he heard her turn over. She switched off the light.

Bond verified that the wedges were in place under the doors. Then he took off his coat and tie and lay down on the bottom berth. He turned off his own light and lay thinking of Solitaire and listening to the steady gallop of the wheels beneath his head and the comfortable small noises in the room, the gentle rattles and squeaks and murmurs in the coachwork that bring sleep so quickly on a train at night-time.

It was eleven o'clock and the train was on the long stretch between Columbia and Savannah, Georgia. There were another six hours or so to Jacksonville, another six hours of darkness during which The Big Man would almost certainly have instructed his agent to make some move, while the whole train was asleep and while a man could use the corridors without interference.

The great train snaked on through the dark, pounding out the miles through the empty plains and mingy hamlets of Georgia, the 'Peach State', the angry moan of its four-toned wind-horn soughing over the wide savannah and the long shaft of its single searchlight ripping the black calico of the night.

Bond turned on his light again and read for a while, but his thoughts were too insistent and he soon gave up and switched the light off. Instead, he thought of Solitaire and of the future and of the more immediate prospects of Jacksonville and St. Petersburg and of seeing Leiter again.

Much later, around one o'clock in the morning, he was

dozing and on the edge of sleep, when a soft metallic noise quite close to his head brought him wide awake with his hand on his gun.

There was someone at the passage door and the lock was being softly tried.

Bond was immediately on the floor and moving silently on his bare feet. He gently pulled the wedge away from under the door to the next compartment and as gently pulled the bolt and opened the door. He crossed the next compartment and softly began to open the door to the corridor.

There was a deafening click as the bolt came back. He tore the door open and threw himself into the corridor, only to see a flying figure already nearing the forward end of the car.

If his two hands had been free he could have shot the man, but to open the doors he had to tuck his gun into the waistband of his trousers. Bond knew that pursuit would be hopeless. There were too many empty compartments into which the man could dodge and quietly close the door. Bond had worked all this out beforehand. He knew his only chance would be surprise and either a quick shot or the man's surrender.

He walked a few steps to Compartment H. A tiny diamond of paper protruded into the corridor.

He went back and into their room, locking the doors behind him. He softly turned on his reading light. Solitaire was still asleep. The rest of the paper, a single sheet, lay on the carpet against the passage door. He picked it up and sat on the edge of his bed.

It was a sheet of cheap ruled notepaper. It was covered with irregular lines of writing in rough capitals, in red ink.

Bond handled it gingerly, without much hope that it would yield any prints. These people weren't like that.

Oh Witch [he read] *do not slay me,*
Spare me. His is the body.

The divine drummer declares that
When he rises with the dawn
He will sound his drums for YOU *in the morning*
Very early, very early, very early, very early.
Oh Witch that slays the children of men before they are fully matured
Oh Witch that slays the children of men before they are fully matured
The divine drummer declares that
When he rises with the dawn
He will sound his drums for YOU *in the morning*
Very early, very early, very early, very early.
We are addressing YOU
And YOU *will understand.*

Bond lay down on his bed and thought.

Then he folded the paper and put it in his pocket-book.

He lay on his back and looked at nothing, waiting for daybreak.

CHAPTER XII

THE EVERGLADES

IT was around five o'clock in the morning when they slipped off the train at Jacksonville.

It was still dark and the naked platforms of the great Florida junction were sparsely lit. The entrance to the subway was only a few yards from Car 245 and there was no sign of life on the sleeping train as they dived down the steps. Bond had told the attendant to keep the door of their compartment locked after they had gone and the blinds drawn and he thought there was quite a chance they would not be missed until the train reached St. Petersburg.

They came out of the subway into the booking-hall. Bond verified that the next express for St. Petersburg would be the Silver Meteor, the sister train of the Phantom, due at about nine o'clock, and he booked two Pullman seats on it. Then he took Solitaire's arm and they walked out of the station into the warm dark street.

There were two or three all-night diners to choose from and they pushed through the door that announced 'Good Eats' in the brightest neon. It was the usual sleazy food-machine – two tired waitresses behind a zinc counter loaded with cigarettes and candy and paper-backs and comics. There was a big coffee percolator and a row of butane gas-rings. A door marked 'Restroom' concealed its dreadful secrets next to a door marked 'Private' which was probably the back entrance. A group of overalled men at one of the dozen stained crueted tables looked up briefly as they came in and then resumed their low conversation. Relief crews for the Diesels, Bond guessed.

There were four narrow booths on the right of the entrance and Bond and Solitaire slipped into one of them. They looked dully at the stained menu card.

After a time, one of the waitresses sauntered over and stood leaning against the partition, running her eyes over Solitaire's clothes.

'Orange juice, coffee, scrambled eggs, twice,' said Bond briefly.

' 'Kay,' said the girl. Her shoes lethargically scuffed the floor as she sauntered away.

'The scrambled eggs'll be cooked with milk,' said Bond. 'But one can't eat boiled eggs in America. They look so disgusting without their shells, mixed up in a tea-cup the way they do them here. God knows where they learned the trick. From Germany, I suppose. And bad American coffee's the worst in the world, worse even than in England. I suppose they can't do much harm to the orange juice. After all we are in Florida now.' He suddenly felt depressed by the thought of their four-hour wait in this unwashed, dog-eared atmosphere.

'Everybody's making easy money in America these days,' said Solitaire. 'That's always bad for the customer. All they want is to strip a quick dollar off you and toss you out. Wait till you get down to the coast. At this time of the year, Florida's the biggest sucker-trap on earth. On the East Coast they fleece the millionaires. Where we're going they just take it off the little man. Serves him right, of course. He goes there to die. He can't take it with him.'

'For heaven's sake,' said Bond, 'what sort of a place are we going to?'

'Everybody's nearly dead in St. Petersburg,' explained Solitaire. 'It's the Great American Graveyard. When the bank clerk or the post-office worker or the railroad conductor reaches sixty he collects his pension or his annuity and goes to St. Petersburg to get a few years' sunshine before he dies. It's called "The Sunshine City". The weather's so good that the evening paper there, *The Independent*, is given away free any day the sun hasn't shone by edition time. It only happens three or four times a year and it's a fine advertisement. Everybody goes to bed around nine o'clock in the evening and during the day the old folks play shuffleboard and bridge, herds of them. There's a couple of baseball teams down there, the "Kids" and the "Kubs", all over seventy-five! Then they play bowls, but most of the time they sit squashed together in droves on things called "Sidewalk Davenports", rows of benches up and down the sidewalks of the main streets. They just sit in the sun and gossip and doze. It's a terrifying sight, all these old people with their spectacles and hearing-aids and clicking false-teeth.'

'Sounds pretty grim,' said Bond. 'Why the hell did Mr. Big choose this place to operate from?'

'It's perfect for him,' said Solitaire seriously. 'There's practically no crime, except cheating at bridge and Canasta. So there's a very small police force. There's quite a big Coastguard Station but it's mainly concerned with smuggling between Tampa and Cuba, and sponge-fishing out of season at Tarpon Springs. I don't really know what he does there except that he's got a big agent called "The Robber". Something to do with Cuba, I expect,' she added thoughtfully. 'Probably mixed up with Communism. I believe Cuba comes under Harlem and runs red agents all through the Caribbean.

'Anyway,' she went on, 'St. Petersburg is probably the most innocent town in America. Everything's very "folksy" and "gracious". It's true there's a place called "The Restorium", a hospital for alcoholics. But very old ones, I suppose,' she laughed, 'and I expect they're past doing anyone any harm. You'll love it,' she smiled maliciously at Bond. 'You'll probably want to settle down there for life and be an "Oldster" too. That's the great word down there . . . "oldster".'

'God forbid,' said Bond fervently. 'It sounds rather like Bournemouth or Torquay. But a million times worse. I hope we don't get into a shooting match with "The Robber" and his friends. We'd probably hurry a few hundred oldsters off to the cemetery with heart-failure. But isn't there anyone young in this place?'

'Oh yes,' laughed Solitaire. 'Plenty of them. All the local inhabitants who take the money off the oldsters, for instance. The people who own the motels and the trailer-camps. You could make plenty of money running the bingo tournaments. I'll be your "barker" – the girl outside who gets the suckers in. Dear Mr. Bond,' she reached over and pressed his hand, 'will you settle down with me and grow old gracefully in St. Petersburg?'

Bond sat back and looked at her critically. 'I want a long time of disgraceful living with you first,' he said with a grin. 'I'm probably better at that. But it suits me that they go to bed at nine down there.'

Her eyes smiled back at him. She took her hand away from his as their breakfast arrived. 'Yes,' she said. 'You go to bed at nine. Then I shall slip out by the back door and go on the tiles with the Kids and the Kubs.'

The breakfast was as bad as Bond had prophesied.

When they had paid they wandered over to the station waiting-room.

The sun had risen and the light swarmed in dusty bars into the vaulted, empty hall. They sat together in a corner and until the Silver Meteor came in Bond plied her with questions about The Big Man and all she could tell him about his operations.

Occasionally he made a note of a date or a name but there was little she could add to what he knew. She had an apartment to herself in the same Harlem block as Mr. Big and she had been kept virtually a prisoner there for the past year. She had two tough negresses as 'companions' and was never allowed out without a guard.

From time to time Mr. Big would have her brought over to the room where Bond had seen him. There she would be told to divine whether some man or woman, generally bound to the chair, was lying or not. She varied her replies according to whether she sensed these people were good or evil. She knew that her verdict might often be a death sentence but she felt indifferent to the fate of those she judged to be evil. Very few of them were white.

Bond jotted down the dates and details of all these occasions.

Everything she told him added to the picture of a very powerful and active man, ruthless and cruel, commanding a huge network of operations.

All she knew of the gold coins was that she had several

times had to question men on how many they had passed and the price they had been paid for them. Very often, she said, they were lying on both counts.

Bond was careful to divulge very little of what he himself knew or guessed. His growing warmth towards Solitaire and his desire for her body were in a compartment which had no communicating door with his professional life.

The Silver Meteor came in on time and they were both relieved to be on their way again and to get away from the dreary world of the big junction.

The train sped on down through Florida, through the forests and swamps, stark and bewitched with Spanish moss, and through the mile upon mile of citrus groves.

All through the centre of the state the moss lent a dead, spectral feeling to the landscape. Even the little townships through which they passed had a grey skeletal aspect with their dried-up, sun-sucked clapboard houses. Only the citrus groves laden with fruit looked green and alive. Everything else seemed baked and desiccated with the heat.

Looking out at the gloomy silent withered forests, Bond thought that nothing could be living in them except bats and scorpions, horned toads and black widow spiders.

They had lunch and then suddenly the train was running along the Gulf of Mexico, through the mangrove swamps and palm groves, endless motels and caravan sites, and Bond caught the smell of the other Florida, the Florida of the advertisements, the land of 'Miss Orange Blossom 1954'.

They left the train at Clearwater, the last station before St. Petersburg. Bond took a cab and gave the address on Treasure Island, half an hour's drive away. It was two o'clock and the sun blazed down out of a cloudless sky. Solitaire insisted on taking off her hat and veil. 'It's sticking to my face,' she said. 'Hardly a soul has ever seen me down here.'

A big negro with a face pitted with ancient smallpox was held up in his cab at the same time as they were checked at the intersection of Park Street and Central Avenue, where the Avenue runs on to the long Treasure Island causeway across the shallow waters of Boca Ciega Bay.

When the negro saw Solitaire's profile his mouth fell open. He pulled his cab into the kerb and dived into a drugstore. He called a St. Petersburg number.

'Dis is Poxy,' he said urgently into the mouthpiece. 'Gimme da Robber 'n step on it. Dat you, Robber? Lissen, Da Big Man muss be n'town. Whaddya mean yuh jes talked wit him 'n New York? Ah jes seen his gal 'n a Clearwater cab, one of da Stassen Company's. Headin' over da Causeway. Sho Ahm sartin. Cross ma heart. Couldn mistake dat eyeful. Wid a man 'n a blue suit, grey Stetson. Seemed like a scar down his face. Whaddya mean, follow 'em? Ah jes couldn believe yuh wouldn tell me da Big Man wuz 'n town ef he wuz. Thought mebbe Ahd better check 'n make sho. Okay, okay. Ah'll ketch da cab when he comes back over da Causeway, else at Clearwater. Okay, okay. Keep yo shirt on. Ah ain't done nuthen wrong.'

The man called 'The Robber' was through to New York in five minutes. He had been warned about Bond but he couldn't understand where Solitaire tied in to the picture. When he had finished talking to The Big Man he still didn't know, but his instructions were quite definite.

He rang off and sat for a while drumming his fingers

on his desk. Ten Grand for the job. He'd need two men. That would leave eight Grand for him. He licked his lips and called a poolroom in a downtown bar in Tampa.

Bond paid off the cab at The Everglades, a group of neat white-and-yellow clapboard cottages set on three sides of a square of Bahama grass which ran fifty yards down to a bone-white beach and then to the sea. From there, the whole Gulf of Mexico stretched away, as calm as a mirror, until the heat-haze on the horizon married it into the cloudless sky.

After London, after New York, after Jacksonville, it was a sparkling transition.

Bond went through a door marked 'Office' with Solitaire demurely at his heels. He rang a bell that said, 'Manageress: Mrs. Stuyvesant', and a withered shrimp of a woman with blue-rinsed hair appeared and smiled with her pinched lips. 'Yes?'

'Mr. Leiter?'

'Oh yes, you're Mr. Bryce. Cabana Number One, right down on the beach. Mr. Leiter's been expecting you since lunchtime. And . . . ?' She heliographed with her pince-nez towards Solitaire.

'Mrs. Bryce,' said Bond.

'Ah yes,' said Mrs. Stuyvesant, wishing to disbelieve. 'Well, if you'd care to sign the register, I'm sure you and Mrs. Bryce would like to freshen up after the journey. The full address, please. Thank you.'

She led them out and down the cement path to the end cottage on the left. She knocked and Leiter appeared. Bond had looked forward to a warm welcome, but Leiter seemed staggered to see him. His mouth hung open. His straw-coloured hair, still faintly black at the roots, looked like a haystack.

'You haven't met my wife, I think,' said Bond.

'No, no, I mean, yes. How do you do?'

The whole situation was beyond him. Forgetting Solitaire, he almost dragged Bond through the door. At the last moment he remembered the girl and seized her with his other hand and pulled her in too, banging the door shut with his heel so that Mrs. Stuyvesant's 'I hope you have a happy . . .' was guillotined before the 'stay'.

Once inside, Leiter could still not take them in. He stood and gaped from one to the other.

Bond dropped his suitcase on the floor of the little lobby. There were two doors. He pushed open the one on his right and held it for Solitaire. It was a small living-room that ran the width of the cottage and faced across the beach to the sea. It was pleasantly furnished with bamboo beach chairs upholstered in foam rubber covered with a red-and-green hibiscus chintz. Palm-leaf matting covered the floor. The walls were duck's-egg blue and in the centre of each was a colour print of tropical flowers in a bamboo frame. There was a large drum-shaped table in bamboo with a glass top. It held a bowl of flowers and a white telephone. There were broad windows facing the sea and to the right of them a door leading on to the beach. White plastic jalousies were drawn half up the windows to cut the glare from the sand.

Bond and Solitaire sat down. Bond lit a cigarette and threw the pack and his lighter on to the table.

Suddenly the telephone rang. Leiter came out of his trance and walked over from the door and picked up the receiver.

'Speaking,' he said. 'Put the Lieutenant on. That you, Lieutenant? He's here. Just walked in. No, all in one piece.' He listened for a moment, then turned to Bond. 'Where did you leave the Phantom?' he asked. Bond told him. 'Jacksonville,' said Leiter into the telephone. 'Yeah, I'll say. Sure. I'll get the details from him and call you back. Will you call off Homicide? I'd sure appreciate it. And New York. Much obliged, Lieutenant. Orlando 9000. Okay. And thanks again. 'Bye.' He put down the receiver. He wiped the sweat off his forehead and sat down opposite Bond.

Suddenly he looked at Solitaire and grinned apologetically. 'I guess you're Solitaire,' he said. 'Sorry for the rough welcome. It's been quite a day. For the second time in around twenty-four hours I didn't expect to see this guy again.' He turned back to Bond. 'Okay to go ahead?' he asked.

'Yes,' said Bond. 'Solitaire's on our side now.'

'That's a break,' said Leiter. 'Well, you won't have seen the papers or heard the radio, so I'll give you the headlines first. The Phantom was stopped soon after Jacksonville. Between Waldo and Ocala. Your compartment was tommy-gunned and bombed. Blown to bits. Killed the Pullman porter who was in the corridor at the time. No other casualties. Bloody uproar going on. Who did it? Who's Mr. Bryce and who's Mrs. Bryce? Where are they? Of course we were sure you'd been snatched. The police at Orlando are in charge. Traced the bookings back to New York. Found the FBI had made them. Everyone comes down on me like a load of bricks. Then you walk in with a pretty girl on your arm looking as happy as a clam.'

Leiter burst out laughing. 'Boy! You should have heard

Washington a while back. Anybody would have thought it was me that bombed the goddam train.'

He reached for one of Bond's cigarettes and lit it.

'Well,' he said. 'That's the synopsis. I'll hand over the shooting script when I've heard your end. Give.'

Bond described in detail what had happened since he had spoken to Leiter from the St. Regis. When he came to the night on the train he took the piece of paper out of his pocket-book and pushed it across the table.

Leiter whistled. 'Voodoo,' he said. 'This was meant to be found on the corpse, I guess. Ritual murder by friends of the men you bumped in Harlem. That's how it was supposed to look. Take the heat right away from The Big Man. They certainly think out all the angles. We'll get after that thug they had on the train. Probably one of the help in the diner. He must have been the man who put the finger on your compartment. You finish. Then I'll tell you how he did it.'

'Let me see,' said Solitaire. She reached across for the paper.

'Yes,' she said quietly. 'It's an *ouanga*, a Voodoo fetish. It's the invocation to the Drum Witch. It's used by the Ashanti tribe in Africa when they want to kill someone. They use something like it in Haiti.' She handed it back to Bond. 'It was lucky you didn't tell me about it,' she said seriously. 'I would still be having hysterics.'

'I didn't care for it myself,' said Bond. 'I felt it was bad news. Lucky we got off at Jacksonville. Poor Baldwin. We owe him a lot.'

He finished the story of the rest of their trip.

'Anyone spot you when you left the train?' asked Leiter.

'Shouldn't think so,' said Bond. 'But we'd better keep

Solitaire under cover until we can get her out. Thought we ought to fly her over to Jamaica tomorrow. I can get her looked after there till we come on.'

'Sure,' agreed Leiter. 'We'll put her in a charter plane at Tampa. Get her down to Miami by tomorrow lunch-time and she can take one of the afternoon services – KLM or Panam. Get her in by dinner-time tomorrow. Too late to do anything this afternoon.'

'Is that all right, Solitaire?' Bond asked her.

The girl was staring out of the window. Her eyes had the faraway look that Bond had seen before.

Suddenly she shivered.

Her eyes came back to Bond. She put out a hand and touched his sleeve.

'Yes,' she said. She hesitated. 'Yes, I guess so.'

CHAPTER XIII

DEATH OF A PELICAN

SOLITAIRE stood up.

'I must go and tidy myself,' she said. 'I expect you've both got plenty to talk about.'

'Of course,' said Leiter, jumping up. 'Crazy of me! You must be dead beat. Guess you'd better take James's room and he can bed down with me.'

Solitaire followed him out into the little hall and Bond heard Leiter explaining the arrangement of the rooms.

In a moment Leiter came back with a bottle of Haig and Haig and some ice.

'I'm forgetting my manners,' he said. 'We could both do with a drink. There's a small pantry next the bathroom and I've stocked it with all we're likely to need!'

He fetched some soda-water and they both took a long drink.

'Let's have the details,' said Bond, sitting back. 'Must have been the hell of a fine job.'

'Sure was,' agreed Leiter, 'except for the shortage of corpses.'

He put his feet on the table and lit a cigarette.

'Phantom left Jacksonville around five,' he began. 'Got to Waldo around six. Just after leaving Waldo – and here I'm guessing – Mr. Big's man comes along to your car, gets into the next compartment to yours and hangs a towel between the drawn blind and the window, meaning – and he must have done a good deal of telephoning at stations on the way down – meaning "the window to the right of this towel is it".

'There's a long stretch of straight track between Waldo and Ocala,' continued Leiter, 'running through forest and swamp land. State highway right alongside the track. About twenty minutes outside Waldo, Wham! goes a dynamite emergency signal under the leading Diesel. Driver comes down to forty. Wham! And another Wham! Three in line! Emergency! Halt at once! He ha s the train wondering what the hell. Straight track. Last signal green over green. Nothing in sight. It's around quarter after six and just getting light. There's a sedan, clouted heap I expect [Bond raised an eyebrow. 'Stolen car,' explained Leiter], grey, thought to have been a Buick, no lights, engine running, waiting on the highway opposite the centre of the train. Three men get out. Coloured. Probably negro. They walk slowly in line abreast along the grass verge between the road and the track. Two on the outside carry rippers – tommy-guns. Man in the centre has something in his hand. Twenty yards and they stop outside Car 245. Men with the rippers give a double squirt at your window. Open it up for the pineapple. Centre man tosses in the pineapple and all three run back to the car. Two seconds fuse. As they reach the car, BOOM! Fricassee of Compartment H. Fricassee, presumably, of Mr. and Mrs. Bryce. In fact fricassee of your Baldwin who runs out and crouches in corridor directly he sees men approaching his car. No other casualties except multiple shock and hysterics throughout train. Car drives away very fast towards limbo where it still is and will probably remain. Silence, mingled with screams, falls. People run to and fro. Train limps gingerly into Ocala. Drops Car 245. Is allowed to proceed three hours later. Scene II. Leiter sits alone in cottage, hoping he has never said an unkind word to his friend James, and wondering how Mr. Hoover will have Mr. Leiter served for his dinner tonight. That's all, folks.'

Bond laughed. 'What an organization!' he said. 'I'm sure it's all beautifully covered up and alibied. What a man! He certainly seems to have the run of this country. Just shows how one can push a democracy around, what with *habeas corpus* and human rights and all the rest. Glad we haven't got him on our hands in England. Wooden truncheons wouldn't make much of a dent in him. Well,' he concluded, 'that's three times I've managed to get away with it. The pace is beginning to get a bit hot.'

'Yes,' said Leiter thoughtfully. 'Before you arrived over here you could have counted the mistakes Mr. Big has ever made on one thumb. Now he's made three all in a row. He won't like that. We've got to put the heat on him while he's still groggy and then get out, quick. Tell you what I've got in mind. There's no doubt that gold gets into the States through this place. We've tracked the *Secatur* again and again and she just comes straight over from Jamaica to St. Petersburg and docks at that worm-and-bait factory – Rubberus or whatever it's called.'

'Ourobouros,' said Bond. 'The Great Worm of mythology. Good name for a worm-and-bait factory.' Suddenly a thought struck him. He hit the glass table-top with the flat of his hand. 'Felix! Of course. Ourobouros – "The Robber" – don't you see? Mr. Big's man down here. It must be the same.'

Leiter's face lit up. 'Christ Almighty,' he exclaimed.

'Of course it's the same. That Greek who's supposed to own it, the man in Tarpon Springs that figures in the reports that blockhead showed us in New York, Binswanger. He's probably just a figurehead. Probably doesn't even know there's anything phoney about it. It's his manager here we've got to get after. "The Robber." Of course that's who it is.'

Leiter jumped up.

'C'mon. Let's get going. We'll go right along and look the place over. I was going to suggest it anyway, seeing the *Secatur* always docks at their wharf. She's in Cuba now, by the way,' he added, 'Havana. Cleared from here a week ago. They searched her good and proper when she came in and when she left. Didn't find a thing, of course. Thought she might have a false keel. Almost tore it off. She had to go into dock before she could sail again. Nix. Not a shadow of anything wrong. Let alone a stack of gold coins. Anyway, we'll go and smell around. See if we can get a look at our Robber friend. I'll just have to talk to Orlando and Washington. Tell 'em all we know. They must catch up quick with The Big Man's fellow on the train. Probably too late by now. You go and see how Solitaire's getting on. Tell her she's not to move till we get back. Lock her in. We'll take her out to dinner in Tampa. They've got the best restaurant on the whole coast, Cuban, "Los Novedades". We'll stop at the airport on the way and fix her flight for tomorrow.'

Leiter reached for the telephone and asked for Long Distance. Bond left him to it.

Ten minutes later they were on their way.

Solitaire had not wanted to be left. She had clung to Bond. 'I want to get away from here,' she said, her eyes frightened. 'I have a feeling . . .' She didn't end the sentence. Bond kissed her.

'It's all right,' he said. 'We'll be back in an hour or so. Nothing can happen to you here. Then I shan't leave you until you're on the plane. We can even stay the night in Tampa and get you off at first light.'

'Yes, please,' said Solitaire anxiously. 'I'd rather do that. I'm frightened here. I feel in danger.' She put her arms round his neck. 'Don't think I'm being hysterical.' She kissed him. 'Now you can go. I just wanted to see you. Come back quickly.'

Leiter had called and Bond had closed the door on her and locked it.

He followed Leiter to his car on the Parkway feeling vaguely troubled. He couldn't imagine that the girl could come to any harm in this peaceful, law-abiding place, or that The Big Man could conceivably have traced her to The Everglades, which was only one of a hundred similar beach establishments on Treasure Island. But he respected the extraordinary power of her intuitions and her attack of nerves made him uneasy.

The sight of Leiter's car put these thoughts out of his mind.

Bond liked fast cars and he liked driving them. Most American cars bored him. They lacked personality and the patina of individual craftsmanship that European cars have. They were just 'vehicles', similar in shape and in colour, and even in the tone of their horns. Designed to serve for a year and then be turned in in part exchange for the next year's model. All the fun of driving had been taken out of them with the abolition of a gear-change, with hydraulic-assisted steering and spongy suspension. All effort had been smoothed away and all of that close contact with the machine and the road that extracts skill and nerve from the European driver. To Bond, American cars were just beetle-shaped Dodgems in which you motored along with one hand on the wheel, the radio full on, and the power-operated windows closed to keep out the draughts.

But Leiter had got hold of an old Cord, one of the few American cars with a personality, and it cheered Bond to climb into the low-hung saloon, to hear the solid bite of the gears and the masculine tone of the wide exhaust. Fifteen years old, he reflected, yet still one of the most modern-looking cars in the world.

They swung on to the causeway and across the wide expanse of unrippled water that separates the twenty miles of narrow island from the broad peninsula sprawling with St. Petersburg and its suburbs.

Already as they idled up Central Avenue on their way across the town to the Yacht Basin and the main harbour and the big hotels, Bond caught a whiff of the atmosphere that makes the town the 'Old Folks Home' of America. Everyone on the sidewalks had white hair, white or blue, and the famous Sidewalk Davenports that Solitaire had described were thick with oldsters sitting in rows like the starlings in Trafalgar Square.

Bond noted the small grudging mouths of the women, the sun gleaming on their pince-nez; the stringy, collapsed chests and arms of the men displayed to the sunshine in Truman shirts. The fluffy, sparse balls of hair on the women showing the pink scalp. The bony bald heads of the men. And, everywhere, a prattling camaraderie, a swapping of news and gossip, a making of folksy dates for the shuffleboard and the bridge-table, a handing round of letters from children and grandchildren, a tut-tutting about prices in the shops and the motels.

You didn't have to be amongst them to hear it all. It was all in the nodding and twittering of the balls of blue fluff, the back-slapping and hawk-an-spitting of the little old baldheads.

'It makes you want to climb right into the tomb and pull the lid down,' said Leiter at Bond's exclamations of horror. 'You wait till we get out and walk. If they see your shadow coming up the sidewalk behind them they jump out of the way as if you were the Chief Cashier coming to look over their shoulders in the bank. It's ghastly. Makes me think of the bank clerk who went home unexpectedly at midday and found the President of the bank sleeping with his wife. He went back and told his pals in the ledger department and said, "Gosh, fellers, he nearly caught me!" '

Bond laughed.

'You can hear all the presentation gold watches ticking in their pockets,' said Leiter. 'Place is full of undertakers, and pawnshops stuffed with gold watches and masonic rings and bits of jet and lockets full of hair. Makes you shiver to think of it all. Wait till you go to "Aunt Milly's Place" and see them all in droves mumbling over their corn-beef hash and cheeseburgers, trying to keep alive till ninety. It'll frighten the life out of you. But they're not all old down here. Take a look at that ad over there.' He pointed towards a big hoarding on a deserted lot.

It was an advertisement for maternity clothes. 'STUTZHEIMER & BLOCK,' it said, 'IT'S NEW! OUR ANTICIPATION

DEPARTMENT, AND AFTER! CLOTHES FOR CHIPS (1–4) AND TWIGS (4–8).'

Bond groaned. 'Let's get away from here,' he said. 'This is really beyond the call of duty.'

They came down to the waterfront and turned right until they came to the seaplane base and the coastguard station. The streets were free of oldsters and here there was the normal life of a harbour – wharves, warehouses, a ship's chandler, some up-turned boats, nets drying, the cry of seagulls, the rather fetid smell coming in off the bay. After the teeming boneyard of the town the sign over the garage: 'Drive-ur-Self. Pat Grady. The Smiling Irishman. Used cars,' was a cheerful reminder of a livelier, bustling world.

'Better get out and walk,' said Leiter. 'The Robber's place is in the next block.'

They left the car beside the harbour and sauntered along past a timber warehouse and some oil-storage tanks. Then they turned left again towards the sea.

The side-road ended at a small weather-beaten wooden jetty that reached out twenty feet on barnacled piles into the bay. Right up against its open gate was a long low corrugated-iron warehouse. Over its wide double doors was painted, black on white, 'Ourobouros Inc. Live Worm and Bait Merchants. Coral, Shells, Tropical Fish. Wholesale only.' In one of the double doors there was a smaller door with a gleaming Yale lock. On the door was a sign: 'Private. Keep Out.'

Against this a man sat on a kitchen chair, its back tilted so that the door supported his weight. He was cleaning a rifle, a Remington 30 it looked like to Bond. He had a wooden toothpick sticking out of his mouth and a battered baseball cap on the back of his head. He was wearing a stained white singlet that revealed tufts of black hair under his arms, and slept-in white canvas trousers and rubber-soled sneakers. He was around forty and his face was as knotted and seamed as the mooring posts on the jetty. It was a thin, hatchet face, and the lips were thin too, and bloodless. His complexion was the colour of tobacco dust, a sort of yellowy-beige. He looked cruel and cold, like the bad man in a film about poker-players and gold mines.

Bond and Leiter walked past him and on to the pier. He didn't look up from his rifle as they went past but Bond sensed that his eyes were following them.

'If that isn't The Robber,' said Leiter, 'it's a blood relation.'

A pelican, grey with a pale yellow head, was hunched on one of the mooring posts at the end of the jetty. He let them get very close, then reluctantly gave a few heavy beats of his wings and planed down towards the water. The two men stood and watched him flying slowly along just above the surface of the harbour. Suddenly he crashed clumsily down, his long bill snaking out and down in front of him. It came up clutching a small fish which he moodily swallowed. Then the heavy bird got up again and went on fishing, flying mostly into the sun so that its big shadow would give no warning. When Bond and Leiter turned to walk back down the jetty it gave up fishing and glided back to its post. It settled with a clatter of wings and resumed its thoughtful consideration of the late afternoon.

The man was still bent over his gun, wiping the mechanism with an oily rag.

'Good afternoon,' said Leiter. 'You the manager of this wharf?'

'Yep,' said the man without looking up.

'Wondered if there was any chance of mooring my boat here. Basin's pretty crowded.'

'Nope.'

Leiter took out his notecase. 'Would twenty talk?'

'Nope.' The man gave a rattling hawk in his throat and spat directly between Bond and Leiter.

'Hey,' said Leiter. 'You want to watch your manners.'

The man deliberated. He looked up at Leiter. He had small, close-set eyes as cruel as a painless dentist's.

'What's a name of your boat?'

'The *Sybil*,' said Leiter.

'Ain't no sich boat in the Basin,' said the man. He clicked the breech shut on his rifle. It lay casually on his lap pointing down the approach to the warehouse, away from the sea.

'You're blind,' said Leiter. 'Been there a week. Sixty-foot twin-screw Diesel. White with a green awning. Rigged for fishing.'

The rifle started to move lazily in a low arc. The man's left hand was at the trigger, his right just in front of the trigger-guard, pivoting the gun.

They stood still.

The man sat lazily looking down at the breech, his chair still tilted against the small door with the yellow Yale lock.

The gun slowly traversed Leiter's stomach, then Bond's. The two men stood like statues, not risking a move of the hand. The gun stopped pivoting. It was pointing down the wharf. The Robber looked briefly up, narrowed his eyes and pulled the trigger. The pelican gave a faint squawk and they heard its heavy body crash into the water. The echo of the shot boomed across the harbour.

'What the hell d'you do that for?' asked Bond furiously.

'Practice,' said the man, pumping another bullet into the breech.

'Guess there's a branch of the A S P C A in this town,' said Leiter. 'Let's get along there and report this guy.'

'Want to be prosecuted for trespass?' asked The Robber, getting slowly up and shifting the gun under his arm. 'This is private property. Now,' he spat the words out, 'git the hell out of here.' He turned and yanked the chair away from the door, opened the door with a key and turned with one foot on the threshold. 'You both got guns,' he said. 'I kin smell 'em. You come aroun' here again and you follow the boid 'n I plead self-defence. I've had a bellyful of you lousy dicks aroun' here lately breathin' down my neck. *Sybil* my ass!' He turned contemptuously through the door and slammed it so that the frame rattled.

They looked at each other. Leiter grinned ruefully and shrugged his shoulders.

'Round One to The Robber,' he said.

They moved off down the dusty sideroad. The sun was setting and the sea behind them was a pool of blood. When they got to the main road, Bond looked back. A big arc light had come on over the door and the approach to the warehouse was stripped of shadows.

'No good trying anything from the front,' said Bond. 'But there's never been a warehouse with only one entrance.'

'Just what I was thinking,' said Leiter. 'We'll save that for the next visit.'

They got into the car and drove slowly home across Central Avenue.

On their way home Leiter asked a string of questions

about Solitaire. Finally he said casually: 'By the way, hope I fixed the rooms like you want them.'

'Couldn't be better,' said Bond cheerfully.

'Fine,' said Leiter. 'Just occurred to me you two might be hyphenating.'

'You read too much Winchell,' said Bond.

'It's just a delicate way of putting it,' said Leiter. 'Don't forget the walls of those cottages are pretty thin. I use my ears for hearing with – not for collecting lip-stick.'

Bond grabbed for a handkerchief. 'You lousy, goddam sleuth,' he said furiously.

Leiter watched him scrubbing at himself out of the corner of his eye. 'What are you doing?' he asked innocently. 'I wasn't for a moment suggesting the colour of your ears was anything but a natural red. However . . .' He put a wealth of meaning into the word.

'If you find yourself dead in your bed tonight,' laughed Bond, 'you'll know who did it.'

They were still chaffing each other when they arrived at The Everglades and they were laughing when the grim Mrs. Stuyvesant greeted them on the lawn.

'Pardon me, Mr. Leiter,' she said. 'But I'm afraid we can't allow music here. I can't have the other guests disturbed at all hours.'

They looked at her in astonishment. 'I'm sorry, Mrs. Stuyvesant,' said Leiter. 'I don't quite get you.'

'That big radiogram you had sent round,' said Mrs. Stuyvesant. 'The men could hardly get the packing-case through the door.'

CHAPTER XIV

'HE DISAGREED WITH SOMETHING THAT ATE HIM'

THE girl had not put up much of a struggle.

When Leiter and Bond, leaving the manageress gaping on the lawn, raced down to the end cottage, they found her room untouched and the bedclothes barely rumpled.

The lock of her room had been forced with one swift wrench of a jemmy and then the two men must have just stood there with guns in their hands.

'Get going, Lady. Get your clothes on. Try any tricks and we'll let the fresh air into you.'

Then they must have gagged her or knocked her out and doubled her into the packing-case and nailed it up. There were tyre-marks at the back of the cottage where the truck had stood. Almost blocking the entrance hall was a huge old-fashioned radiogram. Second-hand it must have cost them under fifty bucks.

Bond could see the expression of blind terror on Solitaire's face as if she was standing before him. He cursed himself bitterly for leaving her alone. He couldn't guess how she had been traced so quickly. It was just another example of The Big Man's machine.

Leiter was talking to the FBI headquarters at Tampa. 'Airports, railroad terminals and the highways,' he was saying. 'You'll get blanket orders from Washington just as soon as I've spoken to them. I guarantee they'll give this top priority. Thanks a lot. Much appreciated. I'll be around. Okay.'

He hung up. 'Thank God they're co-operating,' he said to Bond, who was standing gazing with hard blank eyes out to sea. 'Sending a couple of their men round right away and throwing as wide a net as they can. While I sew this up with Washington and New York, get what you can from that old battle-axe. Exact time, descriptions, etc. Better make out it was a burglary and that Solitaire has skipped with the men. She'll understand that. It'll keep the whole thing on the level of the usual hotel crimes. Say the police are on the way and that we don't blame The Everglades. She'll want to avoid a scandal. Say we feel the same way.'

Bond nodded. 'Skipped with the men?' That was possible too. But somehow he didn't think so. He went back to Solitaire's room and searched it minutely. It still smelled of her, of the 'Vent Vert' that reminded him of their journey together. Her hat and veil were in the cupboard and her few toilet articles on the shelf in the bathroom. He soon found her bag and knew that he was right to have trusted her. It was under the bed and he visualized her kicking it there as she got up with the guns trained on her. He emptied it out on the bed and felt the lining. Then he took out a small knife and carefully cut a few threads. He took out the five thousand dollars and slipped them into his pocket-book. They would be safe with him. If she was killed by Mr. Big, he would spend them on avenging her. He covered up the torn lining as best he could, replaced the other contents of the bag and kicked it back under the bed.

Then he went up to the office.

It was eight o'clock by the time the routine work was finished. They had a stiff drink together and then went to the central dining-room, where the handful of other guests were just finishing their dinner. Everyone looked curiously and rather fearfully at them. What were these two rather dangerous-looking young men doing in this place? Where was the woman who had come with them? Whose wife was she? What had all those goings on meant that evening? Poor Mrs. Stuyvesant running about looking quite distracted. And didn't they realize that dinner was at seven o'clock? The kitchen staff would be just going home. Serve them right if their food was quite cold. People must have consideration for others. Mrs. Stuyvesant had said she thought they were government men, from Washington. Well, what did that mean?

The consensus of opinion was that they were bad news and no credit to the carefully restricted clientele of The Everglades.

Bond and Leiter were shown to a bad table near the service door. The set dinner was a string of inflated English and pidgin French. What it came down to was tomato juice, boiled fish with a white sauce, a strip of frozen turkey with a dab of cranberry, and a wedge of lemon curd surmounted by a whorl of stiff cream substitute. They munched it down gloomily while the dining-room emptied of its oldster couples and the table lights went out one by one. Fingerbowls, in which floated one hibiscus petal, was the final gracious touch to their meal.

Bond ate silently and when they had finished Leiter made a determined effort to be cheerful.

'Come and get drunk,' he said. 'This is the bad end to

a worse day. Or do you want to play bingo with the oldsters? It says there's a bingo tournament in the "romp room" this evening.'

Bond shrugged his shoulders and they went back to their sitting-room and sat gloomily for a while, drinking and staring out across the sand, bonewhite in the light of the moon, towards the endless dark sea.

When Bond had drunk enough to drown his thoughts he said good night and went off to Solitaire's room, which he had now taken over as his bedroom. He climbed between the sheets where her warm body had lain and, before he slept, he had made up his mind. He would go after The Robber as soon as it was light and strangle the truth out of him. He had been too preoccupied to discuss the case with Leiter but he was certain that The Robber must have had a big hand in the kidnapping of Solitaire. He thought of the man's little cruel eyes and the pale thin lips. Then he thought of the scrawny neck rising like a turtle's out of the dirty sweat-shirt. Under the bedclothes the muscles of his arms went taut. Then, his mind made up, he relaxed his body into sleep.

He slept until eight. When he saw the time on his watch he cursed. He quickly took a shower, holding his eyes open into the needles of water until they smarted. Then he put a towel round his waist and went into Leiter's room. The slats of the jalousies were still down but there was light enough to see that neither bed had been slept in.

He smiled, thinking that Leiter had probably finished the bottle of whisky and fallen asleep on the couch in the living-room. He walked through. The room was empty. The bottle of whisky, still half full, was on the table and a pile of cigarette butts overflowed the ash-tray.

Bond went to the window, pulled up the jalousies and opened it. He caught a glimpse of a beautiful clear morning before he turned back into the room.

Then he saw the envelope. It was on a chair in front of the door through which he had come. He picked it up. It contained a note scribbled in pencil.

> Got to thinking and don't feel like sleep. It's about five a.m. Going to visit the worm-and-bait store. All same early bird. Odd that trick-shot artist was sitting there while S. was being snatched. As if he knew we were in town and was ready for trouble in case the snatch went wrong. If I'm not back by ten, call out the militia. Tampa 88. FELIX

Bond didn't wait. While he shaved and dressed he ordered some coffee and rolls and a cab. In just over ten minutes he had got them all and had scalded himself with the coffee. He was leaving the cottage when he heard the telephone ring in the living-room. He ran back.

'Mr. Bryce? Mound Park Hospital speaking,' said a voice. 'Emergency ward. Doctor Roberts. We have a Mr. Leiter here who's asking for you. Can you come right over?'

'God Almighty,' said Bond, gripped with fear. 'What's the matter with him. Is he bad?'

'Nothing to worry about,' said the voice. 'Automobile accident. Looks like a hit-and-run job. Slight concussion. Can you come over? He seems to want you.'

'Of course,' said Bond, relieved. 'Be there right away.'

Now what the hell, he wondered as he hurried across the lawn. Must have been beaten up and left in the road. On the whole, Bond was glad it was no worse.

As they turned across Treasure Island Causeway an ambulance passed them, its bell clanging.

More trouble, thought Bond. Don't seem to be able to move without running into it.

They crossed St. Petersburg by Central Avenue and turned right down the road he and Leiter had taken the day before. Bond's suspicions seemed to be confirmed when he found the hospital was only a couple of blocks from Ourobouros Inc.

Bond paid off the cab and ran up the steps of the impressive building. There was a reception desk in the spacious entrance hall. A pretty nurse sat at the desk reading the ads in the *St. Petersburg Times.*

'Dr. Roberts?' inquired Bond.

'Dr. which?' asked the girl looking at him with approval.

'Dr. Roberts, Emergency ward,' said Bond impatiently. 'Patient called Leiter, Felix Leiter. Brought in this morning.'

'No doctor called Roberts here,' said the girl. She ran a finger down a list on the desk. 'And no patient called Leiter.' Just a moment and I'll call the ward. What did you say your name was?'

'Bryce,' said Bond. 'John Bryce.' He started to sweat profusely although it was quite cool in the hall. He wiped his wet hands on his trousers, fighting to keep from panic. The damn girl just didn't know her job. Too pretty to be a nurse. Ought to have someone competent on the desk. He ground his teeth as she talked cheerfully into the telephone.

She put down the receiver. 'I'm sorry, Mr. Bryce. Must be some mistake. No cases during the night and they've never heard of a Dr. Roberts or a Mr. Leiter. Sure you've got the right hospital?'

Bond turned away without answering her. Wiping the sweat from his forehead, he made for the exit.

The girl made a face at his back and picked up her paper.

Mercifully, a cab was just drawing up with some other visitors. Bond took it and told the driver to get him back quick to The Everglades. All he knew was that they had got Leiter and had wanted to draw Bond away from the cottage. Bond couldn't make it out, but he knew that suddenly everything was going bad on them and that the initiative was back in the hands of Mr. Big and his machine.

Mrs. Stuyvesant hurried out when she saw him leave the cab.

'Your poor friend,' she said without sympathy. 'Really he should be more careful.'

'Yes, Mrs. Stuyvesant. What is it?' said Bond impatiently.

'The ambulance came just after you left.' The woman's eyes were gleaming with the bad news. 'Seems Mr. Leiter was in an accident with his car. They had to carry him to the cottage on a stretcher. Such a nice coloured man was in charge. He said Mr. Leiter would be quite all right but he mustn't be disturbed on any account. Poor boy! Face all covered with bandages. They said they'd make him comfortable and a doctor would be coming later. If there's anything I can . . .'

Bond didn't wait for more. He ran down the lawn to the cottage and dashed through the lobby into Leiter's room.

There was the shape of a body on Leiter's bed. It was covered with a sheet. Over the face, the sheet seemed to be motionless.

Bond gritted his teeth as he leant over the bed. Was there a tiny flutter of movement?

Bond snatched the shroud down from the face. There was no face. Just something wrapped round and round with dirty bandages, like a white wasps' nest.

He softly pulled the sheet down further. More bandages, still more roughly wound, with wet blood seeping through. Then the top of a sack which covered the lower half of the body. Everything soaked in blood.

There was a piece of paper protruding from a gap in the bandages where the mouth should have been.

Bond pulled it away and leant down. There was the faintest whisper of breath against his cheek. He snatched up the bedside telephone. It took minutes before he could make Tampa understand. Then the urgency in his voice got through. They would get to him in twenty minutes.

He put down the receiver and looked vaguely at the paper in his hand. It was a rough piece of white wrapping paper. Scrawled in pencil in ragged block letters were the words:

HE DISAGREED WITH SOMETHING THAT ATE HIM

And underneath in brackets:

(P.S. WE HAVE PLENTY MORE JOKES AS GOOD AS THIS)

With the movements of a sleep-walker, Bond put the piece of paper down on the bedside table. Then he turned back to the body on the bed. He hardly dared touch it for fear that the tiny fluttering breath would suddenly cease. But he had to find out something. His fingers worked softly at the bandages on top of the head. Soon he uncovered some of the strands of hair. The hair was wet and he put his fingers to his mouth. There was a salt taste. He pulled out some strands of hair and looked closely at them. There was no more doubt.

He saw again the pale straw-coloured mop that used to hang down in disarray over the right eye, grey and humorous, and below it the wry, hawk-like face of the Texan with whom he had shared so many adventures. He thought of him for a moment, as he had been. Then he tucked the lock of hair back into the bandages and sat on the edge of the other bed and quietly watched over the body of his friend and wondered how much of it could be saved.

When the two detectives and the police surgeon arrived he told them all he knew in a quiet flat voice. Acting on what Bond had already told them on the telephone they had sent a squad car down to The Robber's place and they waited for a report while the surgeon worked next door.

He was finished first. He came back into the sitting-room looking anxious. Bond jumped to his feet. The police surgeon slumped into a chair and looked up at him.

'I think he'll live,' he said. 'But it's fifty-fifty. They certainly did a job on the poor guy. One arm gone. Half the left leg. Face in a mess, but only superficial. Darned if I know what did it. Only thing I can think of is an animal or a big fish. Something's been tearing at him. Know a bit more when I can get him to the hospital. There'll be traces left from the teeth of whatever it was. Ambulance should be along any time.'

They sat in gloomy silence. The telephone rang intermittently. New York, Washington. The St. Petersburg Police Department wanted to know what the hell was going on down at the wharf and were told to keep out of the case. It was a Federal job. Finally, from a call-box, there was the lieutenant in charge of the squad car reporting.

They had been over The Robber's place with a tooth-comb. Nothing but tanks of fish and bait and cases of coral and shells. The Robber and two men who were down there in charge of the pumps and the water-heating had been taken in custody and grilled for an hour. Their alibis had been checked and found to be solid as the Empire State. The Robber had angrily demanded his mouthpiece and when the lawyer had finally been allowed to get to them they had been automatically sprung. No charge and no evidence to base one on. Dead-ends everywhere except that Leiter's car had been found the other side of the yacht basin, a mile away from the wharf. A mass of fingerprints, but none that fitted the three men. Any suggestions?

'Keep with it,' said the senior man in the cottage who had introduced himself as Captain Franks. 'Be along presently. Washington says we've got to get these men if it's the last thing we do. Two top operatives flying down tonight. Time to get co-operation from the Police. I'll tell 'em to get their stoolies working in Tampa. This isn't only a St. Petersburg job. 'Bye now.'

It was three o'clock. The police ambulance came and left again with the surgeon and the body that was so near to death. The two men left. They promised to keep in touch. They were anxious to know Bond's plans. Bond was evasive. Said he'd have to talk to Washington. Meanwhile, could he have Leiter's car? Yes, it would be brought round directly Records had finished with it.

When they had gone, Bond sat lost in thought. They had made sandwiches from the well-stocked pantry and Bond now finished these and had a stiff drink.

The telephone rang. Long-distance. Bond found himself speaking to the head of Leiter's Section of the Central Intelligence Agency. The gist of it was that they'd be very glad if Bond would move on to Jamaica at once. All very polite. They had spoken to London, who had agreed. When should they tell London that Bond would arrive in Jamaica?

Bond knew there was a Transcarib plane via Nassau due out next day. He said he'd be taking it. Any other news? Oh yes, said the CIA. The gentleman from Harlem and his girl friend had left by plane for Havana, Cuba, during the night. Private charter from a little place up the East coast called Vero Beach. Papers were in order and charter company was such a small one the FBI had not bothered to include them when they put the watch on all airports. Arrival had been reported by the CIA man in Cuba. Yes, too bad. Yes, the *Secatur* was still there. No sailing date. Well, too bad about Leiter. Fine man. Hope he makes out. So Bond would be in Jamaica tomorrow? Okay. Sorry things been so hectic. 'Bye.

Bond thought for a while, then he picked up the telephone and spoke briefly to a man at the Eastern Garden Aquarium at Miami and consulted him about buying a live shark to keep in an ornamental lagoon.

'Only place I ever heard of is right near you now, Mr. Bryce,' said the helpful voice. ' "Ourobouros Worm and Bait." They got sharks. Big ones. Do business with foreign zoos and suchlike. White, Tiger, even Hammerheads. They'll be glad to help you. Costs a lot to feed 'em. You're welcome. Any time you're passing. 'Bye.'

Bond took out his gun and cleaned it, waiting for the night.

CHAPTER XV

MIDNIGHT AMONG THE WORMS

AROUND six Bond packed his bag and paid the check. Mrs. Stuyvesant was glad to see the last of him. The Everglades hadn't experienced such alarums since the last hurricane.

Leiter's car was back on the Boulevard and he drove it over to the town. He visited a hardware store and made various purchases. Then he had the biggest steak, rare, with French fried, he had ever seen. It was a small grill called Pete's, dark and friendly. He drank a quarter of a pint of Old Grandad with the steak and had two cups of very strong coffee. With all this under his belt he began to feel more sanguine.

He spun out the meal and the drinks until nine o'clock. Then he studied a map of the city and took the car and made a wide detour that brought him within a block of The Robber's wharf from the south. He ran the car down to the sea and got out.

It was a bright moonlit night and the buildings and warehouses threw great blocks of indigo shadow. The whole section seemed deserted and there was no sound except the quiet lapping of the small waves against the sea-wall and water gurgling under the empty wharves.

The top of the low sea-wall was about three feet wide. It was in shadow for the hundred yards or more that separated him from the long black outline of the Ourobouros warehouse.

Bond climbed on to it and walked carefully and silently along between the buildings and the sea. As he got nearer a steady, high-pitched whine became louder, and by the time he dropped down on the wide cement parking space at the back of the building it was a muted scream. Bond had expected something of the sort. The noise came from the air-pumps and heating systems which he knew would be necessary to keep the fish healthy through the chill of the night hours. He had also relied on the fact that most of the roof would certainly be of glass to admit sunlight during the day. Also that there would be good ventilation.

He was not disappointed. The whole of the south wall of the warehouse, from just above the level of his head, was of plate glass, and through it he could see the moonlight shining down through half an acre of glass roofing. High up above him, and well out of reach, broad windows were open to the night air. There was, as he and Leiter had expected, a small door low down, but it was locked and bolted and leaded wires near the hinges suggested some form of burglar-alarm.

Bond was not interested in the door. Following his hunch, he had come equipped for an entry through glass. He cast about for something that would raise him an extra two feet. In a land where litter and junk are so much a part of the landscape he soon found what he wanted. It was a discarded heavy gauge tyre. He rolled it to the wall of the warehouse away from the door and took off his shoes.

He put bricks against the bottom edges of the tyre to hold it steady and hoisted himself up. The steady scream of the pumps gave him protection and he at once set to work with a small glass-cutter which he had bought, together with a hunk of putty, on his way to dinner. When he had cut down the two vertical sides of one of the yard-square panes, he pressed the putty against the centre of the glass and worked it to a protruding knob. He then went to work on the lateral edges of the pane.

While he worked he gazed through into the moonlit vistas of the huge repository. The endless rows of tanks stood on wooden trestles with narrow passages between. Down the centre of the building there was a wider passage. Under the trestles Bond could see long tanks and trays let into the floor. Just below him, broad racks covered with regiments of sea-shells jutted out from the walls. Most of the tanks were dark but in some a tiny strip of electric light glimmered spectrally and glinted on little fountains of bubbles rising from the weeds and sand. There was a light metal runway suspended from the roof over each row of tanks and Bond guessed that any individual tank could be lifted out and brought to the exit for shipment or to extract sick fish for quarantine. It was a window into a queer world and into a queer business. It was odd to think of all the worms and eels and fish stirring quietly in the night, the thousands of gills sighing and the multitude of antennae waving and pointing and transmitting their tiny radar signals to the dozing nerve-centres.

After a quarter of an hour's meticulous work there was a slight cracking noise and the pane came away attached to the putty knob in his hand.

He climbed down and put the pane carefully on the ground away from the tyre. Then he stuffed his shoes inside his shirt. With only one good hand they might be vital weapons. He listened. There was no sound but the unfaltering whine of the pumps. He looked up to see if by chance there were any clouds about to cross the moon, but the sky was empty save for its canopy of brightly burning stars. He got back on top of the tyre and with an easy heave half of his body was through the wide hole he had made.

He turned and grasped the metal frame above his head and putting all his weight on his arms he jack-knifed his legs through and down so that they were hanging a few inches above the racks full of shells. He lowered himself until he could feel the backs of the shells with his stockinged toes, then he softly separated them with his toes until he had exposed a width of board. Then he let his whole weight subside softly on to the tray. It held, and in a moment he was down on the floor listening with all his senses for any noise behind the whine of the machinery.

But there was none. He took his steel-tipped shoes out of his shirt and left them on the cleared board, then he moved off on the concrete floor with a pencil flashlight in his hand.

He was in the aquarium-fish section, and as he examined the labels he caught flashes of coloured light from the deep tanks and occasionally a piece of living jewellery would materialize and briefly goggle at him before he moved on.

There were all kinds – Swordtails, Guppies, Platys, Terras, Neons, Cichlids, Labyrinth and Paradise fish, and every variety of exotic Goldfish. Underneath, sunk in the floor, and most of them covered with chicken wire, there were tray upon tray swarming and heaving with worms and baits: white worms, micro worms, Daphnia, shrimp, and thick slimy clam worms. From these ground tanks, forests of tiny eyes looked up at his torch.

There was the fœtid smell of a mangrove swamp in the

air and the temperature was in the high seventies. Soon Bond began to sweat slightly and to long for the clean night air.

He had moved to the central passage-way before he found the poison fish which were one of his objectives. When he had read about them in the files of the Police Headquarters in New York, he had made a mental note that he would like to know more about this sideline of the peculiar business of Ourobouros Inc.

Here the tanks were smaller and there was generally only one specimen in each. Here the eyes that looked sluggishly at Bond were cold and hooded and an occasional fang was bared at the torch or a spined backbone slowly swelled. Each tank bore an ominous skull-and-crossbones in chalk and there were large labels that said VERY DANGEROUS and KEEP OFF.

There must have been at least a hundred tanks of various sizes, from the large ones to hold Torpedo Skates and the sinister Guitar Fish, to smaller ones for the Horse-killer Eel, Mud Fish from the Pacific, and the monstrous West Indian Scorpion Fish, each of whose spines has a poison sac as powerful as a rattlesnake's.

Bond's eyes narrowed as he noticed that in all the dangerous tanks the mud or sand on the bottom occupied nearly half the tank.

He chose a tank containing a six-inch Scorpion Fish. He knew something of the habits of this deadly species and in particular that they do not strike, but poison only on contact.

The top of the tank was on a level with his waist. He took out a strong pocket-knife he had purchased and opened the longest blade. Then he leant over the tank and with his sleeve rolled up he deliberately aimed his knife at the centre of the craggy head between the overhung grottoes of the eye-sockets. As his hand broke the surface of the water the white dinosaur spines stood threateningly erect and the mottled stripes of the fish turned to a uniform muddy brown. Its broad, wing-like pectorals rose slightly, poised for flight.

Bond lunged swiftly, correcting his aim for the refraction from the surface of the tank. He pinned the bulging head down as the tail threshed wildly and slowly drew the fish towards him and up the glass side of the tank. He stood aside and whipped it out on to the floor, where it continued flapping and jumping despite its shattered skull.

He leant over the tank and plunged his hand deep into the centre of the mud and sand.

Yes, they were there. His hunch about the poison fish had been right. His fingers felt the close rows of coin deep under the mud, like counters in a box. They were in a flat tray. He could feel the wooden partitions. He pulled out a coin, rinsing it and his hand in the cleaner surface water as he did so. He shone his torch on it. It was as big as a modern five-shilling piece and nearly as thick and it was gold. It bore the arms of Spain and the head of Philip II.

He looked at the tank, measuring it. There must be a thousand coins in this one tank that no customs officer would think of disturbing. Ten to twenty thousand dollars' worth, guarded by one poison-fanged Cerberus. These must be the cargo brought in by the *Secatur* on her last trip a week ago. A hundred tanks. Say one hundred and fifty thousand dollars' worth of gold per trip. Soon the trucks would be coming for the tanks and somewhere down the road men with rubber-coated tongs would extract the deadly fish and throw them back in the sea or burn them. The water and the mud would be emptied out and the gold coin washed and poured into bags. Then the bags would go to agents and the coins would trickle out on the market, each one strictly accounted for by Mr. Big's machine.

It was a scheme after Mr. Big's philosophy, effective, technically brilliant, almost foolproof.

Bond was full of admiration as he bent to the floor and speared the Scorpion Fish in the side. He dropped it back in the tank. There was no point in divulging his knowledge to the enemy.

It was as he turned away from the tank that all the lights in the warehouse suddenly blazed on and a voice of sharp authority said, 'Don't move an inch. Stick 'em up.'

As Bond took a rolling dive under the tank he caught a glimpse of the lank figure of The Robber squinting down the sights of his rifle about twenty yards away, up against the main entrance. As he dived he prayed that The Robber would miss, but also he prayed that the floor tank which was to take his dive would be one of the covered ones. It was. It was covered with chicken wire. Something snapped up at him as he hit the wire and sprawled clear in the next passage-way. As he dived, the rifle cracked and the Scorpion Fish tank above his head splintered sharply and water gushed down.

Bond sprinted fast between the tanks back towards his only means of retreat. Just as he turned the corner there was a shot and a tank of angel fish exploded like a bomb just beside his ear.

He was now at his end of the warehouse with The Robber

at the other, fifty yards away. There was no possible chance of jumping for his window on the other side of the central passage-way. He stood for a moment gaining his breath and thinking. He realized that the lines of tanks would only protect him to the knees and that between the tanks he would be in full view down the narrow passages. Either way, he could not stand still. He was reminded of the fact as a shot whammed between his legs into a pile of conchs, sending splinters of their hard china buzzing round him like wasps. He ran to his right and another shot came at his legs. It hit the floor and zoomed into a huge carboy of clams that split in half and emptied a hundred shell-fish over the floor. Bond raced back, taking long quick strides. He had his Beretta out and loosed off two shots as he crossed the central passage-way. He saw The Robber jump for shelter as a tank shattered above his head.

Bond grinned as he heard a shout drowned by the crash of glass and water.

He immediately dropped to one knee and fired two shots at The Robber's legs, but fifty yards for his small-calibre pistol was too much. There was the crash of another tank but the second shot clanged emptily into the iron entrance gates.

Then The Robber was shooting again and Bond could only dodge to and fro behind the cases and wait to be caught in the kneecap. Occasionally he fired a shot in return to make The Robber keep his distance, but he knew the battle was lost. The other man seemed to have endless ammunition. Bond had only two shots left in his gun and one fresh clip in his pocket.

As he shuttled to and fro, slipping on the rare fish that flapped wildly on the concrete, he even stooped to snatching up heavy queen conchs and helmet shells and hurling them towards the enemy. Often they burst impressively on top of some tank at The Robber's end and added to the appalling racket inside the corrugated-iron shed. But they were quite ineffective. He thought of shooting out the lights, but there were at least twenty of them in two rows.

Finally Bond decided to give up. He had one ruse to fall back on, and any change in the battle was better than exhausting himself at the wrong end of this deadly coconut-shy.

As he passed a row of cases of which the one near him was shattered, he pushed it on to the floor. It was still half full of rare Siamese Fighting Fish, and Bond was pleased with the expensive crash as the remains of the tank burst in fragments on the floor. A wide space was cleared on the trestle table, and after making two quick darts to pick up his shoes he dashed back to the table and jumped up.

With no target for The Robber to shoot at there was a moment's silence save for the whine of the pumps, the sound of water dripping out of broken tanks and the flapping of dying fish. Bond slipped his shoes on and laced them tight.

'Hey, Limey,' called The Robber patiently. 'Come on out or I start using pineapples. I been expectin' you an' I got plenty ammo.'

'Guess I got to give up,' answered Bond through cupped hands. 'But only because you smashed one of my ankles.'

'I'll not shoot,' called The Robber. 'Drop your gun on the floor and come down the central passage with your hands up. We'll have a quiet little talk.'

'Guess I got no option,' said Bond, putting hopelessness

into his voice. He dropped his Beretta with a clatter on to the cement floor. He took the gold coin out of his pocket and clenched it in his bandaged left hand.

Bond groaned as he put his feet to the floor. He dragged his left leg behind him as he limped heavily up the central passage, his hands held level with his shoulders. He stopped half way up the passage.

The Robber came slowly towards him, half-crouching, his rifle pointed at Bond's stomach. Bond was glad to see that his shirt was soaked and that he had a cut over the left eye.

The Robber walked well to the left of the passage-way. When he was about ten yards away from Bond he paused with one stockinged foot casually resting on a small obstruction in the cement floor.

He gestured with his rifle. 'Higher,' he said harshly.

Bond groaned and lifted his hands a few inches so that they were almost across his face, as if in defence.

Between the fingers he saw The Robber's toes kick something sharply sideways and there was a faint clang as if a bolt had been drawn. Bond's eyes glinted behind his hands and his jaw tightened. He knew now what had happened to Leiter.

The Robber came on, his hard, thin frame obscuring the spot where he had paused.

'Christ,' said Bond, 'I gotta sit down. My leg won't hold me.'

The Robber stopped a few feet away. 'Go ahead and stand while I ask you a few questions, Limey.' He bared his tobacco-stained teeth. 'You'll soon be lying down, and for keeps.' The Robber stood and looked him over. Bond sagged. Behind the defeat in his face his brain was measuring in inches.

'Nosey bastard,' said The Robber. . . .

At that moment Bond dropped the gold coin out of his left hand. It clanged on the cement floor and started to roll.

In the fraction of a second that The Robber's eyes flickered down, Bond's right foot in its steel-capped shoe lashed out to its full length. It kicked the rifle almost out of The Robber's hands. At the same moment that The Robber pulled the trigger and the bullet crashed harmlessly through the glass ceiling, Bond launched himself in a dive at the man's stomach, his two arms flailing.

Both hands connected with something soft and brought a grunt of agony. Pain shot through Bond's left hand and he winced as the rifle crashed down across his back. He bore on into the man, blind to pain, hitting with both hands, his head down between hunched shoulders, forcing the man back and off his balance. As he felt the balance yield he straightened himself slightly and lashed out again with his steel-capped foot. It connected with The Robber's kneecap. There was a scream of agony and the rifle clattered to the ground as The Robber tried to save himself. He was half way to the floor when Bond's uppercut hit him and projected the body another few feet.

The Robber fell in the centre of the passage just opposite what Bond could now see was a drawn bolt in the floor.

As the body hit the ground a section of the floor turned swiftly on a central pivot and the body almost disappeared down the black opening of a wide trap-door in the concrete.

As he felt the floor give under his weight The Robber gave a shrill scream of terror and his hands scrabbled for a hold. They caught the edge of the floor and clutched it just as his whole body slid into space and the six-foot panel of reinforced concrete revolved smoothly until it rested upright on its pivot, a black rectangle yawning on either side.

Bond gasped for air. He put his hands on his hips and got back some of his breath. Then he walked to the edge of the right-hand hole and looked down.

The Robber's terrified face, the lips drawn back from the teeth and the eyes madly distended, jabbered up at him.

Looking beyond him, Bond could see nothing, but he heard the lapping of water against the foundations of the building and there was a faint luminescence on the seaward side. Bond guessed that there was access to the sea through wire or narrow bars.

As The Robber's voice died down to a whimper, Bond could hear something stirring down there, awoken by the light. A Hammerhead or a Tiger Shark, he guessed, with their sharper reactions.

'Pull me out, friend. Give me a break. Pull me out. I can't hold much longer. I'll do anything you want. Tell you anything.' The Robber's voice was a hoarse whisper of supplication.

'What happened to Solitaire?' Bond stared down into the frenzied eyes.

'The Big Man did it. Told me to fix a snatch. Two men in Tampa. Ask for Butch and The Lifer. Poolroom behind the "Oasis". She came to no harm. Lemme out, pal.'

'And the American, Leiter?'

The agonized face pleaded. 'It was his fault. Called me out early this mornin'. Said the place was on fire. Seen it passing in his car. Held me up and brought me back in here. Wanted to search the place. Just fell through the trap. Accident. I swear it was his fault. We pulled him out before he was finished. He'll be okay.'

Bond looked down coldly at the white fingers desperately clinging to the sharp edge of concrete. He knew that The Robber must have got the bolt back and somehow engineered Leiter over the trap. He could hear the man's laugh of triumph as the floor swung open, could see the cruel smile as he pencilled the note and stuck it into the bandages when they had fished the half-eaten body out.

For a moment blind rage seized him.

He kicked out sharply, twice.

One short scream came up out of the depths. There was a splash and then a great commotion in the water.

Bond walked to the side of the trap-door and pushed the upright concrete slab. It revolved easily on its central pivot.

Just before its edges shut out the blackness below, Bond heard one terrible snuffling grunt as if a great pig was getting its mouth full. He knew it for the grunt that a shark makes as its hideous flat nose comes up out of the water and its sickle-shaped mouth closes on a floating carcase. He shuddered and kicked the bolt home with his foot.

Bond collected the gold coin off the floor and picked up his Beretta. He went to the main entrance and looked back for a moment at the shambles of the battlefield.

He reflected that there was nothing to show that the secret of the treasure had been discovered. The top had been shot off the Scorpion Fish tank under which Bond had dived, and when the other men came in the morning they would not be surprised to find the fish dead in the tank. They would get the remains of The Robber out of the Shark tank and report to Mr. Big that he'd been worsted in a gun battle and that there were X thousand dollars' worth of damage which would have to be repaired before the *Secatur* could bring over its next cargo. They would find some of Bond's bullets and soon guess that it was his work.

Bond grimly shut his mind to the horror beneath the floor of the warehouse. He turned off the lights and let himself out by the main entrance.

A small payment had been made on account of Solitaire and Leiter.

CHAPTER XVI

THE JAMAICA VERSION

IT was two o'clock in the morning. Bond eased his car away from the sea-wall and moved off through the town on to 4th Street, the highway to Tampa.

He dawdled along down the four-lane concrete highway through the endless gauntlet of motels, trailer camps and roadside emporia selling beach furniture, sea-shells and concrete gnomes.

He stopped at the 'Gulf Winds Bar and Snacks' and ordered a double Old Grandad on the rocks. While the barman poured it he went into the washroom and cleaned himself up. The bandages on his left hand were covered with dirt and the hand throbbed painfully. The splint had broken on The Robber's stomach. There was nothing Bond could do about it. His eyes were red with strain and lack of sleep. He went back to the bar, drank down the Bourbon and ordered another one. The barman looked like a college kid spending his holidays the hard way. He wanted to talk but there was no talk left in Bond. Bond sat and looked into his glass and thought about Leiter and The Robber and heard the sickening grunt of the feeding shark.

He paid and went out and on again over the Gandy Bridge, and the air of the Bay was cool on his face. At the end of the bridge he turned left towards the airport and stopped at the first motel that looked awake.

The middle-aged couple that owned the place were listening to late rhumba music from Cuba with a bottle of rye between them. Bond told a story of a blow-out on his way from Sarasota to Silver Springs. They weren't interested. They were just glad to take his ten dollars. He drove his car up to the door of Room 5 and the man unlocked the door and turned on the light. There was a double bed and a shower and a chest-of-drawers and two chairs. The motif was white and blue. It looked clean and Bond put his bag down thankfully and said good night. He stripped and threw his clothes unfolded on to a chair. Then he took a quick shower, cleaned his teeth and gargled with a sharp mouthwash and climbed into bed.

He plunged at once into a calm untroubled sleep. It was the first night since he had arrived in America that did not threaten a fresh battle with his stars on the morrow.

He awoke at midday and walked down the road to a cafeteria where the short-order cook fixed him a delicious three-decker western sandwich and coffee. Then he came back to his room and wrote a detailed report to the FBI at Tampa. He omitted all reference to the gold in the poison tanks for fear that The Big Man would close down his operations in Jamaica. The nature of these had still to be discovered. Bond knew that the damage he had done to the machine in America had no bearing on the heart of his assignment – the discovery of the source of the gold, its seizure, and the destruction, if possible, of Mr. Big himself.

He drove to the airport and caught the silver, four-engined plane with a few minutes to spare. He left Leiter's car in the parking space as in his report he had told the

FBI he would. He guessed that he need not have mentioned it to the FBI when he saw a man in an unnecessary raincoat hanging round the souvenir shop, buying nothing. Raincoats seemed almost the badge of office of the FBI. Bond was certain they wanted to see he caught the plane. They would be glad to see the last of him. Wherever he had gone in America he had left dead bodies. Before he boarded the plane he called the hospital in St. Petersburg. He wished he hadn't; Leiter was still unconscious and there was no news. Yes, they would cable him when they had something definite.

It was five in the evening when they circled over Tampa Bay and headed East. The sun was low on the horizon. A big jet from Pensacola swept by, well to port, leaving four trails of vapour that hung almost motionless in the still air. Soon it would complete its training circuit and go in to land, back to the Gulf Coast packed with oldsters in Truman shirts. Bond was glad to be on his way to the soft green flanks of Jamaica and to be leaving behind the great hard continent of Eldollarado.

The plane swept on across the waist of Florida, across the acres of jungle and swamp without sign of human habitation, its wing-lights blinking green and red in the gathering dark. Soon they were over Miami and the monster chump-traps of the Eastern Seaboard, their arteries ablaze with Neon. Away to port, State Highway No. 1 disappeared up the coast in a golden ribbon of motels, gas stations and fruit-juice stands, up through Palm Beach and Daytona to Jacksonville, three hundred miles away. Bond thought of the breakfast he had had at Jacksonville not three days before and of all that had happened since. Soon, after a short stop at Nassau, he would be flying over Cuba, perhaps over the hideout where Mr. Big had put her away. She would hear the noise of the plane and perhaps her instincts would make her look up towards the sky and feel that for a moment he was nearby.

Bond wondered if they would ever meet again and finish what they had begun. But that would have to come later, when his work was over – the prize at the end of the dangerous road that had started three weeks before in the fog of London.

After a cocktail and an early dinner they came in to Nassau and spent half an hour on the richest island in the world, the sandy patch where a thousand million pounds of frightened sterling lies buried beneath the Canasta tables and where bungalows surrounded by a thin scurf of screw-pine and casuarina change hands at fifty thousand pounds a piece.

They left the platinum whistle-stop behind and were soon crossing the twinkling mother-of-pearl lights of Havana, so different in their pastel modesty from the harsh primary colours of American cities at night.

They were flying at fifteen thousand feet when, just after crossing Cuba, they ran into one of those violent tropical storms that suddenly turn aircraft from comfortable drawing-rooms into bucketing death-traps. The great plane staggered and plunged, its screws now roaring in vacuum and now biting harshly into walls of solid air. The thin tube shuddered and swung. Crockery crashed in the pantry and huge rain hammered on the perspex windows.

Bond gripped the arms of his chair so that his left hand hurt and cursed softly to himself.

He looked at the racks of magazines and thought: they won't help much when the steel tires at fifteen thousand feet, nor will the eau-de-cologne in the washroom, nor the personalized meals, the free razor, the 'orchid for your lady' now trembling in the ice-box. Least of all the safety-belts and the life-jackets with the whistle that the steward demonstrates will really blow, nor the cute little rescue-lamp that glows red.

No, when the stresses are too great for the tired metal, when the ground mechanic who checks the de-icing equipment is crossed in love and skimps his job, way back in London, Idlewild, Gander, Montreal; when those or many things happen, then the little warm room with propellers in front falls straight down out of the sky into the sea or on to the land, heavier than air, fallible, vain. And the forty little heavier-than-air people, fallible within the plane's fallibility, vain within its larger vanity, fall down with it and make little holes in the land or little splashes in the sea. Which is anyway their destiny, so why worry? You are linked to the ground mechanic's careless fingers in Nassau just as you are linked to the weak head of the little man in the family saloon who mistakes the red light for the green and meets you head-on, for the first and last time, as you are motoring quietly home from some private sin. There's nothing to do about it. You start to die the moment you are born. The whole of life is cutting through the pack with death. So take it easy. Light a cigarette and be grateful you are still alive as you suck the smoke deep into your lungs. Your stars have already let you come quite a long way since you left your mother's womb and whimpered at the cold air of the world. Perhaps they'll even let you get to Jamaica tonight. Can't you hear those cheerful voices in the control tower that have said quietly all day long, 'Come in BOAC. Come in Panam. Come in

KLM'? Can't you hear them calling you down too: 'Come in Transcarib. Come in Transcarib'? Don't lose faith in your stars. Remember that hot stitch of time when you faced death from The Robber's gun last night. You're still alive, aren't you? There, we're out of it already. It was just to remind you that being quick with a gun doesn't mean you're really tough. Just don't forget it. This happy landing at Palisadoes Airport comes to you by courtesy of your stars. Better thank them.

Bond unfastened his seat-belt and wiped the sweat off his face.

To hell with it, he thought, as he stepped down out of the huge strong plane.

Strangways, the chief Secret Service agent for the Caribbean, was at the airport to meet him and he was quickly through the Customs and Immigration and Finance Control.

It was nearly eleven and the night was quiet and hot. There was the shrill sound of crickets from the dildo cactus on both sides of the airport road and Bond gratefully drank in the sounds and smells of the tropics as the military pick-up cut across the corner of Kingston and took them up towards the gleaming, moonlit foothills of the Blue Mountains.

They talked in monosyllables until they were settled on the comfortable veranda of Strangways's neat white house on the Junction Road below Stony Hill.

Strangways poured a strong whisky-and-soda for both of them and then gave a concise account of the whole of the Jamaica end of the case.

He was a lean, humorous man of about thirty-five, a former Lieutenant-Commander in the Special Branch of the RNVR. He had a black patch over one eye and the sort of aquiline good looks that are associated with the bridges of destroyers. But his face was heavily lined under its tan and Bond sensed from his quick gestures and clipped sentences that he was nervous and highly strung. He was certainly efficient and he had a sense of humour, and he showed no signs of jealousy at someone from headquarters butting in on his territory. Bond felt that they would get on well together and he looked forward to the partnership.

This was the story that Strangways had to tell.

It had always been rumoured that there was treasure on the Isle of Surprise and everything that was known about Bloody Morgan supported the rumour.

The tiny island lay in the exact centre of Shark Bay, a small harbour that lies at the end of the Junction Road that runs across the thin waist of Jamaica from Kingston to the north coast.

The great buccaneer had made Shark Bay his headquarters. He liked to have the whole width of the island between himself and the Governor at Port Royal so that he could slip in and out of Jamaican waters in complete secrecy. The Governor also liked the arrangement. The Crown wished a blind eye to be turned on Morgan's piracy until the Spaniards had been cleared out of the Caribbean. When this was accomplished, Morgan was rewarded with a Knighthood and the Governorship of Jamaica. Till then, his actions had to be disavowed to avoid a European war with Spain.

So, for the long period before the poacher turned gamekeeper, Morgan used Shark Bay as his sallyport. He built three houses on the neighbouring estate, christened Llanrumney after his birthplace in Wales. These houses were called 'Morgan's', 'The Doctor's' and 'The Lady's'. Buckles and coins are still turned up in the ruins of them.

His ships always anchored in Shark Bay and he careened them in the lee of the Isle of Surprise, a precipitous lump of coral and limestone that surges straight up out of the centre of the bay and is surmounted by a jungly plateau of about an acre.

When, in 1683, he left Jamaica for the last time, it was under open arrest to be tried by his peers for flouting the Crown. His treasure was left behind somewhere in Jamaica and he died in penury without revealing its whereabouts. It must have been a vast hoard, the fruits of countless raids on Hispaniola, of the capture of innumerable treasure-ships sailing for The Plate, of the sacking of Panama and the looting of Maracaibo. But it vanished without trace.

It was always thought that the secret lay somewhere on the Isle of Surprise, but for two hundred years the diving and digging of treasure-hunters yielded nothing. Then, said Strangways, just six months before, two things had happened within a few weeks. A young fisherman disappeared from the village of Shark Bay, and had not been heard of since, and an anonymous New York syndicate purchased the island for a thousand pounds from the present owner of the Llanrumney Estate, which was now a rich banana and cattle property.

A few weeks after the sale, the yacht *Secatur* put in to Shark Bay and dropped anchor in Morgan's old anchorage in the lee of the island. It was manned entirely by negroes. They went to work and cut a stairway in the rock face of the island and erected on the summit a number of low-lying shacks in the fashion known in Jamaica as 'wattle-and-daub'.

They appeared to be completely equipped with provisions, and all they purchased from the fishermen of the bay was fresh fruit and water.

They were a taciturn and orderly lot who gave no trouble. They explained to the Customs which they had cleared in the neighbouring Port Maria that they were there to catch tropical fish, especially the poisonous varieties, and collect rare shells for Ourobouros Inc. in St. Petersburg. When they had established themselves they purchased large quantities of these from the Shark Bay, Port Maria and Oracabessa fishermen.

For a week they carried out blasting operations on the island and it was given out that these were for the purpose of excavating a large fish-tank.

The *Secatur* began a fortnightly shuttle-service with the Gulf of Mexico and watchers with binoculars confirmed that, before each sailing, consignments of portable fish-tanks were taken aboard. Always half a dozen men were left behind. Canoes approaching the island were warned off by a watchman, at the base of the steps in the cliff, who fished all day from a narrow jetty alongside which the *Secatur* on her visits moored with two anchors out, well sheltered from the prevailing north-easterly winds.

No one succeeded in landing on the island by daylight and, after two tragic attempts, nobody tried to gain access by night.

The first attempt was made by a local fisherman spurred on by the rumours of buried treasure that no talk of tropical fish could suppress. He had swum out one dark night and his body had been washed back over the reef next day. Sharks and barracuda had left nothing but the trunk and the remains of a thigh.

At about the time he should have reached the island the whole village of Shark Bay was awakened by the most horrible drumming noise. It seemed to come from inside the island. It was recognized as the beating of Voodoo drums. It started softly and rose slowly to a thunderous crescendo. Then it died down again and stopped. It lasted about five minutes.

From that moment the island was ju-ju, or obeah, as it is called in Jamaica, and even in daylight canoes kept at a safe distance.

By this time Strangways was interested and he made a full report to London. Since 1950 Jamaica had become an important strategic target, thanks to the development by Reynolds Metal and the Kaiser Corporation of huge bauxite deposits found on the island. So far as Strangways was concerned, the activities on Surprise might easily be the erection of a base for one-man submarines in the event of war, particularly since Shark Bay was within range of the route followed by the Reynolds ships to the new bauxite harbour at Ocho Rios, a few miles down the coast.

London followed the report up with Washington and it came to light that the New York syndicate that had purchased the island was wholly owned by Mr. Big.

This was three months ago. Strangways was ordered to penetrate the island at all costs and find out what was going on. He mounted quite an operation. He rented a property on the western arm of Shark Bay called Beau Desert. It contained the ruins of one of the famous Jamaican Great Houses of the early nineteenth century and also a modern beach-house directly across from the *Secatur*'s anchorage up against Surprise.

He brought down two very fine swimmers from the naval base at Bermuda and set up a permanent watch on the island through day- and night-glasses. Nothing of a suspicious nature was seen and on a dark calm night he sent out the two swimmers with instructions to make an underwater survey of the foundations of the island.

Strangways described his horror when, an hour after they had left to swim across the three hundred yards of water, the terrible drumming had started up somewhere inside the cliffs of the island.

That night the two men did not return.

On the next day they were both washed up at different parts of the bay. Or rather, the remains left by the shark and barracuda.

At this point in Strangeways's narrative, Bond interrupted him.

'Just a minute,' he said. 'What's all this about shark and barracuda? They're not generally savage in these waters. There aren't very many of them round Jamaica and they don't often feed at night. Anyway, I don't believe either of them attack humans unless there's blood in the water. Occasionally they might snap at a white foot out of curiosity. Have they ever behaved like this round Jamaica before?'

'Never been a case since a girl got a foot bitten off in Kingston harbour in 1942,' said Strangways. 'She was being towed by a speedboat, flipping her feet up and down. The white feet must have looked particularly appetising. Travelling at just the right speed too. Everyone agrees with your theory. And my men had harpoons and knives. I thought I'd done everything to protect them. Dreadful business. You can imagine how I felt about it. Since then we've done nothing except try to get legitimate access to the island via the Colonial Office and Washington. You see, it belongs to an American now. Damn slow business, particularly as there's nothing against these people. They seem to have pretty good protection in Washington and some smart international lawyers. We're absolutely stuck. London told me to hang on until you came.' Strangways took a pull at his whisky and looked expectantly at Bond.

'What are the *Secatur*'s movements?' asked Bond.

'Still in Cuba. Sailing in about a week, according to the CIA.'

'How many trips has she done?'

'About twenty.'

Bond multiplied one hundred and fifty thousand dollars by twenty. If his guess was right, Mr. Big had already taken a million pounds in gold out of the island.

'I've made some provisional arrangements for you,' said Strangways. 'There's the house at Beau Desert. I've got you a car, Sunbeam Talbot coupé. New tyres. Fast. Right car for these roads. I've got a good man to act as your factotum. A Cayman Islander called Quarrel. Best swimmer and fisherman in the Caribbean. Terribly keen. Nice chap. And I've borrowed the West Indian Citrus Company's rest-house at Manatee Bay. It's the other end of the island. You could rest up there for a week and get in a bit of training until the *Secatur* comes in. You'll need to be fit if you're going to try to get over to Surprise, and I honestly believe that's the only answer. Anything else I can do? I'll be about, of course, but I'll have to stay around Kingston to keep up communications with London and Washington. They'll want to know everything we do. Anything else you'd like me to fix up?'

Bond had been making up his mind.

'Yes,' he said. 'You might ask London to get the Admiralty to lend us one of their frogmen suits complete with compressed-air bottles. Plenty of spares. And a couple of good underwater harpoon guns. The French ones called "Champion" are the best. Good underwater torch. A commando dagger. All the dope they can get from the Natural History Museum on barracuda and shark. And some of that shark-repellent stuff the Americans used in the Pacific. Ask B O A C to fly it all out on their direct service.'

Bond paused. 'Oh yes,' he said. 'And one of those things our saboteurs used against ships in the war. Limpet mine, with assorted fuses.'

CHAPTER XVII

THE UNDERTAKER'S WIND

PAW-PAW with a slice of green lime, a dish piled with red bananas, purple star-apples and tangerines, scrambled eggs and bacon, Blue Mountain coffee – the most delicious in the world – Jamaican marmalade, almost black, and guava jelly.

As Bond, wearing shorts and sandals, had his breakfast on the veranda and gazed down on the sunlit panorama of Kingston and Port Royal, he thought how lucky he was and what wonderful moments of consolation there were for the darkness and danger of his profession.

Bond knew Jamaica well. He had been there on a long assignment just after the war when the Communist headquarters in Cuba was trying to infiltrate the Jamaican labour unions. It had been an untidy and inconclusive job but he had grown to love the great green island and its staunch, humorous people. Now he was glad to be back and to have a whole week of respite before the grim work began again.

After breakfast, Strangways appeared on the veranda with a tall brown-skinned man in a faded blue shirt and old brown twill trousers.

This was Quarrel, the Cayman Islander, and Bond liked him immediately. There was the blood of Cromwellian soldiers and buccaneers in him and his face was strong and angular and his mouth was almost severe. His eyes were grey. It was only the spatulate nose and the pale palms of his hands that were negroid.

Bond shook him by the hand.

'Good morning, Captain,' said Quarrel. Coming from the most famous race of seamen in the world, this was the highest title he knew. But there was no desire to please, or humility, in his voice. He was speaking as mate of the ship and his manner was straightforward and candid.

That moment defined their relationship. It remained that of a Scots laird with his head stalker; authority was unspoken and there was no room for servility.

After discussing their plans, Bond took the wheel of the little car Quarrel had brought up from Kingston and they started on up the Junction Road, leaving Strangways to busy himself with Bond's requirements.

They had got off before nine and it was still cool as they crossed the mountains that run along Jamaica's back like the central ridges of a crocodile's armour. The road wound down towards the northern plains through some of the most beautiful scenery in the world, the tropical vegetation changing with the altitude. The green flanks of the uplands, all feathered with bamboo interspersed with the dark, glinting green of breadfruit and the sudden Bengal fire of Flame of the Forest, gave way to the lower forests of ebony, mahogany, mahoe and logwood. And when they reached the plains of Agualta Vale the green sea of sugar-cane and bananas stretched away to where the distant fringe of glittering shrapnel bursts marked the palm-groves along the north coast.

Quarrel was a good companion on the drive and a wonderful guide. He talked about the trap-door spiders as they passed through the famous palm-gardens of Castleton, he told about a fight he had witnessed between a giant centipede and a scorpion and he explained the difference between the male and female paw-paw. He described the poisons of the forest and the healing properties of tropical herbs, the pressure the palm kernel develops to break open its coconut, the length of a humming-bird's tongue, and how crocodiles carry their young in their mouths laid lengthways like sardines in a tin.

He spoke exactly but without expertise, using Jamaican language in which plants 'strive' or 'quail', moths are 'bats', and 'love' is used instead of 'like'. As he talked he would raise his hand in greeting to the people on the road and they would wave back and shout his name.

'You seem to know a lot of people,' said Bond as the driver of a bulging bus with ROMANCE in large letters over the windshield gave him a couple of welcoming blasts on his wind-horn.

'I bin watching Surprise for tree muns, Cap'n,' answered Quarrel, ' 'n I been travelling this road twice a week. Everyone soon know you in Jamaica. They got good eyes.'

By half-past ten they had passed through Port Maria and branched off along the little parochial road that runs down to Shark Bay. Round a turning they suddenly came on it below them and Bond stopped the car and they got out.

The bay was crescent shaped, perhaps three-quarters of a mile wide at its arms. Its blue surface was ruffled by a light breeze blowing from the north-east, the edge of the Trade Winds that are born five hundred miles away in the Gulf of Mexico and then go on their long journey round the world.

A mile from where they stood, a long line of breakers showed the reef just outside the bay and the narrow untroubled waters of the passage which was the only entrance to the anchorage. In the centre of the crescent, the Isle of Surprise rose a hundred feet sheer out of the water, small waves creaming against its easterly base, calm waters in its lee.

It was nearly round, and it looked like a tall grey cake topped with green icing on a blue china plate.

They had stopped about a hundred feet above the little cluster of fishermen's huts behind the palm-fringed beach of the bay and they were level with the flat green top of the island, half a mile away. Quarrel pointed out the thatched roofs of the wattle-and-daub shanties among the trees in the centre of the island. Bond examined them through Quarrel's binoculars. There was no sign of life except a thin wisp of smoke blowing away with the breeze.

Below them, the water of the bay was pale green on the white sand. Then it deepened to dark blue just before the broken brown of a submerged fringe of inner reef that made a wide semicircle a hundred yards from the island. Then it was dark blue again with patches of lighter blue and aquamarine. Quarrel said that the depth of the *Secatur*'s anchorage was about thirty feet.

To their left, in the middle of the western arms of the bay, deep among the trees behind a tiny white sand beach, was their base of operations, Beau Desert. Quarrel described its layout and Bond stood for ten minutes examining the three-hundred-yard stretch of sea between it and the *Secatur*'s anchorage up against the island.

In all, Bond spent an hour reconnoitring the place, then, without going near their house or the village, they turned the car and got back on the main coast road.

They drove on through the beautiful little banana port of Oracabessa and Ocho Rios with its huge new bauxite plant, along the north shore to Montego Bay, two hours away. It was now February and the season was in full swing. The little village and the straggle of large hotels were bathed in the four months gold-rush that sees them through the whole year. They stopped at a rest-house on the other side of the wide bay and had lunch and then drove on through the heat of the afternoon to the western tip of the island, two hours further on.

Here, because of the huge coastal swamps, nothing has happened since Columbus used Manatee Bay as a casual anchorage. Jamaican fishermen have taken the place of the Arawak Indians, but otherwise there is the impression that time has stood still.

Bond thought it the most beautiful beach he had ever seen, five miles of white sand sloping easily into the breakers and, behind, the palm trees marching in graceful disarray to the horizon. Under them, the grey canoes were pulled up beside pink mounds of discarded conch shells, and among them smoke rose from the palm thatch cabins of the fishermen in the shade between the swamp-lands and the sea.

In a clearing among the cabins, set on a rough lawn of Bahama grass, was the house on stilts built as a week-end cottage for the employees of the West Indian Citrus Company. It was built on stilts to keep the termites at bay and it was closely wired against mosquito and sand-fly. Bond drove off the rough track and parked under the house. While Quarrel chose two rooms and made them comfortable Bond put a towel round his waist and walked through the palm trees to the sea, twenty yards away.

For an hour he swam and lazed in the warm buoyant water, thinking of Surprise and its secret, fixing these three hundred yards in his mind, wondering about the shark and barracuda and the other hazards of the sea, that great library of books one cannot read.

Walking back to the little wooden bungalow, Bond picked up his first sandfly bites. Quarrel chuckled when he saw the flat bumps on his back that would soon start to itch maddeningly.

'Can't do nuthen to keep them away, Cap'n,' he said. 'But Ah kin stop them ticklin'. You best take a shower first to git the salt off. They only bites hard for an hour in the evenin' and then they likes salt with their dinner.'

When Bond came out of the shower Quarrel produced an old medicine bottle and swabbed the bites with a brown liquid that smelled of creosote.

'We get more skeeters and sandfly in the Caymans than anywheres else in the world,' he said, 'but we gives them no attention so long as we got this medicine.'

The ten minutes of tropical twilight brought its quick melancholy and then the stars and the three-quarter moon blazed down and the sea died to a whisper. There was the short lull between the two great winds of Jamaica, and then the palms began to whisper again.

Quarrel jerked his head towards the window.

'De "Undertaker's Wind",' he commented.

'How's that?' asked Bond, startled.

'On-and-off shore breeze de sailors call it,' said Quarrel.

'De Undertaker blow de bad air out of de Island night-times from six till six. Then every morning de "Doctor's Wind" come and blow de sweet air in from de sea. Leastwise dat's what we calls dem in Jamaica.'

Quarrel looked quizzically at Bond.

'Guess you and de Undertaker's Wind got much de same job, Cap'n,' he said half-seriously.

Bond laughed shortly. 'Glad I don't have to keep the same hours,' he said.

Outside, the crickets and the tree-frogs started to zing and tinkle and the great hawkmoths came to the wire-netting across the windows and clutched it, gazing with trembling ecstasy at the two oil lamps that hung from the cross-beams inside.

Occasionally a pair of fishermen, or a group of giggling girls, would walk by down the beach on their way to the single tiny rum-shop at the point of the bay. No man walked alone for fear of the duppies under the trees, or the rolling calf, the ghastly animal that comes rolling towards you along the ground, its legs in chains and flames coming out of its nostrils.

While Quarrel prepared one of the succulent meals of fish and eggs and vegetables that were to be their staple diet, Bond sat under the light and pored over the books that Strangways had borrowed from the Jamaica Institute, books on the tropical sea and its denizens by Beebe and Allyn and others, and on sub-marine hunting by Cousteau and Hass. When he set out to cross those three hundred yards of sea, he was determined to do it expertly and to leave nothing to chance. He knew the calibre of Mr. Big and he guessed that the defences of Surprise would be technically brilliant. He thought they would not involve simple weapons like guns and high explosives. Mr. Big needed to work undisturbed by the police. He had to keep out of reach of the law. He guessed that somehow the forces of the sea had been harnessed to do The Big Man's work for him and it was on these that he concentrated, on murder by shark and barracuda, perhaps by Manta Ray and octopus.

The facts set out by the naturalists were chilling and awe-inspiring, but the experiences of Cousteau in the Mediterranean and of Hass in the Red Sea and Caribbean were more encouraging.

That night Bond's dreams were full of terrifying encounters with giant squids and sting rays, hammerheads and the saw-teeth of barracuda, so that he whimpered and sweated in his sleep.

On the next day he started his training under the critical, appraising eyes of Quarrel. Every morning he swam a mile up the beach before breakfast and then ran back along the firm sand to the bungalow. At about nine they would set out in a canoe, the single triangular sail taking them fast through the water up the coast to Bloody Bay and Orange Bay where the sand ends in cliffs and small coves and the reef is close in against the coast.

Here they would beach the canoe and Quarrel would take him out with spears and masks and an old underwater harpoon gun on breathtaking expeditions in the sort of waters he would encounter in Shark Bay.

They hunted quietly, a few yards apart, Quarrel moving effortlessly in an element in which he was almost at home.

Soon Bond too learned not to fight the sea but always to give and take with the currents and eddies and not to struggle against them, to use judo tactics in the water.

On the first day he came home cut and poisoned by the coral and with a dozen sea-egg spines in his side. Quarrel grinned and treated the wounds with merthiolate and Milton. Then, as every evening, he massaged Bond for half an hour with palm oil, talking quietly the while about the fish they had seen that day, explaining the habits of the carnivores and the ground-feeders, the camouflage of fish and their machinery for changing colour through the blood stream.

He also had never known fish to attack a man except in desperation or because there was blood in the water. He explained that fish are rarely hungry in tropical waters and that most of their weapons are for defence and not for attack. The only exception, he admitted, was the barracuda. 'Mean fish,' he called them, fearless since they knew no enemy except disease, capable of fifty miles an hour over short distances, and with the worst battery of teeth of any fish in the sea.

One day they shot a ten-pounder that had been hanging round them, melting into the grey distances and then reappearing, silent, motionless in the upper water, its angry tiger's eyes glaring at them so close that they could see its gills working softly and the teeth glinting like a wolf's along its cruel underslung jaw.

Quarrel finally took the harpoon gun from Bond and shot it, badly, through the streamlined belly. It came straight for them, its jaws on their great hinges wide open like a striking rattlesnake. Bond made a wild lunge at it with his spear just as it was on to Quarrel. He missed but the spear went between its jaws. They immediately snapped shut on the steel shaft, and as the fish tore the spear out of Bond's hand, Quarrel stabbed at it with his knife and it went mad, dashing through the water with its entrails hanging out, the spear clenched between its teeth, and the harpoon dangling from its body. Quarrel could scarcely hold the line as the fish tried to tear the wide barb through the walls of its stomach, but he moved with it towards a piece of submerged reef and climbed on to it and slowly pulled the fish in.

When Quarrel had cut its throat and they twisted the spear out of its jaws they found bright, deep scratches in the steel.

They took the fish ashore and Quarrel cut its head off and opened the jaws with a piece of wood. The upper jaw rose in an enormous gape, almost at right angles to the lower, and revealed a fantastic battery of razor-sharp teeth, so crowded that they overlapped like shingles on a roof. Even the tongue had several runs of small pointed recurved teeth and, in front, there were two huge fangs that projected forward like a snake's.

Although it only weighed just over ten pounds, it was over four feet long, a nickel bullet of muscle and hard flesh.

'We shoot no more cudas,' said Quarrel. 'But for you I been in hospital for a month and mebbe lost ma face. It was foolish of me. If we swim towards it, it gone away. Dey always do. Dey cowards like all fish. Doan you worry bout those,' he pointed at the teeth. 'You never see dem again.'

'I hope not,' said Bond. 'I haven't got a face to spare.'

By the end of the week, Bond was sunburned and hard. He had cut his cigarettes down to ten a day and had not had a single drink. He could swim two miles without tiring, his hand was completely healed and all the scales of big city life had fallen from him.

Quarrel was pleased. 'You ready for Surprise, Cap'n,' he said, 'and I not like be de fish what tries to eat you.'

Towards nightfall on the eighth day they came back to the rest-house to find Strangways waiting for them.

'I've got some good news for you,' he said: 'your friend Felix Leiter's going to be all right. At all events he's not going to die. They've had to amputate the remains of an arm and a leg. Now the plastic surgery chaps have started building up his face. They called me up from St. Petersburg yesterday. Apparently he insisted on getting a message to you. First thing he thought of when he could think at all. Says he's sorry not to be with you and to tell you not to get your feet wet – or at any rate, not as wet as he did.'

Bond's heart was full. He looked out of the window. 'Tell him to get well quickly,' he said abruptly. 'Tell him I miss him.' He looked back into the room. 'Now what about the gear? Everything okay?'

'I've got it all,' said Strangways, 'and the *Secatur* sails tomorrow for Surprise. After clearing at Port Maria, they should anchor before nightfall. Mr. Big's on board – only the second time he's been down here. Oh and they've got a woman with them. Girl called Solitaire, according to the CIA. Know anything about her?'

'Not much,' said Bond. 'But I'd like to get her away from him. She's not one of his team.'

'Sort of damsel in distress,' said the romantic Strangways. 'Good show. According to the CIA she's a corker.'

But Bond had gone out on the veranda and was gazing up at his stars. Never before in his life had there been so much to play for. The secret of the treasure, the defeat of a great criminal, the smashing of a Communist spy ring, and the destruction of a tentacle of SMERSH, the cruel machine that was his own private target. And now Solitaire, the ultimate personal prize.

The stars winked down their cryptic morse and he had no key to their cipher.

CHAPTER XVIII

BEAU DESERT

STRANGEWAYS went back alone after dinner and Bond agreed that they would follow at first light. Strangways left him a fresh pile of books and pamphlets on shark and barracuda and Bond went through them with rapt attention.

They added little to the practical lore he had picked up from Quarrel. They were all by scientists and much of the data on attacks was from the beaches of the Pacific where a flashing body in the thick surf would excite any inquisitive fish.

But there seemed to be general agreement that the danger to underwater swimmers with breathing equipment was far less than to surface swimmers. They might be attacked by almost any of the shark family, particularly when the shark was stimulated and excited by blood in the water, by the smell of a swimmer or by the sensory vibration set up by an injured person in the water. But they could sometimes be frightened off, he read, by loud noises in the water – even by shouting below the surface, and they would often flee if a swimmer chased them.

The most successful form of shark repellent, according to U.S. Naval Research Laboratory tests, was a combination of copper acetate and a dark nigrosine dye, and cakes of this mixture were apparently now attached to the Mae Wests of all the U.S. Armed Forces.

Bond called in Quarrel. The Cayman Islander was scornful until Bond read out to him what the Navy Department had to say about their researches at the end of the war among packs of sharks stimulated by what was described as 'extreme mob behaviour conditions' : '. . . Sharks were attracted to the back of the shrimp boat with trash fish,' read out Bond. 'Sharks appeared as a slashing, splashing shoal. We prepared a tub of fresh fish and another tub of fish mixed with repellent powder. We got up to the shoal of sharks and the photographer started his camera. I shovelled over the plain fish for 30 seconds while the sharks, with much splashing, ate them. Then I started on the repellent fish and shovelled for 30 seconds repeating the procedure 3 times. On the first trial the sharks were quite ferocious in feeding on plain fish right at the stern of the boat. They cut fish for only about 5 seconds after the repellent mixture was thrown over. A few came back when the plain fish were put out immediately following the repellent. On a second trial 30 minutes later, a ferocious school fed for the 30 seconds that plain fish were supplied, but left as soon as the repellent struck the water. There were no attacks on fish while the repellent was in the water. On the third trial we could not get the sharks nearer than 20 yards of the stern of the boat.'

'What do you make of that?' asked Bond.

'You better have some of dat stuff,' said Quarrel, impressed against his will.

Bond was inclined to agree with him. Washington had cabled that cakes of the stuff were on the way. But they had not yet arrived and were not expected for another forty-eight hours. If the repellent did not arrive, Bond was not dismayed. He could not imagine that he would encounter such dangerous conditions in his underwater swim to the island.

Before he went to bed, he finally decided that nothing would attack him unless there was blood in the water or unless he communicated fear to a fish that threatened. As for octopus, scorpion fish and morays, he would just have to watch where he put his feet. To his mind, the three-inch spines of the black sea-eggs were the greatest hazard to normal underwater swimming in the tropics and the pain they caused would not be enough to interfere with his plans.

They left before six in the morning and were at Beau Desert by half-past ten.

The property was a beautiful old plantation of about a thousand acres with the ruins of a fine Great House commanding the bay. It was given over to pimento and citrus inside a fringe of hardwoods and palms and had a history dating back to the time of Cromwell. The romantic name was in the fashion of the eighteenth century, when Jamaican properties were called Bellair, Bellevue, Boscobel, Harmony, Nymphenburg or had names like Prospect, Content or Repose.

A track, out of sight of the island in the bay, led them among the trees down to the little beach-house. After the week's picnic at Manatee Bay, the bathrooms and comfortable bamboo furniture seemed very luxurious and the brightly coloured rugs were like velvet under Bond's hardened feet.

Through the slats of the jalousies Bond looked across the little garden, aflame with hibiscus, bougainvillea and roses, which ended in the tiny crescent of white sand half obscured by the trunks of the palms. He sat on the arm of a chair and let his eyes go on, inch by inch, across the different blues and browns of sea and reef until they met the base of the island. The upper half of it was obscured by the dipping feathers of the palm trees in the foreground, but the stretch of vertical cliff within his vision looked grey and formidable in the half-shadow cast by the hot sun.

Quarrel cooked lunch on a primus stove so that no smoke would betray them, and in the afternoon Bond slept and then went over the gear from London that had been sent across from Kingston by Strangways. He tried on the thin black rubber frogman's suit that covered him from the skull-tight helmet with the perspex window to the long black flippers over his feet. It fitted like a glove and Bond blessed the efficiency of M's 'Q' Branch.

They tested the twin cylinders each containing a thousand litres of free air compressed to two hundred atmospheres and Bond found the manipulation of the demand valve and the reserve mechanism simple and fool-proof. At the depth he would be working the supply of air would last him for nearly two hours under water.

There was a new and powerful Champion harpoon gun and a commando dagger of the type devised by Wilkinsons during the war. Finally, in a box covered with danger-labels, there was the heavy limpet mine, a flat cone of explosive on a base, studded with wide copper bosses, so powerfully magnetized that the mine would stick like a clam to any metal hull. There were a dozen pencil-shaped metal and glass fuses set for ten minutes to eight hours and a careful memorandum of instructions that were as simple as the rest of the gear. There was even a box of benzedrine tablets to give endurance and heightened perception during the operation and an assortment of underwater torches, including one that threw only a tiny pencil-thin beam.

Bond and Quarrel went through everything, testing joints and contacts until they were satisfied that nothing further remained to be done, then Bond went down among the trees and gazed and gazed at the waters of the bay, guessing at depths, tracing routes through the broken reef and estimating the path of the moon, which would be his only point of reckoning on the tortuous journey.

At five o'clock, Strangways arrived with news of the *Secatur*.

'They've cleared Port Maria,' he said. 'They'll be here in ten minutes at the outside. Mr. Big had a passport in the name of Gallia and the girl in the name of Latrelle, Simone Latrelle. She was in her cabin, prostrate with what the negro captain of the *Secatur* described as sea-sickness. It may have been. Scores of empty fish-tanks on board. More than a hundred. Otherwise nothing suspicious and they were given a clean bill. I wanted to go on board as one of the Customs team but I thought it best that the show should be absolutely normal. Mr. Big stuck to his cabin. He was reading when they went to see his papers. How's the gear?'

'Perfect,' said Bond. 'Guess we'll operate tomorrow night. Hope there's a bit of a wind. If the air-bubbles are spotted we shall be in a mess.'

Quarrel came in. 'She's coming through the reef now, Cap'n.'

They went down as close to the shore as they dared and put their glasses on her.

She was a handsome craft, black with a grey superstructure, seventy foot long and built for speed – at least twenty knots, Bond guessed. He knew her history, built for a millionaire in 1947 and powered with twin General Motors Diesels, steel hull and all the latest wireless gadgets, including ship-to-shore telephone and Decca navigator. She was wearing the Red Ensign at her cross-trees and the Stars and Stripes aft and she was making about three knots through the twenty-foot opening of the reef.

She turned sharply inside the reef and came down to seaward of the island. When she was below it, she put her helm hard over and came up with the island to port. At the same time three negroes in white ducks came running down the cliff steps to the narrow jetty and stood by to catch lines. There was a minimum of backing and filling before she was made fast just opposite to the watchers ashore, and the two anchors roared down among the rocks and coral scattered round the island's foundations in the sand. She lay well secured even against a 'Norther'. Bond estimated there would be about twenty feet of water below her keel.

As they watched, the huge figure of Mr. Big appeared on deck. He stepped on to the jetty and started slowly to climb the steep cliff steps. He paused often, and Bond thought of the diseased heart pumping laboriously in the great grey-black body.

He was followed by two negro members of the crew hauling up a light stretcher on which a body was strapped. Through his glasses Bond could see Solitaire's black hair. Bond was worried and puzzled and he felt a tightening of the heart at her nearness. He prayed the stretcher was only a precaution to prevent Solitaire from being recognized from the shore.

Then a chain of twelve men was established up the steps

and the fish-tanks were handed up one by one. Quarrel counted a hundred and twenty of them.

Then some stores went up by the same method.

'Not taking much up this time,' commented Strangways when the operation ceased. 'Only half a dozen cases gone up. Generally about fifty. Can't be staying long.'

He had hardly finished speaking before a fish-tank, which their glasses showed was half full of water and sand, was being gingerly passed back to the ship, down the human ladder of hands. Then another and another, at about five-minute intervals.

'My God,' said Strangways. 'They're loading her up already. That means they'll be sailing in the morning. Wonder if it means they've decided to clean the place out and that this is the last cargo.'

Bond watched carefully for a while and then they walked quietly up through the trees, leaving Quarrel to report developments.

They sat down in the living-room, and while Strangways mixed himself a whisky-and-soda, Bond gazed out of the window and marshalled his thoughts.

It was six o'clock and the fireflies were beginning to show in the shadows. The pale primrose moon was already high up in the eastern sky and the day was dying swiftly at their backs. A light breeze was ruffling the bay and the scrolls of small waves were unfurling on the white beach across the lawn. A few small clouds, pink and orange in the sunset, were meandering by overhead and the palm trees clashed softly in the cool Undertaker's Wind.

'Undertaker's Wind,' thought Bond and smiled wryly. So it would have to be tonight. The only chance, and the conditions were so nearly perfect. Except that the shark-repellent stuff would not arrive in time. And that was only a refinement. There was no excuse. This was what he had travelled two thousand miles and five deaths to do. And yet he shivered at the prospect of the dark adventure under the sea that he had already put off in his mind until tomorrow. Suddenly he loathed and feared the sea and everything in it. The millions of tiny antennae that would stir and point as he went by that night, the eyes that would wake and watch him, the pulses that would miss for the hundredth of a second and then go beating quietly on, the jelly tendrils that would grope and reach for him, as blind in the light as in the dark.

He would be walking through thousands of millions of secrets. In three hundred yards, alone and cold, he would be blundering through a forest of mystery towards a deadly citadel whose guardians had already killed three men. He, Bond, after a week's paddling with his nanny beside him in the sunshine, was going out tonight, in a few hours, to walk alone under that black sheet of water. It was crazy, unthinkable. Bond's flesh cringed and his fingers dug into his wet palms.

There was a knock on the door and Quarrel came in. Bond was glad to get up and move away from the window to where Strangways was enjoying his drink under a shaded reading light.

'They're working with lights now, Cap'n,' Quarrel said with a grin. 'Still a tank every five minutes. I figure that'll be ten hours' work. Be through about four in the morning. Won't sail before six. Too dangerous to try the passage without plenty light.'

Quarrel's warm grey eyes in the splendid mahogany face were looking into Bond's, waiting for orders.

'I'll start at ten sharp,' Bond found himself saying. 'From the rocks to the left of the beach. Can you get us some dinner and then get the gear out on to the lawn? Conditions are perfect. I'll be over there in half an hour.' He counted on his fingers. 'Give me fuses for five to eight hours. And the quarter-hour one in reserve in case anything goes wrong. Okay?'

'Aye aye, Cap'n,' said Quarrel. 'You jes leave 'em all to me.'

He went out.

Bond looked at the whisky bottle, then he made up his mind and poured half a glass on top of three ice cubes. He took the box of benzedrine tablets out of his pocket and slipped a tablet between his teeth.

'Here's luck,' he said to Strangways and took a deep swallow. He sat down and enjoyed the tough hot taste of his first drink for more than a week. 'Now,' he said, 'tell me exactly what they do when they're ready to sail. How long it takes them to clear the island and get through the reef. If it's the last time, don't forget they'll be taking off an extra six men and some stores. Let's try to work it out as closely as we can.'

In a moment Bond was immersed in a sea of practical details and the shadow of fear had fled back to the dark pools under the palm trees.

Exactly at ten o'clock, with nothing but anticipation and excitement in him, the shimmering black bat-like figure slipped off the rocks into ten feet of water and vanished under the sea.

'Go safely,' said Quarrel to the spot where Bond had disappeared. He crossed himself. Then he and Strangways moved back through the shadows to the house to sleep uneasily in watches and wait fearfully for what might come.

CHAPTER XIX

VALLEY OF SHADOWS

BOND was carried straight to the bottom by the weight of the limpet mine that he had secured to his chest with tapes and by the leaded belt which he wore round his waist to correct the buoyancy of the compressed-air cylinders.

He didn't pause for an instant but immediately streaked across the first fifty yards of open sand in a fast crawl, his face just above the sand. The long webbed feet would almost have doubled his normal speed if he had not been hampered by the weight he was carrying and by the light harpoon gun in his left hand, but he travelled fast and in under a minute he came to rest in the shadow of a mass of sprawling coral.

He paused and examined his sensations.

He was warm in the rubber suit, warmer than he would have been swimming in the sunshine. He found his movements very easy and breathing perfectly simple so long as his breath was even and relaxed. He watched the tell-tale bubbles streaming up against the coral in a fountain of silver pearls and prayed that the small waves were hiding them.

In the open he had been able to see perfectly. The light was soft and milky but not strong enough to melt the mackerel shadows of the surface waves that chequered the sand. Now, up against the reef, there was no reflection from the bottom, and the shadows under the rocks were black and impenetrable.

He risked a quick glance with his pencil torch and immediately the underbelly of the mass of brown tree-coral came alive. Anemones with crimson centres waved their velvet tentacles at him, a colony of black sea-eggs moved their toledo-steel spines in sudden alarm and a hairy sea-centipede halted in its hundred strides and questioned with its eyeless head. In the sand at the base of the tree a toad-fish softly drew its hideous warty head back into its funnel and a number of flower-like sea-worms whisked out of sight down their gelatinous tubes. A covey of bejewelled butterfly and angel fish flirted into the light and he marked the flat spiral of a Long-spined Star Shell.

Bond tucked the light back in his belt.

Above him the surface of the sea was a canopy of quicksilver. It crackled softly like fat frying in a saucepan. Ahead the moonlight glinted down into the deep crooked valley that sloped down and away on the route he had to follow. He left his sheltering tree of coral and walked softly forward. Now it was not so easy. The light was tricky and bad and the petrified forest of the coral reef was full of culs-de-sac and tempting but misleading avenues.

Sometimes he had to climb almost to the surface to get over a tangled scrub of tree- and antler-coral and when this happened he profited by it to check his position with the moon that glowed like a huge pale rocket-burst through the broken water. Sometimes the hourglass waist of a niggerhead gave him shelter and he rested for a few moments knowing that the small froth of his air-bubbles would be hidden by the jagged knob protruding above the surface. Then he would focus his eyes on the phosphorescent scribbles of the minute underwater night-life and perceive whole colonies and populations about their microscopic business.

There were no big fish about, but many lobsters were out of their holes looking huge and prehistoric in the magnifying lens of the water. Their stalk-like eyes glared redly at him and their foot-long spined antennae asked him for the password. Occasionally they scuttled nervously backwards into their shelters, their powerful tails kicking up the sand, and crouched on the tips of their eight hairy feet, waiting for the danger to pass. Once the great streamers of a portuguese man-of-war floated slowly by. They almost reached his head from the surface, fifteen feet away, and he remembered the whiplash of a sting from the contact of one of their tendrils that had burned for three of his days at Manatee Bay. If they caught a man across the heart they could kill him. He saw several green and speckled moray eels, the latter moving like big yellow and black snakes along patches of sand, the green ones baring their teeth from some hole in the rock, and several West Indian blowfish, like brown owls with huge soft green eyes. He poked at one with the end of his gun and it swelled out to the size of a football and became a mass of dangerous white spines. Wide sea fans swayed and beckoned in the eddies, and in the grey valleys they caught the light of the moon and waved spectrally, like fragments of the shrouds of men buried at sea. Often in the shadows there were unexplained, heavy movements and swirls in the water and the sudden glare of large eyes at once extinguished. Then Bond would whirl round, thumbing up the safety-catch on his harpoon gun, and stare back into the darkness. But he shot at nothing and nothing attacked him as he scrambled and slithered through the reef.

The hundred yards of coral took him a quarter of an hour. When he got through and rested on a round lump of brain-coral under the shelter of a last niggerhead, he was glad that nothing but a hundred yards of grey-white water lay in front of him. He still felt perfectly fresh and the elation and clarity of mind produced by the benzedrine were still with him, but the gauntlet of hazards through the reef had been a constant fret, with the risk of tearing his rubber skin always on his mind. Now the forest of razor-blade coral was behind, to be exchanged for shark and barracuda or perhaps a sudden stick of dynamite dropped into the centre of the little flower of his bubbles on the surface.

It was while he was measuring the dangers ahead that the octopus got him. Round both ankles.

He had been sitting with his feet on the sand and suddenly they were manacled to the base of the round toadstool of coral on which he was resting. Even as he realized what had happened a tentacle began to snake up his leg and another one, purple in the dim light, wandered down his webbed left foot.

He gave a start of fear and disgust and at once he was on his feet, shuffling and straining to get away. But there was no inch of yield and his movements only gave the octopus an opportunity to pull his heels tighter under the overhang of the round rock. The strength of the brute was prodigious and Bond could feel his balance going fast. In a moment he would be pulled down flat on his face and then, hampered by the mine on his chest and the cylinders on his back, it might be almost impossible to get at the beast.

Bond snatched his dagger out of his belt and jabbed down between his legs. But the overhang of the rock impeded him and he was terrified of cutting his rubber skin. Suddenly he was toppled over, lying on the sand. At once his feet began to be drawn into a wide lateral cleft under the rock. He scrabbled at the sand and tried to curl round to get within range with the dagger. But the thick hump of the mine protruding from his chest prevented him. On the edge of panic, he remembered the harpoon gun. Before, he had dismissed it as being a hopeless weapon at that short range, but now it was the only chance. It lay on the sand where he had left it. He reached for it and put up the safety-catch. The mine prevented him from aiming. He slid the barrel along his legs and probed each of his feet with the tip of the harpoon to find the gap between them. At once a tentacle seized the steel tip and began tugging. The gun slipped between his manacled feet and he pulled the trigger blindly.

Immediately a great cloud of viscous, stringy ink rolled out of the cleft towards his face. But one leg was free and then the other and he whipped them round and under him and seized the haft of the three-foot harpoon where it disappeared under the rock. He pulled and strained until, with a rending of flesh, it came away from the black fog that hung over the hole. Panting, he got up and stood away from the rock, the sweat pouring down his face under the mask. Above him, the tell-tale stream of silver bubbles rose straight to the surface and he cursed the wounded 'pus-feller' in its lair.

But there was no time to worry further with it and he

re-loaded his gun and struck out with the moon over his right shoulder.

Now he made good going through the misty grey water and he concentrated only on keeping his face a few inches above the sand and his head well down to streamline his body. Once, out of the corner of his eye, he saw a sting-ray as big as a ping-pong table shuffle out of his path, the tip of its great speckled wings beating like a bird's, its long horned tail streaming out behind it. But he paid it no attention, remembering that Quarrel had said that rays never attack except in self-defence. He reflected that it had probably come in over the outer reef to lay its eggs, or 'Mermaids' Purses' as the fishermen call them, because they are shaped like a pillow with a stiff black string at each corner, on the sheltered sandy bottom.

Many shadows of big fish lazed across the moonlit sand, some as long as himself. When one followed beside him for at least a minute he looked up to see the white belly of a shark ten feet above him like a glaucous tapering air-ship. Its blunt nose was buried inquisitively in his stream of air-bubbles. The wide sickle slit of its mouth looked like a puckered scar. It leant sideways and glanced down at him out of one hard pink naked eye, then it wobbled its great scythe-shaped tail and moved slowly into the wall of grey mist.

He frightened a family of squids, ranging from about six pounds down to an infant of six ounces, frail and luminous in the half-light, hanging almost vertical in a diminishing chorus-line. They righted themselves and shot off with streamlined jet propulsion.

Bond rested for a moment about half way and then went on. Now there were barracuda about, big ones of up to twenty pounds. They looked just as deadly as he had remembered them. They glided above him like silver submarines, looking down out of their angry tigers' eyes. They were curious about him and about his bubbles and they followed him, around and above him, like a pack of silent wolves. By the time Bond met the first bit of coral that meant he was coming up with the island there must have been twenty of them moving quietly, watchfully in and out of the opaque wall that enclosed him.

Bond's skin cringed under the black rubber but he could do nothing about them and he concentrated on his objective.

Suddenly there was a long metallic shape hanging in the water above him. Behind it there was a jumble of broken rock leading steeply upwards.

It was the keel of the *Secatur* and Bond's heart thumped in his chest.

He looked at the Rolex watch on his wrist. It was three minutes past eleven o'clock. He selected the seven-hour fuse from the handful he extracted from a zipped side-pocket and inserted it in the fuse pocket of the mine and pushed it home. The rest of the fuses he buried in the sand so that if he was captured the mine would not be betrayed.

As he swam up, carrying the mine between his hands, bottom upwards, he was aware of a commotion in the water behind him. A barracuda flashed by, its jaws half open, almost hitting him, its eyes fixed on something at his back. But Bond was intent only on the centre of the ship's keel and on a point about three feet above it.

The mine almost dragged him the last few feet, its huge magnets straining for the metallic kiss with the hull.

Bond had to pull hard against it to prevent the clang of contact. Then it was silently in place and with its weight removed Bond had to swim strongly to counter his new buoyancy and get down again and away from the surface.

It was as he turned to swim towards the twin propellers on his way to the shelter of the rocks that he suddenly saw the terrible things that had been going on behind him.

The great pack of barracudas seemed to have gone mad. They were whirling and snapping in the water like hysterical dogs. Three sharks that had joined them were charging through the water with a clumsier frenzy. The water was boiling with the dreadful fish and Bond was slammed in the face and buffeted again and again within a few yards. At any moment he knew his rubber skin would be torn with the flesh below it and then the pack would be on him.

'Extreme mob behaviour conditions.' The Navy Department's phrase flashed into his mind. This was just when he might have saved himself with the shark-repellent stuff. Without it he might only have a few more minutes to live.

In desperation he threshed through the water along the ship's keel, the safety-catch up on the harpoon gun that was now only a toy in the face of this drove of maddened cannibal fish.

He reached the two big copper screws and clung to one of them, panting, his lips drawn back from his teeth in a snarl of fear, his eyes distended as he faced the frenzy of the boiling sea around him.

He at once saw that the mouths of the hurtling, darting

fish were half open and that they were plunging in and out of a brownish cloud, spreading downwards from the surface. Close to him a barracuda hung for an instant, something brown and glittering in its jaws. It gave a great swallow and then swirled back into the mêlée.

At the same time he noticed that it was getting darker. He looked up and saw with dawning comprehension that the quicksilver surface of the sea had turned red, a horrible glinting crimson.

Threads of the stuff drifted within his reach. He hooked some towards him with the end of his gun. Held the end close up against his glass mask.

There was no doubt about it.

Up above, someone was spraying the surface of the sea with blood and offal.

CHAPTER XX

BLOODY MORGAN'S CAVE

IMMEDIATELY Bond understood why all these barracuda and shark were lurking round the island, how they were kept frenzied with bloodlust by this nightly banquet, why, against all reason, the three men had been washed up half-eaten by the fish.

Mr. Big had just harnessed the forces of the sea for his protection. It was a typical invention – imaginative, technically foolproof and very easy to operate.

Even as Bond's mind grasped it all, something hit him a terrific blow in the shoulder and a twenty-pound barracuda backed away, black rubber and flesh hanging from its jaws. Bond felt no pain as he let go of the bronze propeller and threshed wildly for the rocks, only a horrible sickness in the pit of his stomach at the thought of part of himself between those hundred razor-sharp teeth. Water started to ooze between the close-fitting rubber and his skin. It would not be long before it penetrated up his neck and into the mask.

He was just going to give up and shoot the twenty feet to the surface when he saw a wide fissure in the rocks in front of him. Beside it a great boulder lay on its side and somehow he got behind it. He turned from the partial shelter it gave just in time to see the same barracuda coming at him again, its upper jaw held at right angles to the lower for its infamous gaping strike.

Bond fired almost blind with the harpoon gun. The rubber thongs whammed down the barrel and the barbed harpoon caught the big fish in the centre of its raised upper jaw, pierced it and stuck with half the shaft and the line still free.

The barracuda stopped dead in its tracks, three feet from Bond's stomach. It tried to get its jaws together and then gave a mighty shake of its long reptile's head. Then it shot away, zigzagging madly, the gun and line, jerked from Bond's hand, streaming behind it. Bond knew that the other fish would be on to it, tearing it to bits, before it had gone a hundred yards.

Bond thanked God for the diversion. His shoulder was now surrounded by a cloud of blood. In a matter of seconds the other fish would catch the scent. He slipped round the boulder with the thought that he would scramble up under the shelter of the jetty and somehow hide himself above the level of the sea until he had made a fresh plan.

Then he saw the cave that the boulder had hidden.

It was really almost a door into the base of the island. If Bond had not been swimming for his life he could have walked in. As it was, he dived straight through the opening and only stopped when several yards separated him from the glimmering entrance.

Then he stood upright on the soft sand and switched on his torch. A shark might conceivably come in after him but in the confined space it would be almost impossible for it to bring its underslung mouth to bear on him. It would certainly not come in with a rush for even the shark is frightened of hazarding its tough skin among rocks, and he would have plenty of chance of going for its eyes with his dagger.

Bond shone his torch on the ceiling and sides of the cave. It had certainly been fashioned or finished by man. Bond guessed that it had been dug outwards from somewhere in the centre of the island.

'At least another twenty yards to go, men,' Bloody Morgan must have said to the slave overseers. And then the picks would have burst suddenly through to the sea and a welter of arms and legs and screaming mouths, gagged for ever with water, would have hurtled back into the rock to join the bodies of other witnesses.

The great boulder at the entrance would have been put in position to seal the seaward exit. The Shark Bay fisherman who suddenly disappeared six months before must have one day found it rolled away by a storm or by the tidal wave following a hurricane. Then he had found the treasure and had known he would need help to dispose of it. A white man would cheat him. Better go to the great negro gangster in Harlem and make the best terms he could. The gold belonged to the black men who had died to hide it. It should go back to the black men.

Standing there, swaying in the slight current in the tunnel, Bond guessed that one more barrel of cement had splashed into the mud of the Harlem River.

It was then that he heard the drums.

Out amongst the big fish he had heard a soft thunder in the water that had grown as he entered the cave. But he had thought it was only the waves against the base of the island, and anyway he had had other things to think about.

But now he could distinguish a definite rhythm and the sound boomed and swelled around him in a muffled roar as if he himself was imprisoned inside a vast kettle-drum.

The water seemed to tremble with it. He guessed its double purpose. It was a great fish-call used, when intruders were about, to attract and excite the fish still further. Quarrel had told him how the fishermen at night beat the sides of their canoes with the paddle to wake and bring the fish. This must be the same idea. And at the same time it would be a sinister Voodoo warning to the people on shore, made doubly effective when the dead body was washed up on the following day.

Another of Mr. Big's refinements, thought Bond. Another spark thrown off by that extraordinary mind.

Well, at least he knew where he was now. The drums meant that he had been spotted. What would Strangways and Quarrel think as they heard them? They would just have to sit and sweat it out. Bond had guessed the drums were some sort of trick and he had made them promise not to interfere unless the *Secatur* got safely away. That would mean that all Bond's plans had failed. He had told Strangways where the gold was hidden and the ship would have to be intercepted on the high seas.

Now the enemy was alerted, but would not know who he was nor that he was still alive. He would have to go on if only to stop Solitaire at all costs from sailing in the doomed ship.

Bond looked at his watch. It was half an hour after midnight. So far as Bond was concerned, it might have been a week since he started his lonely voyage through the sea of dangers.

He felt the Beretta under his rubber skin and wondered if it was already ruined by the water that had got in through the rent made by the barracuda's teeth.

Then, the roar of the drums getting louder every moment,

he moved on into the cave, his torch throwing a tiny pin-point of light ahead of him.

He had gone about ten yards when a faint glimmer showed in the water ahead of him. He dowsed the torch and went cautiously towards it. The sandy floor of the cave started to move upwards and with every yard the light grew brighter. Now he could see dozens of small fish playing around him and ahead the water seemed full of them, attracted into the cave by the light. Crabs peered from the small crevices in the rocks and a baby octopus flattened itself into a phosphorescent star against the ceiling.

Then he could make out the end of the cave and a wide shining pool beyond it, the white sandy bottom as bright as day. The throb of the drums was very loud. He stopped in the shadow of the entrance and saw that the surface was only a few inches away and that lights were shining down into the pool.

Bond was in a quandary. Any further step and he would be in full view of anyone looking at the pool. As he stood, debating with himself, he was horrified to see a thin red cloud of blood spreading beyond the entrance from his shoulder. He had forgotten the wound, but now it began to throb, and when he moved his arm the pain shot through it. There was also the thin stream of bubbles from the cylinders, but he hoped these were just creeping up to burst unnoticed at the lip of the entrance.

Even as he drew back a few inches into his hole, his future was settled for him.

Above his head there was a single huge splash and two negroes, naked except for the glass masks over their faces, were on to him, long daggers held like lances in their left hands.

Before his hand reached the knife at his belt they had seized both his arms and were hauling him to the surface.

Hopelessly, helplessly, Bond let himself be man-handled out of the pool on to flat sand. He was pulled to his feet and the zips of his rubber suit were torn open. His helmet was snatched off his head and his holster from his shoulder and suddenly he was standing among the debris of his black skin, like a flayed snake, naked except for his brief swimming-trunks. Blood oozed down from the jagged hole in his left shoulder.

When his helmet came off Bond was almost deafened by the shattering boom and stutter of the drums. The noise was in him and all around him. The hastening syncopated rhythm galloped and throbbed in his blood. It seemed enough to wake all Jamaica. Bond grimaced and clenched his senses against the buffeting tempest of noise. Then his guards turned him round and he was faced with a scene so extraordinary that the sound of the drums receded and all his consciousness was focused through his eyes.

In the foreground, at a green baize card-table, littered with papers, in a folding chair, sat Mr. Big, a pen in his hand, looking incuriously at him. A Mr. Big in a well-cut fawn tropical suit, with a white shirt and black knitted silk tie. His broad chin rested on his left hand and he looked up at Bond as if he had been disturbed in his office by a member of the staff asking for a raise in salary. He looked polite but faintly bored.

A few steps away from him, sinister and incongruous, the scarecrow effigy of Baron Samedi, erect on a rock, gaped at Bond from under its bowler hat.

Mr. Big took his hand off his chin, and his great golden eyes looked Bond over from top to toe.

'Good morning, Mister James Bond,' he said at last, throwing his flat voice against the dying crescendo of the drums. 'The fly has indeed been a long time coming to the spider, or perhaps I should say "the minnow to the whale". You left a pretty wake of bubbles after the reef.'

He leant back in his chair and was silent. The drums softly thudded and boomed.

So it was the fight with the octopus that had betrayed him. Bond's mind automatically registered the fact as his eyes moved on past the man at the table.

He was in a rock chamber as big as a church. Half the floor was taken up with the clear white pool from which he had come and which verged into aquamarine and then blue near the black hole of the underwater entrance. Then there was the narrow strip of sand on which he was standing and the rest of the floor was smooth flat rock dotted with a few grey and white stalagmites.

Some way behind Mr. Big, steep steps mounted towards a vaulted ceiling from which short limestone stalactites hung down. From their white nipples water dripped intermittently into the pool or on to the points of the young stalagmites that rose towards them from the floor.

A dozen bright arc lights were fixed high up on the walls and reflected golden highlights from the naked chests of a group of negroes standing to his left on the stone floor rolling their eyes and watching Bond, their teeth showing in delighted cruel grins.

Round their black and pink feet, in a debris of broken timber and rusty iron hoops, mildewed strips of leather and disintegrating canvas, was a blazing sea of gold coin –

yards, piles, cascades of round golden specie from which the black legs rose as if they had been halted in the middle of a walk through flame.

Beside them were piled row upon row of shallow wooden trays. There were some on the floor partly filled with gold coin, and at the bottom of the steps a single negro had stopped on his way up and he was holding one of the trays in his hands and it was full of gold coin, four cylindrical rows of it, held out as if for sale between his hands.

Further to the left, in a corner of the chamber, two negroes stood by a bellying iron cauldron suspended over three hissing blow-lamps, its base glowing red. They held iron skimmers in their hands and these were splashed with gold half way up the long handles. Beside them was a towering jumble of gold objects, plate, altar pieces, drinking vessels, crosses, and a stack of gold ingots of various sizes. Along the wall near them were ranged rows of metal cooling trays, their segmented surfaces gleaming yellow, and there was an empty tray on the floor near the cauldron and a long gold-spattered ladle, its handle bound with cloth.

Squatting on the floor not far from Mr. Big, a single negro had a knife in one hand and a jewelled goblet in the other. Beside him on a tin plate was a pile of gems that winked dully, red and blue and green, in the glare of the arcs.

It was warm and airless in the great rock chamber and yet Bond shivered as his eyes took in the whole splendid scene, the blazing violet-white lights, the shimmering bronze of the sweating bodies, the bright glare of the gold, the rainbow pool of jewels and the milk and aquamarine of the pool. He shivered at the beauty of it all, at this fabulous petrified ballet in the great treasure-house of Bloody Morgan.

His eyes came back to the square of green baize and the great zombie face and he looked at the face and into the wide yellow eyes with awe, almost with reverence.

'Stop the drums,' said The Big Man to no one in particular. They had died almost to a whisper, a lisping beat right on the pulse of the blood. One of the negroes took two softly clanging steps amongst the gold coin and bent down. There was a portable phonograph on the floor and a powerful amplifier leant beside it against the rock wall. There was a click and the drums stopped. The negro shut the lid of the machine and went back to his place.

'Get on with the work,' said Mr. Big, and at once all the figures started moving as if a penny had been put in a slot. The cauldron was stirred, the gold was picked up and clicked into the boxes, the man picked busily at his jewelled goblet and the negro with the tray of gold moved on up the stairs.

Bond stood and dripped sweat and blood.

The Big Man bent over the lists on his table and wrote one or two figures with his pen.

Bond stirred and felt the prick of a dagger over his kidneys.

The Big Man put down his pen and got slowly to his feet. He moved away from the table.

'Take over,' he said to one of Bond's guards and the naked man walked round the table and sat down in Mr. Big's chair and picked up the pen.

'Bring him up.' Mr. Big walked over to the steps in the rock and started to climb them slowly.

Bond felt a prick in his side. He stepped out of the debris of his black skin and followed the slowly climbing figure.

No one looked up from his work. No one would slacken when Mr. Big was out of sight. No one would put a jewel or a coin in his mouth.

Baron Samedi was left in charge.

Only his Zombie had gone from the cave.

CHAPTER XXI

'GOOD NIGHT TO YOU BOTH'

THEY climbed slowly up, past an open door near the ceiling, for about forty feet and then paused on a wide landing in the rock. Here a single negro with an acetylene light beside him was fitting trays full of gold coin into the centre of the fish-tanks, scores of which were stacked against the wall.

As they waited, two negroes came down the steps from the surface, picked up one of the prepared tanks and went back up the steps with it.

Bond guessed the tanks were stocked with sand and weed and fish somewhere up above and then passed to the human chain that stretched down the cliff face.

Bond noticed that some of the waiting tanks had gold ingots fitted in the centre, and others a gravel of jewels, and he revised his estimate of the treasure, quadrupling it to around four million sterling.

Mr. Big stood for a few moments with his eyes on the stone floor. His breathing was deep but controlled. Then they went on up.

Twenty steps higher there was another landing, smaller and with a door leading off it. The door had a new chain and padlock on it. The door itself was made of platted iron slats, brown and corroded with rust.

Mr. Big paused again and they stood side by side on the small platform of rock.

For a moment Bond thought of escape, but, as if reading his mind, the negro guard crowded him up against the stone wall away from The Big Man. And Bond knew his first duty was to stay alive and get to Solitaire and somehow keep her away from the doomed ship where the acid was slowly eating through the copper of the time-fuse.

From above, a strong draught of cold air was coming down the shaft and Bond felt the sweat drying on him. He put his right hand up to the wound in his shoulder, undeterred by the prick of the guard's dagger in his side. The blood was dry and caked and most of the arm was numb. It ached viciously.

Mr. Big spoke.

'That wind, Mister Bond,' he pointed up the shaft, 'is known in Jamaica as "The Undertaker's Wind".'

Bond shrugged his right shoulder and saved his breath.

Mr. Big turned to the iron door, took a key from his pocket and unlocked it. He went through and Bond and his guard followed.

It was a long, narrow passage of a room with rusty shackles low down in the walls at less than yard intervals.

At the far end, where a hurricane light hung from the stone roof, there was a motionless figure under a blanket on the floor. There was one more hurricane light over their heads near the door, otherwise nothing but a smell of damp rock, and ancient torture, and death.

'Solitaire,' said Mr. Big softly.

Bond's heart leapt and he started forward. At once a huge hand grasped him by the arm.

'Hold it, white man,' snapped his guard and twisted his wrist up between his shoulder-blades, hefting it higher until

Bond lashed out with his left heel. It hit the other man's shin, and hurt Bond more than the guard.

Mr. Big turned round. He had a small gun almost covered by his huge hand.

'Let him go,' he said, quietly. 'If you want an extra navel, Mister Bond, you can have one. I have six of them in this gun.'

Bond brushed past The Big Man. Solitaire was on her feet, coming towards him. When she saw his face she broke into a run, holding out her two hands.

'James,' she sobbed. 'James.'

She almost fell at his feet. Their hands clutched at each other.

'Get me some rope,' said Mr. Big in the doorway.

'It's all right, Solitaire,' said Bond, knowing that it wasn't. 'It's all right. I'm here now.'

He picked her up and held her at arm's length. It hurt his left arm. She was pale and dishevelled. There was a bruise on her forehead and black circles under her eyes. Her face was grimy and tears had made streaks down the pale skin. She had no make-up. She wore a dirty white linen suit and sandals. She looked thin.

'What's the bastard been doing to you?' said Bond. He suddenly held her tightly to him. She clung to him, her face buried in his neck.

Then she drew away and looked at her hand.

'But you're bleeding,' she said. 'What is it?'

She turned him half round and saw the black blood on his shoulder and down his arm.

'Oh my darling, what is it?'

She started to cry again, forlornly, hopelessly, realizing suddenly that they were both lost.

'Tie them up,' said The Big Man from the door. 'Here under the light. I have things to say to them.'

The negro came towards them and Bond turned. Was it worth a gamble? The negro had nothing but rope in his hands. But The Big Man had stepped sideways and was watching him, the gun held loosely, half pointing at the floor.

'No, Mister Bond,' he said simply.

Bond eyed the big negro and thought of Solitaire and his own wounded arm.

The negro came up and Bond allowed his arms to be tied behind his back. They were good knots. There was no play in them. They hurt.

Bond smiled at Solitaire. He half closed one eye. It was nothing but bravado, but he saw a hopeful awareness dawn through her tears.

The negro led him back to the doorway.

'There,' said The Big Man, pointing at one of the shackles.

The negro cut Bond's legs from under him with a sudden sweep of his shin. Bond fell on his wounded shoulder. The negro pulled him by the rope up to the shackle, tested it, and put the rope through and then down to Bond's ankles which he bound securely. He had stuck his dagger in a crevice in the rock. He pulled it out and cut the rope and went back to where Solitaire was standing.

Bond was left sitting on the stone floor, his legs straight out in front, his arms hoisted up and secured behind him. Blood dripped down from his freshly opened wound. Only the remains of the benzedrine in his system kept him from fainting.

Solitaire was bound and placed almost opposite him. There was a yard between their feet.

When it was done, The Big Man looked at his watch.

'Go,' he said to the guard. He closed the iron door behind the man and leant against it.

Bond and the girl looked at each other and The Big Man gazed down on both of them.

After one of his long silences he addressed Bond. Bond looked up at him. The great grey football of a head under the hurricane lamp looked like an elemental, a malignant spectre from the centre of the earth, as it hung in mid air, the golden eyes blazing steadily, the great body in shadow. Bond had to remind himself that he had heard its heart pumping in its chest, had heard it breathe, had seen sweat on the grey skin. It was only a man, of the same species as himself, a big man, with a brilliant brain, but still a man who walked and defecated, a mortal man with a diseased heart.

The wide rubbery mouth split open and the flat slightly everted lips drew back from the big white teeth.

'You are the best of those that have been sent against me,' said Mr. Big. His quiet flat voice was thoughtful, measured. 'And you have achieved the death of four of my assistants. My followers find this incredible. It was fully time that accounts should be squared. What happened to the American was not sufficient. The treachery of this girl,' he still looked at Bond, 'whom I found in the gutter and whom I was prepared to put on my right hand, has also brought my infallibility in question. I was wondering how she should die, when providence, or Baron Samedi as my followers will believe, brought you also to the altar with your head bowed ready for the axe.'

The mouth paused, with the lips parted. Bond saw the teeth come together to form the next word.

'So it is convenient that you should die together. That will happen, in an appropriate fashion,' The Big Man looked at his watch, 'in two and a half hours' time. At six o'clock, give or take,' he added, 'a few minutes.'

'Let's give those minutes,' said Bond. 'I enjoy my life.'

'In the history of negro emancipation,' Mr. Big continued in an easy conversational tone, 'there have already appeared great athletes, great musicians, great writers, great doctors and scientists. In due course, as in the developing history of other races, there will appear negroes great and famous in every other walk of life.' He paused. 'It is unfortunate for you, Mister Bond, and for this girl, that you have encountered the first of the great negro criminals. I use a vulgar word, Mister Bond, because it is the one you, as a form of policeman, would yourself use. But I prefer to regard myself as one who has the ability and the mental and nervous equipment to make his own laws and act according to them rather than accept the laws that suit the lowest common denominator of the people. You have doubtless read Trotter's *Instincts of the Herd in War and Peace*, Mister Bond. Well, I am by nature and predilection a wolf and I live by a wolf's laws. Naturally the sheep describe such a person as a "criminal".

'The fact, Mister Bond,' The Big Man continued after a pause, 'that I survive and indeed enjoy limitless success, although I am alone against countless millions of sheep, is attributable to the modern techniques I described to you on the occasion of our last talk, and to an infinite capacity for taking pains. Not dull, plodding pains, but artistic, subtle pains. And I find, Mister Bond, that it is not difficult to outwit sheep, however many of them there may be, if one is dedicated to the task and if one is by nature an extremely well-equipped wolf.

'Let me illustrate to you, by an example, how my mind works. We will take the method I have decided upon by which you are both to die. It is a modern variation on the method used in the time of my kind patron, Sir Henry Morgan. In those days it was known as "keel-hauling".'

'Pray continue,' said Bond, not looking at Solitaire.

'We have a paravane on board the yacht,' continued Mr. Big as if he was a surgeon describing a delicate operation to a body of students, 'which we use for trawling for shark and other big fish. This paravane, as you know, is a large buoyant torpedo-shaped device, which rides on the end of a cable, away from the side of a ship, and which can be used for sustaining the end of a net, and drawing it through the water when the ship is in motion, or if fitted with a cutting device, for severing the cables of moored mines in time of war.

'I intend,' said Mr. Big, in a matter-of-fact discursive tone of voice, 'to bind you together to a line streamed from this paravane and to tow you through the sea until you are eaten by sharks.'

He paused, and his eyes looked from one to the other. Solitaire was gazing wide-eyed at Bond and Bond was thinking hard, his eyes blank and his mind boring into the future. He felt he ought to say something.

'You are a big man,' he said, 'and one day you will die a big, horrible death. If you kill us, that death will come soon. I have arranged for it. You are going mad very fast or you would see what our murder will bring down on you.'

Even as he spoke Bond's mind was working fast, counting hours and minutes, knowing that The Big Man's own death was creeping, with the acid in the fuse, round the minute hand towards his personal hour of final rendezvous. But would he and Solitaire be dead before that hour struck? There would not be more than minutes, perhaps seconds in it. The sweat poured off his face on to his chest. He smiled across at Solitaire. She looked back at him opaquely, her eyes not seeing him.

Suddenly she gave an agonized cry that made Bond's nerves jerk.

'I don't know,' she cried. 'I can't see. It's so near, so close. There is much death. But . . .'

'Solitaire,' shouted Bond, terrified that whatever strange things she saw in the future might give a warning to The Big Man. 'Pull yourself together.'

There was an angry bite in his voice.

Her eyes cleared. She looked dumbly at him, without comprehension.

The Big Man spoke again.

'I am not going mad, Mister Bond,' he said evenly, 'and nothing you have arranged will affect me. You will die beyond the reef and there will be no evidence. I shall tow the remains of your bodies until there is nothing left. That is part of the dexterity of my intentions. You may also know that shark and barracuda play a role in Voodooism. They will have their sacrifice and Baron Samedi will be appeased. That will satisfy my followers. I wish also to continue my experiments with carnivorous fish. I believe they only attack when there is blood in the water. So your bodies will be towed from the island. The paravane will take them over the reef. I believe you will not be harmed inside the reef. The blood and offal that is thrown into these waters every night will have dispersed or been consumed. But when your bodies have been dragged over the reef, then I'm afraid you will bleed, your bodies will be very raw. And then we will see if my theories are correct.'

The Big Man put his hand behind him and pulled the door open.

'I will leave you now,' he said, 'to reflect on the excellence of the method I have invented for your death together. Two necessary deaths are achieved. No evidence is left behind. Superstition is satisfied. My followers pleased. The bodies are used for scientific research.

'That is what I meant, Mister James Bond, by an infinite capacity for taking artistic pains.'

He stood in the doorway and looked at them.

'A short, but very good night to you both.'

CHAPTER XXII

TERROR BY SEA

IT was not yet light when their guards came for them. Their leg ropes were cut and with their arms still pinioned they were led up the remaining stone stairs to the surface.

They stood amongst the sparse trees and Bond sniffed the cool morning air. He gazed through the trees towards the east and saw that there the stars were paler and the horizon luminous with the breaking dawn. The night-song of the crickets was almost done and somewhere on the island a mocking bird bubbled its first notes.

He guessed that it was either side of half-past five.

They stood there for several minutes. Negroes brushed past them carrying bundles and jippa-jappa holdalls, talking in cheerful whispers. The doors of the handful of thatched huts among the trees had been left swinging open. The men filed to the edge of the cliff to the right of where Bond and Solitaire were standing and disappeared over the edge. They didn't come back. It was evacuation. The whole garrison of the island was decamping.

Bond rubbed his naked shoulder against Solitaire and she pressed against him. It was cold after the stuffy dungeon and Bond shivered. But it was better to be on the move than for the suspense down below to be prolonged.

They both knew what had to be done, the nature of the gamble.

When The Big Man had left them, Bond had wasted no time. In a whisper, he had told the girl of the limpet mine against the side of the ship timed to explode a few minutes after six o'clock and he had explained the factors that would decide who would die that morning.

First, he gambled on Mr. Big's mania for exactitude and efficiency. The *Secatur* must sail on the dot of six o'clock. Then there must be no cloud, or visibility in the half-light of dawn would not be sufficient for the ship to make the passage through the reef and Mr. Big would postpone the sailing. If Bond and Solitaire were on the jetty alongside the ship, they would then be killed with Mr. Big.

Supposing the ship sailed dead on time, how far behind and to one side of her would their bodies be towed? It would have to be on the port side for the paravane to clear the island. Bond guessed the cable to the paravane would be fifty yards and that they would be towed twenty or thirty yards behind the paravane.

If he was right, they would be hauled over the outer reef about fifty yards after the *Secatur* had cleared the passage. She would probably approach the passage at about three knots and then put on speed to ten or even twenty. At first their bodies would be swept away from the island in a slow arc, twisting and turning at the end of the tow-rope. Then the paravane would straighten out and when the ship had got through the reef, they would still be approaching it. The paravane would then cross the reef when the ship was about forty yards outside it and they would follow.

Bond shuddered to think of the mauling their bodies would suffer being dragged at any speed over the razor-sharp ten yards of coral rocks and trees. The skin on their backs and legs would be flayed off.

Once over the reef they would be just a huge bleeding bait and it would be only a matter of minutes before the first shark or barracuda was on to them.

And Mr. Big would sit comfortably in the stern sheets, watching the bloody show, perhaps with glasses, and ticking off the seconds and minutes as the living bait got smaller and smaller and finally the fish snapped at the bloodstained rope.

Until there was nothing left.

Then the paravane would be hoisted inboard and the yacht would plough gracefully on towards the distant Florida Keys, Cape Sable and the sun-soaked wharf in St. Petersburg Harbour.

And if the mine exploded while they were still in the water, only fifty yards away from the ship? What would be the effect of the shock-waves on their bodies? It might not be deadly. The hull of the ship should absorb most of it. The reef might protect them.

Bond could only guess and hope.

Above all they must stay alive to the last possible second. They must keep breathing as they were hauled, a living bundle, through the sea. Much depended on how they would be bound together. Mr. Big would want them to stay alive. He would not be interested in dead bait.

If they were still alive when the first shark's fin showed on the surface behind them Bond had coldly decided to drown Solitaire. Drown her by twisting her body under his and holding her there. Then he would try and drown himself by twisting her dead body back over his to keep him under.

There was nightmare at every turn of his thoughts, sickening horror in every grisly aspect of the monstrous torture and death this man had invented for them. But Bond knew he must remain cold and absolutely resolved to fight for their lives to the end. There was at least warmth in the knowledge that Mr. Big and most of his men would also die. And there was a glimmer of hope that he and Solitaire would survive. Unless the mine failed, there was no such hope for the enemy.

All this, and a hundred other details and plans went through Bond's mind in the last hour before they were brought up the shaft to the surface. He shared all his hopes with Solitaire. None of his fears.

She had lain opposite him, her tired blue eyes fixed on him, obedient, trusting, drinking in his face and his words, pliant, loving.

'Don't worry about me, my darling,' she had said when the men came for them. 'I am happy to be with you again. My heart is full of it. For some reason I am not afraid although there is much death very close. Do you love me a little?'

'Yes,' said Bond. 'And we shall have our love.'

'Giddap,' said one of the men.

And now, on the surface, it was getting lighter, and from below the cliff Bond heard the great twin Diesels stutter and roar. There was a light flutter of breeze to windward, but to leeward, where the ship lay, the bay was a gunmetal mirror.

Mr. Big appeared up the shaft, a businessman's leather brief-case in his hand. He stood for a moment looking round, gaining his breath. He paid no attention to Bond and Solitaire nor to the two guards standing beside them with revolvers in their hands.

He looked up at the sky, and suddenly called out, in a loud clear voice, towards the rim of the sun:

'Thank you, Sir Henry Morgan. Your treasure will be well spent. Give us a fair wind.'

The negro guards showed the whites of their eyes.

'The Undertaker's Wind it is,' said Bond.

The Big Man looked at him.

'All down?' he asked the guards.

'Yassuh, Boss,' answered one of them.

'Take them along,' said The Big Man.

They went to the edge of the cliff and down the steep steps, one guard in front, one behind. Mr. Big followed.

The engines of the long graceful yacht were turning over quietly, the exhaust bubbling glutinously, a thread of blue vapour rising astern.

There were two men on the jetty at the guide ropes. There were only three men on deck besides the Captain and the navigator on the grey streamlined bridge. There was no room for more. All the available deckspace, save for a fishing chair rigged right aft, was covered with fish-tanks. The Red Ensign had been struck and only the Stars and Stripes hung motionless at the stern.

A few yards clear of the ship the red torpedo-shaped paravane, about six foot long, lay quietly on the water, now aquamarine in the early dawn. It was attached to a thick pile of wire cable, coiled up on the deck aft. To Bond there looked to be a good fifty yards of it. The water was crystal clear and there were no fish about.

The Undertaker's Wind was almost dead. Soon the Doctor's Wind would start to breathe in from the sea. How soon? wondered Bond. Was it an omen?

Away beyond the ship he could see the roof of Beau Desert among the trees, but the jetty and the ship and the cliff path were still in deep shadow. Bond wondered if night-glasses would be able to pick them out. And if they could, what Strangways would be thinking.

Mr. Big stood on the jetty and supervised the process of binding them together.

'Strip her,' he said to Solitaire's guard.

Bond flinched. He stole a glance at Mr. Big's wrist watch. It said ten minutes to six. Bond kept silence. There must not be even a minute's delay.

'Throw the clothes on board,' said Mr. Big. 'Tie some strips round his shoulder. I don't want any blood in the water, yet.'

Solitaire's clothes were cut off her with a knife. She stood pale and naked. She hung her head and the heavy black hair fell forward over her face. Bond's shoulder was roughly bound with strips of her linen skirt.

'You bastard,' said Bond through his teeth.

Under Mr. Big's direction, their hands were freed. Their bodies were pressed together, face to face, and their arms held round each other's waists and then bound tightly again.

Bond felt Solitaire's soft breasts pressed against him. She leant her chin on his right shoulder.

'I didn't want it to be like this,' she whispered tremulously.

Bond didn't answer. He hardly felt her body. He was counting seconds.

On the jetty there was a pile of rope to the paravane. It hung down off the jetty and Bond could see it lying along the sand until it rose to meet the belly of the red torpedo.

The free end was tied under their armpits and knotted tightly between them in the space between their necks. It was all very carefully done. There was no possible escape.

Bond was counting the seconds. He made it five minutes to six.

Mr. Big had a last look at them.

'Their legs can stay free,' he said. 'They'll make appetizing bait.' He stepped off the jetty on to the deck of the yacht.'

The two guards went aboard. The two men on the jetty unhitched their lines and followed. The screws churned up the still water and with the engines at half speed ahead the *Secatur* slid swiftly away from the island.

Mr. Big went aft and sat down in the fishing chair. They could see his eyes fixed on them. He said nothing. Made no gesture. He just watched.

The *Secatur* cut through the water towards the reef. Bond could see the cable to the paravane snaking over the side. The paravane started to move softly after the ship. Suddenly it put its nose down, then righted itself and sped away, its rudder pulling out and away from the wake of the ship.

The coil of rope beside them leapt into life.

'Look out,' said Bond urgently, holding tighter to the girl.

Their arms were pulled almost out of their sockets as they were jerked together off the jetty into the sea.

For a second they both went under, then they were on the surface, their joined bodies smashing through the water.

Bond gasped for breath amongst the waves and spray that dashed past his twisted mouth. He could hear the rasping of Solitaire's breath next to his ear.

'Breathe, breathe,' he shouted through the rushing of the water. 'Lock your legs against mine.'

She heard him and he felt her knees pressing between his thighs. She had a paroxysm of coughing, then her breath became more even against his ear and the thumping of her heart eased against his breast. At the same time their speed slackened.

'Hold your breath,' shouted Bond. 'I've got to have a look. Ready?'

A pressure of her arms answered him. He felt her chest heave as she filled her lungs.

With the weight of his body he swung her round so that his head was now quite out of water.

They were ploughing along at about three knots. He twisted his head above the small bow-wave they were throwing up.

The *Secatur* was entering the passage through the reef, about eighty yards away, he guessed. The paravane was skimming slowly along almost at right angles to her. Another thirty yards and the red torpedo would be crossing the broken water over the reef. A further thirty yards behind, they were riding slowly across the surface of the bay.

Sixty yards to go to the reef.

Bond twisted his body and Solitaire came up, gasping.

Still they moved slowly along through the water.

Five yards, ten, fifteen, twenty.

Only forty yards to go before they hit the coral.

The *Secatur* would be just through. Bond gathered his breath. It must be past six now. What had happened to the blasted mine? Bond thought a quick fervent prayer. God save us, he said into the water.

Suddenly he felt the rope tighten under his arms.

'Breathe, Solitaire, breathe,' he shouted as they got under way and the water started to hiss past them.

Now they were flying over the sea towards the crouching reef.

There was a slight check. Bond guessed that the paravane had fouled a niggerhead or a piece of surface coral. Then their bodies hurtled on again in their deadly embrace.

Thirty yards to go, twenty, ten.

Jesus Christ, thought Bond. We're for it. He braced his muscles to take the crashing, searing pain, edged Solitaire further above him to protect her from the worst of it.

Suddenly the breath whistled out of his body and a giant fist thumped him into Solitaire so that she rose right out of the sea above him and then fell back. A split second later lightning flashed across the sky and there was the thunder of an explosion.

They stopped dead in the water and Bond felt the weight of the slack rope pulling them under.

His legs sank down beneath his stunned body and water rushed into his mouth.

It was this that brought him back to consciousness. His legs pounded under him and brought their mouths to the surface. The girl was a dead weight in his arms. He trod water desperately and looked round him, holding Solitaire's lolling head on his shoulder above the surface.

The first thing he saw was the swirling waters of the reef not five yards away. Without its protection they would both have been crushed by the shock-wave of the explosion. He felt the tug and eddy of its currents round his legs. He backed desperately towards it, catching gulps of air when he could. His chest was bursting with the strain and he saw the sky through a red film. The rope dragged him down and the girl's hair filled his mouth and tried to choke him.

Suddenly he felt the sharp scrape of the coral against the back of his legs. He kicked and felt frantically with his feet for a foothold, flaying the skin off with every movement.

He hardly felt the pain.

Now his back was being scraped and his arms. He floundered clumsily, his lungs burning in his chest. Then there was a bed of needles under his feet. He put all his weight on it, leaning back against the strong eddies that tried to dislodge him. His feet held and there was rock at his back. He leant back panting, blood streaming up around him in the water, holding the girl's cold, scarcely breathing body against him.

For a minute he rested, blessedly, his eyes shut and the blood pounding through his limbs, coughing painfully, waiting for his senses to focus again. His first thought was for the blood in the water around him. But he guessed the big fish would not venture into the reef. Anyway there was nothing he could do about it.

Then he looked out to sea.

There was no sign of the *Secatur*.

High up in the still sky there was a mushroom of smoke, beginning to trail, with the Doctor's Wind, in towards the land.

There were things strewn all over the water and a few heads bobbing up and down and the whole sea was glinting with the white stomachs of fish stunned or killed by the explosion. There was a strong smell of explosive in the air. On the fringe of the debris, the red paravane lay quietly, hull down, anchored by the cable whose other end must lie somewhere on the bottom. Fountains of bubbles were erupting on the glassy surface of the sea.

On the edge of the circle of bobbing heads and dead fish a few triangular fins were cutting fast through the water. More appeared as Bond watched. Once he saw a great snout come out of the water and smash down on something. The fins threw up spray as they flashed among the tidbits. Two black arms suddenly stuck up in the air and then disappeared. There were screams. Two or three pairs of arms started to flail the water towards the reef. One man stopped to bang the water in front of him with the flat of his hand. Then his hands disappeared under the surface. Then he too began to scream and his body jerked to and fro in the water. Barracuda hitting into him, said Bond's dazed mind.

But one of the heads was getting nearer, making for the bit of reef where Bond stood, the small waves breaking under his armpits, the girl's black hair hanging down his back.

It was a large head and a veil of blood streamed down over the face from a wound in the great bald skull.

Bond watched it come on.

The Big Man was executing a blundering breast-stroke, making enough flurry in the water to attract any fish that wasn't already occupied.

Bond wondered whether he would make it. Bond's eyes narrowed and his breath became calmer as he watched the cruel sea for its decision.

The surging head came nearer. Bond could see the teeth showing in a rictus of agony and frenzied endeavour. Blood half veiled the eyes that Bond knew would be bulging in their sockets. He could almost hear the great diseased heart thumping under the grey-black skin. Would it give out before the bait was taken?

The Big Man came on. His shoulders were naked, his clothes stripped off him by the explosion, Bond supposed, but the black silk tie had remained and it showed round the thick neck and streamed behind the head like a Chinaman's pigtail.

A splash of water cleared some blood away from the eyes. They were wide open, staring madly towards Bond. They held no appeal for help, only a fixed glare of physical exertion.

Even as Bond looked into them, now only ten yards away, they suddenly shut and the great face contorted in a grimace of pain.

'Aarrh,' said the distorted mouth.

Both arms stopped flailing the water and the head went under and came up again. A cloud of blood welled up and darkened the sea. Two six-foot thin brown shadows backed out of the cloud and then dashed back into it. The body in the water jerked sideways. Half of The Big Man's left arm came out of the water. It had no hand, no wrist, no wrist watch.

But the great turnip head, the drawn-back mouth full of white teeth almost splitting it in half, was still alive. And now it was screaming, a long gurgling scream that only broke each time a barracuda hit into the dangling body.

There was a distant shout from the bay behind Bond. He paid no attention. All his senses were focused on the horror in the water in front of him.

A fin split the surface a few yards away and stopped.

Bond could feel the shark pointing like a dog, the short-sighted pink button eyes trying to pierce the cloud of blood and weigh up the prey. Then it shot in towards the chest and the screaming head went under as sharply as a fisherman's float.

Some bubbles burst on the surface.

There was the swirl of a sharp brown-spotted tail as the huge Leopard shark backed out to swallow and attack again.

The head floated back to the surface. The mouth was closed. The yellow eyes seemed still to look at Bond.

Then the shark's snout came right out of the water and it drove in towards the head, the lower curved jaw open so that light glinted on the teeth. There was a horrible grunting scrunch and a great swirl of water. Then silence.

Bond's dilated eyes went on staring at the brown stain that spread wider and wider across the sea.

Then the girl moaned and Bond came to his senses.

There was another shout from behind him and he turned his head towards the bay.

It was Quarrel, his brown gleaming chest towering above the slim hull of a canoe, his arms flailing at the paddle, and a long way behind him all the other canoes of Shark Bay skimming like water-boatmen across the small waves that had started to ripple the surface.

The fresh north-east trade winds had started to blow and the sun was shining down on the blue water and on the soft green flanks of Jamaica.

The first tears since his childhood came into James Bond's blue-grey eyes and ran down his drawn cheeks into the bloodstained sea.

CHAPTER XXIII

PASSIONATE LEAVE

Like dangling emerald pendants the two humming-birds were making their last rounds of the hibiscus and a mocking bird had started on its evening song, sweeter than a nightingale's, from the summit of a bush of night-scented jasmine.

The jagged shadow of a man-of-war bird floated across the green Bahama grass of the lawn as it sailed on the air currents up the coast to some distant colony, and a slate-blue kingfisher chattered angrily as it saw the man sitting in the chair in the garden. It changed its flight and swerved off across the sea to the island. A brimstone butterfly flirted among the purple shadows under the palms.

The graded blue waters of the bay were quite still. The cliffs of the island were a deep rose in the light of the setting sun behind the house.

There was a smell of evening and of coolness after a hot day and a slight scent of peat-smoke that came from cassava being roasted in one of the fishermen's huts in the village away to the right.

Solitaire came out of the house and walked on naked feet across the lawn. She was carrying a tray with a cocktail shaker and two glasses. She put it down on a bamboo table beside Bond's chair.

'I hope I've made it right,' she said. 'Six to one sounds terribly strong. I've never had Vodka Martinis before.'

Bond looked up at her. She was wearing a pair of his white silk pyjamas. They were far too large for her. She looked absurdly childish.

She laughed. 'How do you like my Port Maria lipstick?' she asked, 'and the eyebrows made up with an HB pencil. I couldn't do anything with the rest of me except wash it.'

'You look wonderful,' said Bond. 'You're far the prettiest girl in the whole of Shark Bay. If I had some legs and arms I'd get up and kiss you.'

Solitaire bent down and kissed him long on the lips, one arm tightly round his neck. She stood up and smoothed back the comma of black hair that had fallen down over his forehead.

They looked at each other for a moment, then she turned to the table and poured him out a cocktail. She poured half a glass for herself and sat down on the warm grass and put her head against his knee. He played with her hair with his right hand and they sat for a while looking out between the trunks of the palm trees at the sea and the light fading on the island.

The day had been given over to licking wounds and cleaning up the remains of the mess.

When Quarrel had landed them on the little beach at Beau Desert, Bond had half carried Solitaire across the lawn and into the bathroom. He had filled the bath full of warm water. Without her knowing what was happening he had soaped and washed her whole body and her hair. When he had cleaned away all the salt and coral slime he helped her out, dried her and put merthiolate on the coral cuts that striped her back and thighs. Then he gave her a sleeping draught and put her naked between the sheets in his own bed. He kissed her. Before he had finished closing the jalousies she was asleep.

Then he got into the bath and Strangways soaped him down and almost bathed his body in merthiolate. He was raw and bleeding in a hundred places and his left arm was numb from the barracuda bite. He had lost a mouthful of muscle at the shoulder. The sting of the merthiolate made him grind his teeth.

He put on a dressing-gown and Quarrel drove him to the hospital at Port Maria. Before he left he had a Lucullian breakfast and a blessed first cigarette. He fell asleep in the car and he slept on the operating table and in the cot where they finally put him, a mass of bandages and surgical tape.

Quarrel brought him back in the early afternoon. By that time Strangways had acted on the information Bond had given him. There was a police detachment on the Isle of Surprise, the wreck of the *Secatur*, lying in about twenty fathoms, was buoyed and the position being patrolled by the Customs launch from Port Maria. The salvage tug and divers were on their way from Kingston. Reporters from the local press had been given a brief statement and there was a police guard on the entrance to Beau Desert prepared to repel the flood of newspapermen who would arrive in Jamaica when the full story got out to the world. Meanwhile a detailed report had gone to M, and to Washington, so that The Big Man's team in Harlem and St. Petersburg could be rounded up and provisionally held on a blanket gold-smuggling charge.

There were no survivors from the *Secatur*, but the local fishermen had brought in nearly a ton of dead fish that morning.

Jamaica was aflame with rumours. There were serried

ranks of cars on the cliffs above the bay and along the beach below. Word had got out about Bloody Morgan's treasure, but also about the packs of shark and barracuda that had defended it, and because of them there was not a swimmer who was planning to get out to the scene of the wreck under cover of darkness.

A doctor had been to visit Solitaire but had found her chiefly concerned about getting some clothes and the right shade of lipstick. Strangways had arranged for a selection to be sent over from Kingston next day. For the time being she was experimenting with the contents of Bond's suitcase and a bowl of hibiscus.

Strangways got back from Kingston shortly after Bond's return from hospital. He had a signal for Bond from M. It read:

PRESUME YOU HAVE FILED CLAIM TO TREASURE IN YOUR NAME BEHALF UNIVERSAL EXPORT STOP PROCEED IMMEDIATELY WITH SALVAGE STOP HAVE ENGAGED COUNSEL TO PRESS OUR RIGHTS WITH TREASURY AND COLONIAL OFFICE STOP MEANWHILE VERY WELL DONE STOP FORTNIGHT'S PASSIONATE LEAVE GRANTED ENDIT

'I suppose he means "Compassionate".' said Bond.

Strangways looked solemn. 'I expect so,' he said. 'I made a full report of the damage to you. And to the girl,' he added.

'Hm,' said Bond. 'M's cipherenes don't often pick a wrong group. However.'

Strangways looked carefully out of the window with his one eye.

'It's so like the old devil to think of the gold first,' said Bond. 'Suppose he thinks he can get away with it and somehow dodge a reduction in the Secret Fund when the next parliamentary estimates come round. I expect half his life is taken up with arguing with the Treasury. But still he's been pretty quick off the mark.'

'I filed your claim at Government House directly I got the signal,' said Strangways. 'But it's going to be tricky. The Crown will be after it and America will come in somewhere as he was an American citizen. It'll be a long business.'

They had talked some more and then Strangways had left and Bond had walked painfully out into the garden to sit for a while in the sunshine with his thoughts.

In his mind he ran once more the gauntlet of dangers he had entered on his long chase after The Big Man and the fabulous treasure, and he lived again through the searing flashes of time when he had looked various deaths in the face.

And now it was over and he sat in the sunshine among the flowers with the prize at his feet and his hand in her long black hair. He clasped the moment to him and thought of the fourteen tomorrows that would be theirs between them.

There was a crash of broken crockery from the kitchen at the back of the house and the sound of Quarrel's voice thundering at someone.

'Poor Quarrel,' said Solitaire. 'He's borrowed the best cook in the village and ransacked the markets for surprises for us. He's even found some black crabs, the first of the season. Then he's roasting a pitiful little sucking pig and making an avocado pear salad and we're to finish up with guavas and coconut cream. And Commander Strangways has left a case of the best champagne in Jamaica. My mouth's watering already. But don't forget it's supposed to be a secret. I wandered into the kitchen and found he had almost reduced the cook to tears.'

'He's coming with us on our passionate holiday,' said Bond. He told her of M's cable. 'We're going to a house on stilts with palm trees and five miles of golden sand. And you'll have to look after me very well because I shan't be able to make love with only one arm.'

There was open sensuality in Solitaire's eyes as she looked up at him. She smiled innocently.

'What about my back?' she said.

Ian Fleming

CASINO ROYALE	30p
MOONRAKER	30p
DIAMONDS ARE FOREVER	30p
FROM RUSSIA WITH LOVE	30p
DR NO	30p
THUNDERBALL	30p
GOLDFINGER	30p
YOU ONLY LIVE TWICE	30p
ON HER MAJESTY'S SECRET SERVICE	30p
THE SPY WHO LOVED ME	25p
OCTOPUSSY	25p
FOR YOUR EYES ONLY	30p
THE MAN WITH THE GOLDEN GUN	30p

These and other PAN Books are obtainable from all booksellers and newsagents. If you have any difficulty please send purchase price plus 7p postage to PO Box 11, Falmouth, Cornwall.

While every effort is made to keep prices low, it is sometimes necessary to increase prices at short notice. PAN Books reserve the right to show new retail prices on covers which may differ from those previously advertised in the text or elsewhere.